PENGUIN BOOKS

CASUALTIES

Lynne Reid Banks, the daughter of a Scottish doctor and an Irish actress, was born in London and was evacuated to the Canadian prairies during the war. On her return to England she studied for the stage at RADA and then had several years' experience with repertory companies all over the country. The first play she wrote was produced by a number of rep companies and later performed on BBC television. She wrote and had published several other plays; one was put on in a London 'little theatre', and others have been performed on radio and television. She was one of the first two women reporters on British television. She worked for ITN for seven years – from its inception until 1962 – initially as a reporter and later as a scriptwriter. After leaving ITN she emigrated to Israel, where she married a sculptor. They lived on a kibbutz for nine years and have three sons. She now lives in Dorset and writes full-time.

Lynne Reid Banks's first novel, *The L-Shaped Room*, appeared in 1960, was made into a successful film and has been in print ever since. It was followed by *An End to Running* (1962), *Children at the Gate* (1968), the second and third books in *The L-Shaped Room* trilogy – *The Backward Shadow* (1970) and *Two is Lonely* (1974) – *Defy the Wilderness* (1981) and *The Warning Bell* (1984), all published by Penguin.

Dark Quartet: The Story of the Brontës (1976) won the Yorkshire Arts Association Award in 1977 and was followed by its sequel, *Path to the Silent Country: Charlotte Brontë's Years of Fame*, in the same year. Both are now reissued by Penguin.

Lynne Reid Banks has also written a number of books for children and young adults. Her children's books include *The Adventures of King Midas*, *The Farthest-Away Mountain*, *Maura's Angel*, *The Indian in the Cupboard*, *Return of the Indian* and *The Fairy Rebel*. Her books for teenagers include *One More River*, *Sarah and After*, *My Darling Villain* and *The Writing on the Wall*. In addition, she has written two historical books about Israel, *Letters to My Israeli Sons* and *Torn Country*.

Lynne Reid Banks

CASUALTIES

PENGUIN BOOKS

PENGUIN BOOKS

Published by the Penguin Group
27 Wrights Lane, London W8 5TZ, England
Viking Penguin Inc., 40 West 23rd Street, New York, New York 10010, USA
Penguin Books Australia Ltd, Ringwood, Victoria, Australia
Penguin Books Canada Ltd, 2801 John Street, Markham, Ontario, Canada L3R 1B4
Penguin Books (NZ) Ltd, 182–190 Wairau Road, Auckland 10, New Zealand

Penguin Books Ltd, Registered Offices: Harmondsworth, Middlesex, England

First published by Hamish Hamilton 1986
Published in Penguin Books 1987
3 5 7 9 10 8 6 4

Made and printed in Great Britain by
Richard Clay Ltd, Bungay, Suffolk

For Marijcke
with love

With grateful acknowledgements to Marjolijn Anstey (for the use of her name, among other things!), Ivan Mindel, Truus Menger, Kees Veenstra, Henry van der Zee and, last but not least, Nan Winton.

Chapter 1

———— ∿ ————

I would not have remembered that particular row with my husband, if the phone call hadn't interrupted it. There were so many rows at that time that I couldn't remember that our marriage had ever been any good. I doubt if I could have called to mind one reason why I'd stuck with Cal. I sank into such a pit of despair that I wrote to an Australian friend (one can loose oneself from the formal bonds of loyalty more easily the further away a correspondent lives): "I wouldn't take a crock of gold to relive one hour of my marriage." She showed me the letter recently.

This precise row, which was interrupted, was about Cal's father, who was expected to arrive in London from the States in a matter of days. Cal had read the letter to himself, announced the bald fact of Calvin McClusky Senior's imminence in astringent tones, and then torn the airgraph up into small bits before I could find out the exact date. I didn't have to ask whether 'Dad' wanted to see us – despite everything, I knew he did. I understood him, after our brief and fraught acquaintance, better than his son did, and I knew, I knew with absolute clarity and certainty, that this brief note – couched no doubt in terse and businesslike terms – was the old monster's way of holding out to his estranged son the hand of forgiveness.

I didn't start anything *then*. The tinder was too perennially dry to risk the slightest spark. Not that I was one to back off from shouting-matches (Cal said I throve on them) but I was tireder than usual after a full day with the children and a bit of writing thrown in. I like to be on top of my form when a row starts, and I scented a real lulu coming over this. So I waited till Cal had gone into the garden and then hastily picked as many scraps of blue airgraph as I could out of the wastepaper basket, hurried up to my study with them, and, pushing my typewriter back, began piecing them together in the dust where it had been standing.

It was a fiddly, infuriating task, and I had only got the edge-pieces in place when he burst in, giving me such a guilty fright that I scattered them.

"What in hell do you think you're doing?"

I tried to appear calm. "Piecing your father's letter together. Did you have to put it through a shredder?"

I looked at him, and wished I hadn't.

He reached round me and grabbed up the bits of paper, as many as he could, and started out of the room. I grabbed him, which was foolhardy when he had those small white bumps all over his face, but I was angry too, and this was very important to us. One of us had to rise above pride and anger and old scores. We had two children and very little money at that time.

"Cal, will you listen?"

"It's my goddamned father. It's my goddamned letter."

"It's *both* our goddamned lives and the goddamned grandfather of our kids!"

He turned to face me. The hand screwing up the blue scraps was trembling with the effort, as if he were crushing a scorpion which had already stung him.

"You can't imagine I'd take a red cent from him after he kicked me out of the firm and the family on my ass – "

This distorted version of past events made me gape, but he rode over me.

"I happen to be the *only sane person* around here, and evidently I'm also the only one with a shred of honesty *or integrity*."

That went home, and not just because Daniel had recently

2

been caught with a hot Mars Bar. But without giving me time to recover, Cal forged straight on.

"We don't happen to be starving. But even if we were I wouldn't crawl, and if you were any kind of true wife and not *just* the bloody breadwinner around here, you'd know better than to ask me to."

In rows of this sort, there are words which give a passing pang – usually four-letter ones, which sting briefly because you think: *How could he speak to me like that?* – not because they carry any actual meaning. What really matters is words that do have meaning, personal meaning rooted deep in the marriage. For me, the worst was the word 'integrity'. Had he known how much of a lance to the vitals that would be? Looking into the face I'd once loved so much, now plague-lumped, sour, full of sullen angry malice, I thought, and for the first time really meant: *We must separate. I can't stand any more.*

That was when the phone rang.

I had an extension in my office. We both looked at it, sharing a reaction (I could always tell, even when things were at their worst, when we did). Both angry. And both relieved to be interrupted.

I picked up the receiver. "Hallo." Flat. Sitting on my fury in case it should be business.

"Sue?"

Even on that one syllable, the accent was patent. But no bells rang, not yet.

"Yes?"

"It's Mariolain."*

Something jumped in my head. *Mariolain*? My eyes went to Cal who was still standing there. The white bumps were fading, inevitably. The raging tension had been, for the moment, blurred at its edges.

"Mariolain? It can't be!"

"You remember me?" Her voice had a high, pleased note, incredulous.

---

* I'm aware that this name should be spelt MARJOLIJN. I have modified the spelling to make it easier to pronounce.

3

"Of course I remember you – if it's really you. Is it really you?"

"I think it must be, don't you?"

"Where are you calling from?"

"Hilversum."

"Where?"

"Hilversum. In Holland." She laughed, and the infectious sound of it brought her back more clearly than the name. "You haven't forgotten that I wear a white cap and clogs and carry everywhere a big red cheese?"

I felt such a wave of sheer nostalgic happiness for the young days when I had known her that a bit of my smile spilled onto Cal. It was so unsuited to his mood – perhaps it even hurt, not being meant for him – that he turned on his heel and left the room. I didn't care. I sank down on my hard office chair.

"Mariolain, this is the most marvellous surprise! What possessed you suddenly to get in touch? My God, it's been so many years!"

"Twenty. Nearly. I'll tell you why, but first I ask some things and you ask back. Okay?"

"Okay!"

"Are you well? Are you married? Have you any kids?"

"I'm well. I'm married. I have kids, two, both boys. What about you?"

"I am married with two, too! How old are yours?"

"George is thirteen and Daniel's eleven. We were late starters."

"But Suky, this is absolutely fantastic! Mine are the same only that one is a girl!"

And now memory focused. It was the Suky that did it. Suky had been left far behind. Nobody had called me that since my mother died. When she had been around to call me that, I introduced myself to new people as Suky, because if she said I was a Suky I wanted to be a Suky. And now the memory cassette had slid into its slot. A motoscarfia was churning along the Grand Canal. It was full of all of us, ten or more student holiday-makers, in love with Venice to the point of ecstasy, and almost in love with each other because we were together in it. It was night, the undark Venetian

4

night, with a full moon apart from all the little lights . . . In the stern, which I, or rather Suky who had been me, was facing, sat a petite red-curly-haired Dutch girl with a guitar. One boy at her feet with his head in her lap, defying the guitar which kept giving him knocks, two more on either side of her, adoringly gazing. No spectacular clothes or special tarting-up – none needed. She wore what I wore – what all the girls wore – a white cotton blouse with puffed sleeves and a wide broderie-anglaise ruffle, that year's boutique special, a bright dirndl skirt with a petticoat, and rope-soles taped in crosses up her tanned legs. A cheeky, snubby face. And clever hands bringing music out of the strings, just what we needed to complete the mood, to transform the setting into total otherness from what we had each come from.

"Suky," she was saying, now, "what I am ringing you for is this. I read your book. The one they translated into Dutch. And I found out your phone number. Now I am asking a big, enormous favour. Niels, my husband, is coming to London next week, and I want to ask you to put up him."

"Put up with him, or put him up?"

She laughed excitedly. "Both. But you'll like him. Everyone does. He is so handsome and charming. And we are just a little bit broke just now and I want that he won't waste money on a hotel, even though it's what he loves. What can you answer but yes? – Except you must say if it's no."

It should, of course, have been no. With the atmosphere between Cal and me? With the question of Calvin Senior still unresolved and only one spare bedroom, at present crammed to the gunwales with junk so that you couldn't even tell if it contained a bed? But I said yes to Mariolain, and she rushed on:

"Thank you, Suky! I knew. And don't think I am terrible and pushy. I am able to pay you back. Niels will tell you how. And I won't say goodbye, only ciao, because soon we'll see each other. When we do . . . please don't tell me how I've got fat with the years. And old."

Old? She was much younger than me, five years at least. I caught a glimpse of my forty-five-year-old face in the uncurtained attic window.

"We'll both have to be merciful," I said drily.

5

*

Niels was as advertised, handsome and charming. I felt he
made a profession of it, a bit, like a lot of media men.
Because that's what it turned out that he was. His current
medium was TV commercials, but he considered himself an
artist and wanted to make feature films. That's what he was
doing in London, trying to package up a film deal.

He was with us for just under a week. He was no trouble,
being out most of the time, and there were several other
advantages about having him to stay. Cal and I postponed
our quarrels for the duration. Cal is deeply opposed – it
amounts to an inhibition – to rowing in front of people, or
even allowing ill feelings to prickle the atmosphere. The let-
it-all-hang-out brigade might attribute this to hypocrisy, but
I call it deeply engrained good manners. He applied it even
to the boys: if he felt a quarrel coming on between us when
the children were around he would hold back until we were
alone. (I recently asked George if he hadn't suffered
through that awful period and he looked at me blankly and
asked what I was on about. He didn't even register that our
marriage was tearing its bottom out on about five kinds of
rocks, and George is the sensitive one.)

Sometimes Niels would phone politely and ask if he could
come back for supper, and then I would make a special
effort because he was a guest and Mariolain's husband. So
we had some fancy meals during that week, and Cal glow-
ered because of the expense but he didn't say anything
because, even without overt quarrelling, he was still punish-
ing me. If we'd been friends, he would have said something
casually about there being no need to push the boat out for a
stranger, but what his silence was saying was: It's your
money, if you want to show off with it, I've no right to say
anything. And I punished him back, by buying steak instead
of chicken and then almost choked eating it. We absolutely
never bought steak.

Meanwhile, during that same week, Calvin Senior presumably came and went and Cal and I were both jumpy,
knowing he was in London somewhere waiting for a phone

call. I was sorry for the old bastard and several times I nearly opened the subject again with Cal because of the pressure of feeling 'Dad' waiting for his only son to grab the hand that had been held out after twelve years. But that last row we'd had in my study still hurt and I didn't want another one, not with a guest in the house, a stranger we had to look happily married in front of.

Instead we cursorily discussed Niels when he was out.

"This film deal is obviously pie in the sky," remarked Cal. "Nobody who really has anything going for him puffs himself so hard."

"Oh, I don't know," I said. I wasn't sure why I was standing up for Niels. Perhaps loyalty to Mariolain had something to do with it. Niels made me feel uneasy. I don't go for these tall, wildly good-looking men with flashing smiles and wavy dark hair and all that, despite the contrary evidence contained in my alleged novels. As a matter of fact, now I think of it, that's probably the precise reason why I was put off him: he was like a living prototype of half my heroes. (The other half are bronzed blond beasts, of course.) I prefer witty, loving, cuddly little men with more hair on their chins and chests than on their heads. Of course if they stop being loving and cuddly and their darling bearded faces get plague-ridden and they start employing their wits to lacerate you instead of making you laugh, that's just too bad; then in your mind you may start calling them short and bald.

But that doesn't mean you could ever start trusting the tall dark and conventionally handsome ones.

Niels was about thirty-seven, I reckoned, and that made him a few years younger than Mariolain, who must be over forty. That didn't make me any more sanguine about her being married to this gorgeous philandering creature.

How did I know he was philandering? Call it intuition. At first. But on the fourth day he was with us he asked me, very nicely, if I'd mind putting some of his laundry in my washing machine. One of his shirts had make-up smudges on it. Nothing blatant, just a trace of foundation, but still. So that was why Mariolain hadn't wanted him to be on the loose in a hotel.

I mentioned this to Cal. It's a relief when you're unhappy about your own marriage to speculate about someone else's.

"For God's sake," he said, "don't get yourself steamed up about Mario Lanza or whatever she's called. Haven't you enough drama-riddled girlfriends in the immediate vicinity?" He's always been baffled by my burning interest in people. He was strictly a places person himself, or so I thought.

On his last night with us, Niels invited our whole family to visit his family in Hilversum at Easter.

Holidays are a problem when you're hard up and have children. Having them at home between terms is obviously pure torment, especially if most of their friends are away and their chief diversion is fighting. Things being as they were between Cal and me, it was highly desirable that we get out of the house and, preferably, the country. We both saw that, even Cal, who is just like a cat about leaving home. So we did our sums and came to the conclusion that taking kids and car to Amsterdam via Harwich and the Hook was not as extravagant, taken all in all, as it sounded at first. It would be educational for the boys to go abroad. And I wanted to see my friend again. The idea had a strong appeal, even without the appeal Mariolain herself was to make, a week after Niels had left. She phoned again, ostensibly to thank me for having him, but actually to beg me to accept the invitation.

"I *need* you to come," she said. Why she needed *me*, us, I don't suppose I'll ever really know. Perhaps it was something about that book of mine she'd read which made her think I might be a good listener.

As for Niels, I think now that he invited us, not just out of politeness or because Mariolain had told him to. I think he too needed some sort of *deus ex machina* to descend from afar onto his world. There are certain situations so deeply rooted, so complex, of such long and tortuous history, that close friends or relatives who have followed the situation through its evolution are no use any more.

Before this, I had driven Niels to the airport. It was the only time I had been alone with him during his stay. Cal and I hadn't then decided whether we could go to Holland.

"It would be great to see Mariolain again," I said. "I wonder if we'll recognise each other after all these years."

"Oh, you'll recognise her all right," said Niels. "She has hardly changed. A little fatter perhaps. Everything else the same."

"How long have you been married?"

"Fourteen years."

"*You* must have been very young."

"Twenty-two." (So I'd guessed more or less right about his age.)

We drove in silence for a while, and then I asked: "Does she still play?"

He turned to me. "What?"

"Does she still play?"

"Play what?"

"The guitar," I said. "She used to play so beautifully. I've always remembered it."

He stared at me for a moment through his beautiful dark eyes. He reminded me uncomfortably of a nauseating recent creation of mine called Darcy Beaumont.

"I didn't know that," he said shortly. But after another few minutes' silence, he added, "Now you mention it, I do seem to think she had a guitar at one time, long ago, before the children. But no, she doesn't play any more."

"I suppose she hasn't time," I murmured. But that was a flat lie. I supposed no such thing. I felt a sudden coldness toward Niels. He had spoken with such deadly casualness. If in the intervening years Mariolain had lost her sight, I felt he might have said: *No, she doesn't see any more,* in the same matter-of-fact tone.

9

Chapter 2

———— ✑ ————

I shouldn't be writing this.

I don't mean it shouldn't be written. It ought to be written – I feel that very strongly. I just mean that now I'm actually on the verge of getting down to it, after brooding about it for years and putting it off, I'm scared. I don't know if I'm the right person, or rather, the right writer.

I'm not sure I'm entitled even to call myself a writer. If I can, it's only with a very small 'w'. It says 'author' in my passport. I put that there before I'd had a word published, as a sort of self-fulfilling prophecy. Then I wrote my first book, which was the one Mariolain read which was translated (not only into Dutch), and which was the classic first novel that every writer's supposed to write, about the most interesting (to them) episode in their own early life, thinly disguised. Mine is about a young girl who has her leg off for cancer. I didn't actually have my leg off, but I very nearly did – I mean it was touch and go (though it wasn't cancer, it was blood poisoning). I went through the whole agony of *thinking* I was going to lose my leg, and then, when they'd saved it and it was all over, I realised I'd effectively lived through the whole trauma and I needed to get that out of my system just as if the worst had really happened. So I sat down and wrote this book, which was a very short-lived bestseller, and which I should have followed up with another novel and another, in which case I might now be an established novelist in my prime. But it seemed that what I really was was a one-book author. Even though that word in my passport had been justified technically, as a writer I seemed to be a burnt-out case.

Then I married Cal, who was then in the London branch of his family banking enterprise. He'd been dragooned into it by his high-powered American father. In defiance of Cal's subsequent twisted version, what actually happened was that we jointly and very shortly decided that that couldn't go on. I mean, it just wasn't Cal. He hated every hour of it. So we swallowed hard, but not too hard because we had only George then – and George was such a little poozle, never let a peep out of him, lived in his sling, slept in our bed with us, hoovered away at my tits and thrived cost- and trouble-free till he was eighteen months old – and in our dim-witted impractical way we thought that this would go on forever (not the sling and the tits of course, but the cost-freedom). I mean, we thought three could live as cheaply as two. Cal had some cushioning savings from his banking years which had been pretty plummy, and we two, Cal and I, *liked* pigging it in our top-floor pad in Paddington and living on lentils and cauli-greens. We were staunch socialists in those days, one reason why Cal hated being a banker. So he quit his job. Which brought Calvin Senior rampaging over in a fury, but Cal had me to back him up and fortunately 'Dad' didn't have too much time to waste on recalcitrant heirs and had to rush back again to New York before the business foundered without his attention.

Thus we found ourselves free, high on integrity, but job-less, not to say cut off without a dollar.

Of course Cal had no intention of just idling his life away (though theoretically I have nothing against such a course, unburdened as I am by the work ethic, provided it doesn't involve starving to death). He bought a rackety old van and set himself up as a freelance small mover. There was lots of work around at that time; in the early sixties everyone was flush and swinging, moving house at yearly intervals apparently. Cal is short and stocky and strong as a Highland bull, or he was then. People liked him – it tickled them to have

11

this bearded bantam Yank turning up on their doorsteps and proving he could move all but the most enormous bits of furniture single-handed with the aid of his hand-crafted trolley, a wondrous device invented by himself. When he needed a mate, he recruited his pal Martin, a weird contrast to Cal physically, being tall and wand-like but also amazingly strong. They made a marvellous team; in fact I often privately thought they'd have made a good comedy duo if only either of them could act. I once saw the pair of them shifting a vast, antiquated fridge, weighing about a ton and leaking unspeakable fluids all the way, down four narrow flights of stairs and out to the council chomper-upper, while the two massive council men, who had refused to tackle the job on account of it being impossible, stood there with their apelike jaws almost coming off their hinges.

During this phase in our lives Daniel appeared, unplanned but offered a qualified welcome, the qualification being that he turn out like George, which is to say no trouble to anyone. Daniel, however, proved to be a perfect little pain in the ass. He screamed without cease from the moment he was born and threw not only our household, but the whole house, of which it formed the top layer, into such an uproar that we had to leave our lovely Paddington pad and find somewhere detached and soundproof.

Thus to Wembley. The unsmartest sector, need I say, which was unsmart enough to suit Cal (who loathes smart) but a bit beyond the pale for me. Pads in Paddington during the onset of married life are one thing – exciting, romantic even. Characterful. Nasty little jerrybuilt semis (it wasn't fully detached, of course – we couldn't run to that) in Wembley are something else. I had to fight against a creeping conviction that we had jointly sunk – or do I mean risen? – to a level which somehow impugned our socialist ideals, rendering us practically petty-bourgeois. I never felt ashamed of living in Paddington. My mother would have relished the fun of that, as we did. But I secretly felt déclassé in Wembley. I was sure of this the first time I realised that I was glad my mother hadn't lived to see me there.

While I was developing a rat-trap mouth and some measure of control over my hands, which were itching to wrap themselves round Daniel's well-stretched little throat, two bad things happened more or less simultaneously. Cal's savings, on which we had been liberally falling back, gave out, and so did his back. Martin, God love him, kept the moving business just moving with one-man jobs for the several months I had Cal disc-slipped and raging with helplessness in one bedroom and Daniel shrieking in another, while George pottered about, loving living in a house with a garden and forgivably confusing the one with the other, taking all the cooking utensils outside and bringing most of the earth in. But then Martin got married and generally 'settled down' which effectively meant he was lost to us, because his wife expected a good deal more, financially speaking, of her man than I did of mine and shoehorned him into a steady job. We still saw him (them) from time to time, but it wasn't anything like the same. And, when it turned out that Cal's back-weakness was permanent, something had to be done. And that was when I turned to my only known talent, which was words.

Someone I knew put me on to Mills and Boon. My first reaction was umbrage. I tried to read their books and couldn't, and then the bills started piling up and I tried again and found I could. Next I tried writing one. It was awful. I mean, really bad. I tried another, and that wasn't much better. I'm not pretending I finished them, I just tried. At last I made an appointment with one of their executives, and she told me that what I had to do was take a suitable writing name and begin to think of myself as that sort of person. Like acting, a bit, not that I can act. But just as I'd been able to project myself into the situation of having my leg off, even though I hadn't, I thought perhaps I could project myself into being Cynthia Smooch or whoever. But, when I said that tentatively to the publisher's woman, she looked shocked and said whatever happened I mustn't take a flippant attitude to the writing of romances or they would never come right. Cynthia Smooch was a *silly* name. I must choose a sensible, beautiful name, like – well, like Drucilla Summers. I said that was the most idiotic name I'd ever heard. She smiled thinly and said I had better go away and forget it.

But I couldn't forget it because we began to get really

strapped. Cal felt *terrible* because, though the pain got better, he was forbidden to lift heavy things and so he was planning to beg back into the banking rat-race and looking as if he'd rather jump off Battersea Bridge. I didn't want him to be unhappy, and I didn't want him to be out all the time because he was the only person who could stop Daniel being a fiend. Daniel responded to him, but only when he, Cal, wasn't tensed. Also, Cal was a wonderful cook, and apart from that the house and garden were practically derelict and I needed him to do just about everything to both of them. Between eight and five I wanted him home and happy, not out and miserable.

So I went into a corner and thought about names and finally I came up with one which was soppy but which I liked, the way one likes certain soppy films or pieces of music. I'm not revealing it because someone might read the books I wrote, and continue to write, under that name. I'm not ashamed of them. Not exactly. One ought not to earn one's living by means one finds shameful. I've thought a lot about it and I've almost decided that I don't have to be ashamed, that my writing is giving a lot of pleasure, that there's no harm in it, that within the genre my books are better than most and while I'm writing them I am able to convince myself that the events are happening and that the characters are real people.

So what is there to feel ashamed of? *Nothing.* So why haven't I ever told anyone whose good opinion I care about, that I do this? Except Cal of course, he has to know, but I've sure as hell never, ever let him catch a glimpse of one of them. I lock them up like severed heads. The boys know that Mum 'writes books for ladies' (of late I've changed it to 'books for women' though somehow that sticks in my throat too – after all, I'm a woman and I wouldn't read them, not for choice). So that lets *them* out, little male chauvinist piglets that they are. The whole business (and I use the word advisedly) has always caused me intense inner problems. The fact that I've just invested nearly £3,000 in a word processor and printer, complete with all the floppy trimmings, which should make me feel better about it *somehow*, has only made everything worse because now I can turn out

14

four books a year with as little effort as I formerly took to write three.

Effort. There. That's the key to much of my disquiet. It's become effortless, and writing shouldn't be. My first (I nearly said my real) book was written in blood, sweat and tears. Now I sit down for a regular three-hour stint most days and out it pours. I see it coming up in those little eerie green letters on the screen and wonder where it's all coming from and feel like a conduit running between that costly machine and some over-embellished silver-gilt cornucopia on a chypre-scented pink cloud somewhere.

It isn't me. It isn't me.

I'd better face it. I'm going to try and write the story of Mariolain and Niels, not only because I feel strongly about it and about them, but for myself. Any *real* writer would say, so what? What else does any writer write for but himself? But since my leg-off book *I've* never written for myself. I've written for us, my family, Cal and me and the boys. And the gerbils and the goldfish and Jonas the dog who eats enough to keep me in hairdos, if I ever had any. I've waited years because I was scared, scared that I wouldn't have the depth, the *quality* to do it justice, because it's a much bigger subject than just one marriage. It goes back a long way and it'll go forward a long way. I can already see it going forward in their children, whom I've just seen for the first time since that fateful Easter holiday. I see now that Cal is right when he says that the worst thing about wars is not the casualties that happen on the battlefield, but the ripples going out from them, on and on toward some shore so impossibly remote in terms of time that effectively it doesn't exist.

Chapter 3

We made arrangements concerning the dog and gerbils and goldfish, piled our cold-weather clobber in the boot and set out for Harwich. The boys were very good for the first part of the journey because they were looking forward passionately to the boat-trip (their first). But the boat proved a disappointment after its lightning nose-to-tail exploration was completed and they then demanded diversions. Diversions, on a boat! It was one of those times when I looked at my sons and wondered whether they were really related to me. Unnatural as this may seem to talented mothers (I mean, of course, women who have a talent for motherhood) these moments of alienation have recurred at frequent intervals ever since Daniel was born. (George was perfect only until then.) By the time we went to Holland, when the boys were thirteen and eleven, I could hardly remember anything about either of them that remotely resembled perfection. Being the same sex and not far apart in age, they were enemies and rivals when together and united only in opposing anything I wanted from them. During most of their growing up I lived for night-time, not simply for the rest, peace and silence that attended the boys' eventual falling asleep, but because of the gentle inflow of my motherlove, which trickled gradually and healingly back to fill the emptied lock left by the noise and turmoil that seemed to expel

16

all vestige of recognisable love during the hours of daylight. Of course by the same token I thrilled to school hours and shrank before the holidays.

We disembarked at the Hook what seemed like a week later (at Dutch snack-bar prices it cost like a week too), all in our various ways apprehensive about the coming drive to Amsterdam. Our family has never been good in cars. First of all because, for some reason I have never been able adequately to explain or excuse, I cannot drive, so all the driving, all our married life, has been done by Cal. Thus he always worries before long journeys that he will get sleepy or cranky and that he will then begin to resent me for not being able to take over. I have the same anxieties in mirror-image. George, at that time, worried that he would be car-sick – *we* worried about that, too – while Daniel worried frenziedly that he would be bored. Daniel's boredom-threshold was preternaturally low – he often reached it after about three minutes of inactivity or lack of outside distractions – and the results for all of us do not bear writing about. (He is marginally better now.)

However, on this occasion we managed all right. The sun was out for one thing, which it hadn't been in England, and what with the dykes and the blossom and the superabundance of water and the different shape to the houses, plus a well delineated road system which helped Cal with the driving and me with the navigating, the journey passed pleasantly. We stopped once to attend to a slipping suitcase on the roof and once for a meal (Tourist Menu – "*Apple sauce* with sausage! UGH!" But there were chips), arriving at Hilversum as evening fell.

At this point I was abruptly, and (typically) belatedly aware that the enterprise was fraught with risks. After all, Mariolain and Niels were effectively strangers to us. Our children might hate their children quite as violently as they often seemed to hate each other, and now I came to think about it, which incredibly I only did when we'd already reached Hilversum and were hunting for the address, how were they going to talk to each other? I hoped that the Dutch kids spoke a bit of English, because nothing was surer than that ours couldn't say so much as piss off, which they'd

17

just joyfully arrived at in their native tongue, in Dutch.

Anyway, I was far too tired to do more than give such potential hazards an anxious thought, because here was the street, and here ("Holy shit, I thought you said they were hard up?") was the house.

It was beautiful. Not magnificent, though God knows it would have made three or four of our Wembley establishment, but beautiful. White-painted board with a green tiled roof, a portico'd porch, three storeys and a half-basement, and all sorts of little odd bits sticking out, including several balconies and a half-circular turret effect on one corner with a pointed roof and a weathercock on top. All the windows, instead of net curtains, had a living curtain of green trailing leaves from houseplants of every sort set on shelves across the middles of the windows. The front door was old oak with brass studs. And there was a lovely big garden on three sides.

"It's like a castle!" said George, looking at the turret and the door.

"No it's not," said Daniel, looking at everything else.

The oak door opened and there was Mariolain running to meet us, trailing kids.

Of course she wasn't fat. She'd just put on that bit of weight most normal women do after childbirth. It suited her. She hadn't changed at all, really. Her hair was still that wonderful russet red, short and curly, though when she came near enough I saw the touch of grey at the roots just before she hugged me. When she drew back though, and we looked into each other's eyes, I saw something different there, something I didn't like. Not that I didn't like *in* her, but about her – stress, hidden things. Masked pain. It scared me and I must have reacted.

"I know," she whispered under her breath. "Don't say." She hugged me again, and breathed into my ear. "I will tell you everything, but just now, pretend."

The next patch of time was the usual chaos of introductions. "This is Anna and this is Pieter – " "This is George and this is Daniel – " Staunch Dutch hands were stretched out, blue Dutch eyes were unshyly levelled; limp English hands shook and retired behind squirming backs, brown

18

Anglo-American eyes were uneasily averted. Then Anna and Pieter led the way up the steps into the house.

At once we all felt better. It was that kind of house. If the outside was beautiful and intriguing, it was nothing to what awaited us inside. Cal-the-places-person gazed round in a way I've never seen him gaze round anywhere except a completely vacant field or the empty reaches of the ocean. I was astonished. It seemed there *were* man-made locations to which he reacted as instinctively as he did to untrammelled nature. And in this case I saw why.

It is very hard to achieve absolute beauty and integrity of design in a house without calling in the professionals, and then the result never seems to belong to the people who paid for it. No designer had had his hand on this place, I could see – it was too handpicked, too organic, too lived-in. All this is the stranger because of what I learnt later about the marriage, because if ever I saw a home which bore every evidence of having been lovingly put together by two talented, artistic, unconventional people who loved it and each other and saw eye to eye in all matters of taste, it was that one. (This is one reason why romance-books are such rubbish. You have to make everything tidy and consistent.)

The hall was large and had plenty of hanging and storage space, none of which obscured the main wall, on which was a striking mural featuring exotic birds and flowers in Gauguin-esque colours. Among the flora and fauna, in naive perspective, appeared Niels, Pieter and Anna, not just once but in various places, at various ages and engaged in different activities. Pieter, unmistakable although with much blonder hair than he had now, could be seen as a plump four-year-old up a hugely flowering tree, reaching for a stranded kitten whose come-and-save-me mew stretched its mouth into a big pink diamond. Anna was below, playing croquet with Niels; the hoop was another cat, or perhaps the kitten grown up, standing obligingly with arched back. Another Niels was off in a corner digging a trench, while Anna, aged about nine, followed on her knees dropping in knobbly potatoes with worried faces and shoots coming out of their ears. In the distance was the house, with Anna waving from the turret window and Pieter again, sitting on the steps with a book.

Other people, friends and relations no doubt, were to be descried, strolling on the lawns or having tea under the trees or playing games with the family and an assortment of pets. There was no sign of Mariolain.

Of course I only had a chance to look closely at this painting, and take in its implications, later. As we passed through the hall that first evening, it was nothing but a huge eye-catching mass of colour, but its ambience prepared us for the big living-room we were led into, the room which caused Cal to stop in his tracks and let out one of his rare accolades, a little grunt of joy. The boys pushed past us and, after a brief pause, began buzzing round the room like bluebottles, all but bumping into the many fascinating objects they found.

The room was double-ended, with a bow window full of leaves looking to the front and french windows at the far end leading to the back garden. The ceiling was high and had crossed beams and the floor was sand-polished, that beautiful reddish colour old pine boards go, partly hidden by a collection of rugs ranging from old Persian to new Spanish. The walls were papered with a lovely greeny print like a spring forest with occasional delicate white birds flying through it. All the woodwork was white except the doors, which were stripped and rubbed to a gloss with wax, which you could smell. Near the french windows almost from ceiling to floor hung a huge elaborately-woven wicker bird-cage of the kind made in the Far East, with four or five brilliantly coloured birds in it. They were made of glass and the setting sun shone through them, turning them to jewels and casting spots of jade and ruby and sapphire light onto the floor and walls.

There was an assortment of furniture, all unusual and beautiful, some looking antique and some obviously modern, and a number of other fascinating *objets trouvés* (and *achetés*). But the main feature of the room was the fireplace. It stood in the front half, away from any wall, on a sort of white pillar which opened out into the petals of a huge flower. The fire itself was made on a grate half-hidden in the flower, and over it was an answering lily-like shape

20

upside down to catch the smoke. The stem of this lily, appropriately painted green, and with fairly graceful metal leaves winding down it, formed the chimney pipe. It vanished into the ceiling, which was dark brown, like earth. Following the lily-chimney into its upside-down bed gave me a strange feeling of inversion as if the world were all around us instead of only under our feet.

I'm aware, rereading this, that the fireplace sounds affectedly art deco. It wasn't. It might have been, if some interior designer had had it manufactured and put it there arbitrarily as part of his pre-ordained Scheme. But this had obviously been hand-made, if not actually by Niels and Mariolain, by some friendly neighbourhood blacksmith. The children had helped in the painting of the lily leaves, and their hands could be seen in quite a number of other items around the rooms, including several framed pictures and clay artifacts, none of which were as awful as most children's school artwork. One embroidered representation of the sun, in bright yellow, pink and orange, contributed to the vividness of the room. I found out afterwards Anna had done it almost alone as a birthday-present for Niels.

The two Dutch children were standing in the doorway, bright-eyed, watching our reaction. Anna now said, in very reasonable English, "You like our house?"

"And how!" said Cal-the-taciturn before I could speak. "In fact this room is just too much."

"He means he likes it," I explained.

"What's this? What're these? Can we ride the horse?" chorused George and Daniel. For them, the main attraction was a gorgeous unpainted rocking-horse which stood at the garden end, its layered and dovetailed hardwood body echoing the glowing polished boards under it. Its face was a msterpiece of galloper art, with stern bunched brows below pricked ears, and wrinkled lips showing wild slabby teeth. Its flaring nostrils were the only painted part – deep red inside. The mane and tail, instead of being of hair, were also carved wood, stylised, the smooth clumps twisting and flowing over each other. I didn't blame my two for standing there in a daze of admiration, irresistibly stroking and feeling.

21

"We don't ride on him now we are big. He is for look at," said Anna.

She firmly removed Daniel's exploring finger from up the painted nostril as if he had been picking his own nose.

"Who made him?" Cal asked Mariolain.

"Oh," she said, "I don't know. He isn't old. He was the star for one of Niels's commercials. Afterwards Niels bought him for the children. But he is really mine."

Pieter asked her to repeat this in Dutch and when she did he jumped up and down saying (I gathered) that he wasn't hers, he was theirs. Mariolain smiled and answered him and he crowed derisively and ran the length of the room, rammed the French windows open with both hands and exited with a flying leap down three steps into the garden.

"Go on," said Cal to our two. "You go too."

They glanced at each other and then at us, decided they couldn't make a stand in front of strangers and finally trailed away reluctantly.

"What did you say to him?" I asked Mariolain. "About the horse."

"I just said horses and other animals belong to the people who are good to them. I am the one who puts polish on him and invisibly mended his ear when Pieter knocked it off."

"By that rule, all our animals belong to me," I said grimly.

"What have you got?" she asked, like a little girl.

I enumerated the goldfish and the gerbils and the dog and was getting on to the rat (which is a very long, sad story) when Cal cut in. He was bursting with things to ask. They were all connected with the room and its contents. He actually took Mariolain by the elbow and began piloting her around her own premises, asking, like the boys, "What's this? Where did you get that?" So uncharacteristic was all this that I had an odd feeling I would shortly hear him asking if he could play with the glass birds or have a ride on the horse, so I said, aside, to Anna, "Look, why don't you show me where we're going to sleep?" Her little pointed face brightened. "Yes! Why we don't?" And she bore me, and a surprising amount of our luggage, upstairs.

Upstairs was as good as downstairs, if nothing like as tidy. If it had been, I think I would have turned against the whole house, because very orderly homes (which contain children) give me a terrible sense of inferiority. While my children were very young, and before we could afford someone to come in and clean, I used to believe that the chief reason friends seemed to enjoy coming to our home was because its state made them feel so much better about their own. I don't blame the kids. At least, I didn't until they were old enough to share the load and signally failed to do so. And nobody forced us to have that stream of animals, hopping, scampering, crapping, peeing, clawing and shedding hair all over the carpets, walls and furniture.

There was nothing sordid about the untidiness in Mariolain's house. It was just normal human muddle, which displayed signs instantly recognisable to a housewife that it was no more than a day or two deep. The children's rooms moved me to swiftly-repressed envy, bearing as they did signs of active minds as well as bodies, and being above all full of *books*, articles which merely gather dust on the shelves of our boys. Anna's room was in addition deliciously feminine.

I must admit at this point that I frequently feel very outnumbered as a woman in our household. If I had contrived a daughter to keep me company – someone who might not jeer if I burst into song in the kitchen, or tears in sad films, with whom I could have chats – I'm sure I wouldn't be so ill-tempered. Sometimes I feel as if I were expected to be a sort of imitation male, and, pressed into this role, I even find myself fulfilling it. As soon as I saw Anna's room with its gaily painted furniture and every vertical and horizontal surface encrusted with feminine objects, I knew at once that, whoever might fail to get on with whom in her family or mine, I was going to get along with Anna.

"I love your room," I said. "What a lot of pretty things. This is nice – " I paused beside a kind of frame made of dark wood, hanging on the wall like a three-dimensional picture. It had about twenty little partitions, each containing some tiny object: a minute painted vase, a shell, a brass gnome, a miniature Spanish doll, a costume ring, a butterfly made of beads.

"It's my collection," said Anna, looking pleased. "I collect from when I am five years. When Papi goes away, he brings me things, and Mami makes and paints."

Pieter's room was bigger than Anna's. Apart from the books and some more normal boyish impedimenta, it boasted a model train set-up with tressels. I could see Niels's hand in a lot of the detail, but it was all a bit dusty and neglected-looking now.

"My boys will love this," I said.

"Pieter will show them, but he will not let them play."

"Why?"

She shrugged. "He is like that. He is tired of his trains now, but he won't let another child. Also they are broken."

"Maybe Dan could fix them. He's good with electric things." I stood a train upright on the track and urged it along. "Couldn't your Dad fix it?"

"Papi is tired of it too. He get tired very quick of toys."

A thick column passed vertically through the room. It was warm to the touch. "What's this?"

"It come from the fire." Of course! The chimney pipe. What an endlessly intriguing house.

Cal and I were to sleep in the attic, reached by steep open-backed steps. It had a skylight on one plane of the roof and a poke-bonnetted dormer in the other. I stood at this, looking over the red and green rooftops. I felt mysteriously at peace and glad we'd made the effort, whatever came of it . . .

"Can I open?"

Anna received my nod and opened my case. Its contents were unexciting enough, but she seemed to enjoy helping me to unpack and put things away in a lovely old chest-of-drawers, thickly painted with flowers.

"I love this," I said, admiring the handles to the drawers which each represented a fat daisy.

"My mother did do it."

"Did she do the painting in the hall, too?"

"Her and me. I helped. She draw the flowers and leaves and I put the paint."

"And the people?"

"They are us. And special friends."

She helped me hang my dresses on hangers and put them

24

away in a wardrobe pushed in under the slope. The bed was wide and old-fashioned, with a big wooden head that you could sit up against. We'd bought a cheap divan, which slithered, a decision I spent years regretting. This bed had a thick white cover on it with a fringe, and masses of pillows. Anna put the suitcase underneath and then sat and bounced.

"It's a nice bed. Pieter and me sleeped here on Christmas when we were small."

"Only at Christmas?"

"Yes. For St Claus." I looked my question. She pursed her lips in a characteristic way she had when she thought you were being slow, and explained. "We think then that he can't drop presents down that small – " she gestured – "you know, the green one, downstairs, and that he is so fat he break the – " Her hands were busy showing me, as if I were deaf. Her movements were delightfully graceful and precise, she hardly needed to talk – Santa's bulk, the narrow chimney pipe, the lotus-like fireplace, all were expressed with turning, flowing hand and arm movements. "In our bedrooms, we have no fire, no . . . Here is a big – " She walked to the attic fireplace and gestured a large, square chimney above it. "Down this he can easy. So we put our – " She raised a leg.

" – Stockings – "

"No! Shoes – in the fireplace, with straw, and wait, and stay awake, but then we cannot more awake. And always he would take the straw and leave us presents!" She finished with a dancing look.

Just then I heard Cal from below. "Sue!"

Anna and I exchanged a look of complicity, as if we'd been hiding together, and went downstairs.

Chapter 4

———— ✸ ————

That night we all had dinner together, the eight of us. Niels
came late, but when he came he was every inch the good
host, making a great deal of small talk, opening wine for us
and fussing because it was 'not *chambré*', while Mariolain
and Anna dished up the spaghetti bolognese. The sauce was
delicious, but different from mine, slightly sweet and nutty.
Later I discovered she augmented the mince with lots of
grated carrot, and that she eschewed garlic because Niels
didn't like it.

Our boys sat together (ever a mistake) and eyed the
Dutch pair warily. Every now and then Daniel would give
George a kick under the table to set him off. I had to deal
with this as best I could because Cal was at the far end and
deep in conversation with Niels about the technicalities of
filming commercials. It was not a topic I would have
expected him to show the slightest interest in, but it seems
that a number of the more intriguing items in the house,
besides the wooden horse, had originated in commercials
that Niels had worked on (or had come across in the course
of his work, which took him abroad a lot) and this had
temporarily raised Cal's low opinion of TV advertising, as a
career anyway. At home he regarded the ads with obsessive
nausea, and would drive the boys wild by leaping up to
switch over for the few minutes they lasted. This usually led

to one or other getting hooked on whatever was showing on the channel he switched to, and refusing to let him switch back. This in turn often led to violence.

Mariolain sat on one side of me, Daniel on the other. Striving to restrain Daniel's far-side (George-side) leg without moving a muscle above table level, which involved swivelling my arm out at right angles while keeping my elbow glued to my side, I tried to give my attention to Mariolain.

"It is so good for him to have an older man to talk to," she murmured. She had a trick of talking so that only one person could hear, like an actor carrying on a conversation on stage between his lines. "All his friends are so young. And most of them are so silly."

"Are they all from the studios?"

"No. Yes. I'm not sure. I can't always tell which is which. There are so many, they change so often. He brings them here in crowds. I am introduced to them and then they have a big party and go away and I don't see them again. Or if I do, I don't recognise them, and if it turns out that I have met them, Niels gets very annoyed. But they all seem so alike, they all talk gossip and nonsense, at least it is nonsense to me. Does Cal gossip?"

"Never," I said.

Mariolain gave a little sigh.

"I think I wish that Niels was a little more serious in his mind," she said. It sounded strange to hear her say this in her rather floaty, little-girl voice which had not changed at all from the time she was seventeen.

I never, ever criticise Cal to other people. It is one of my few good points. I was thus able to say without hesitation, "Oh, Cal is very serious-minded," without even being tempted to add: I wish he were a little more frivolous. The gossipy parties sounded rather fun to me. Writing books, even bad ones, does not tend to bring one into contact with shoals of lively, chatty people. More's the pity . . . I glanced down the table (a lovely old Dutch refectory one) at Cal, talking earnestly with Niels, and tried to imagine him coming home like the Pied Piper trailing a glittering comet's tail of amusing people all waving bottles and looking set for a

27

good time, but I couldn't.

"What are your friends like?" I asked, releasing Daniel's leg long enough to butter another roll. I was having to eat my spaghetti with my left hand. George was shovelling his down with his nose poised about three inches above his plate. Daniel, released from bondage, gave him a hard knee-nudge which caused his rising laden fork to come into contact with his face, which emerged red with sauce. I delivered a short, sharp pinch to Daniel's nearside arm.

"What did you say?" I then asked.

"I said, I really haven't very many."

"Many what?" I asked, having forgotten my own question.

She smiled at me with heart-touching brightness. "Friends."

I stared at her. "How can that possibly be?" I asked her.

"Oh," she said, "I don't think it's because I'm not a friendly person."

"Of course it isn't!"

"I think it's because I am nearly always at home."

"Why are you?" I persisted.

"Well," she said, "for a lot of reasons. For one thing I still have asthma, and some other allergies which often make it difficult for me to breathe easily. Then I get very bad headaches."

"Migraine?" I asked, appalled. My mother used to suffer from migraine.

She nodded, and at the same moment called down the table, "Who would like more spaghetti?" The spaghetti was housed in a large Pyrex bowl, so it was obvious to anyone who looked that there wasn't much left.

"Me!" shouted Daniel.

"Me!" shouted George simultaneously.

Cal glared. I flushed. Mariolain smiled, without a trace of maternal smugness.

"I like big appetites," she remarked. "My two eat so little, and they are such fussies about their food." Pieter didn't understand, but Anna did. After Mariolain had generously served my two bottomless pits, Anna held out her plate almost defiantly.

"I will have more, Mami," she said.

"You haven't finished what you have," said her mother.

"It's only the onions – "

"That's what I mean. Clean your plate, like Sue's boys."

These four speeches were of course in Dutch, but I understood them easily because on this level mother-and-child talk has an international quality. Anna put her plate back in front of her and bent her head. Her dark, straight hair swung forward to hide her face. After a second she took her fork in her hand and started resolutely tackling the onions.

As soon as the sun had gone down, it had become very cold, and I had then noticed that there was no central heating in the house. Both Cal and I had put on warm sweaters before dinner, and our boys had complained to us that their room (on the floor below our attic, next to Pieter's) was freezing. I told them not to fuss, but it was true – our attic was colder still, but there was a little electric fire up there that could be plugged in. Cal had done this immediately, when we went up after dinner, but I was worried about it, and when we were ready to leave the room, I switched it off.

Cal said, "Leave it on, why don't you. There's no electric blanket."

"I don't think we ought to waste their electricity," I said.

"Oh, come on . . . They're obviously loaded."

"On the contrary," I said sharply, "they're quite obviously strapped."

"I don't know why you say that. The whole house is stuffed with treasures. Did you notice the glass and cutlery, and those extraordinary plates? I think they're old ironware. And Niels has a fantastic collection of ivory miniatures. Apart from – "

"Cal," I said, "beautiful objects don't necessarily imply a lot of available cash."

"They damn well would with us."

There was a minute pause. He hadn't said 'us' for a long time. Then I said, "If they had loose money, they'd do all sorts of things to this place. Mariolain may seem a little vague but she's got a very practical nature underneath. How does she manage with a fridge so old it looks as if it should have a block of ice in its belly – for instance?"

"There's nothing wrong with this house," said Cal truculently. "It's perfect."

"Perfectly enchanting. Not perfectly comfortable."

"Maybe you'd rather shog off back to our little wooden hut?"

"Well, at least it's warm." I caught his eye. It used to be our joke that our home was so small that four people breathing in it obviated the need for further heating.

"Any other complaints?"

I sighed impatiently. He was only ever obtuse on purpose.

"I'm not *complaining*," I said. "I'm deducing. There's very little of what your dad would call liquidity around here, that's all I'm saying. Niels's career is hanging fire."

"And all the treasures?"

"Inherited. I bet you. Niels has all the earmarks of a rich man's son."

"You mean he's spoilt rotten, like me?" Cal, as an ideological egalitarian, is naturally a bit touchy on this subject. But there was an added note of defensiveness, possibly on Niels's behalf.

"I wonder if he's really in a position to collect ivory and rocking horses, while his wife has to cook in a kitchen out of the ark," I said. Then, trying to redress the balance by saying something nice, I remarked, "The kids are very sweet, anyway."

He glared. I knew at once I'd said the wrong thing again.

"*Sweet*? Well, *chacun* on that one, I must say! Pieter's got the makings of a howling neurotic."

"*Huh*?"

"That maddening perpetual sniffling – "

"Probably an allergy – "

"And drumming the table the whole time – William Tell Overture, wasn't it? As for that Anna, she's a right little crawler! Catch Daniel forcing down his onions just because his mum told him to."

So that was it. Every time I ventured to say a good word

about someone else's kids, Cal took it for granted I was comparing them unfavourably to ours.

"Listen, Cal," I said bluntly. "I think we shouldn't backbite while we're here."

"Who the hell's backbiting? Maybe we'd just better not *talk* if you think normal conversation's backbiting."

I said nothing. I switched everything off and we went down the stairs. Backwards. I was glad I'd put on tights, because Pieter was at the bottom.

"Goodnight," he said, and put out his hand. I shook it somewhat bemusedly.

"Are you going to bed?"

"Yes, sleep now," he said, and gave a juicy sniff. Cal nudged me, not matily.

I looked at my watch. It was barely quarter to nine.

"Already?"

He nodded and went into his room. Anna came up the main stairs.

"Are you going to bed too?" I asked incredulously. She said she was. A deep guilty anxiety came over me and I glanced uneasily at my fellow-parent.

"It wouldn't hurt ours to get an early night for once," he said blandly.

"Who's going to make them, you or me?"

"If the others are going, perhaps they'll just tag along."

"At a quarter to *nine*? You must be joking!"

We proceeded down to the big living-room. The lily-fire had been lit before dinner and was now in full blaze, throwing warm fiery patterns all round the room. The glass birds in their cage coruscated. All the vivid patterns and colours in the room took on a new charm by fire and lamp-light.

Niels had drawn up an assortment of seating. There was a lovely hooded basket chair which hung from the ceiling, already in position; I headed for that, but was deflected to a white-painted wicker chair with peppermint green cushions and padded arm-rests. As soon as I had sat in this, Niels brought up a wooden footstool and a small metal and glass table, to which he soon added a twinkling glass of crème de menthe. Definitely not my drink in the normal course of events, but it matched the chair and my mood. I felt entirely

31

different here. I watched to see what Cal would be given. It was one of Niels's rich-man's-son attributes that he didn't ask people what they wanted, but just bestowed. When a schooner of advocaat was presented to Cal, I winced. He has been known to refer to it as a faggot's drink. I saw him turn the glass about in his small, hairy hands as if not sure what it was meant for, and then, out of good manners, take a minute sip. An expression of some surprise crossed his face. A short time later, the glass was empty. Evidently the otherness of the house was getting to him, too. Amazing. Perhaps before long I would come upon him surrounded by Niels's frivolous young friends, waving bottles and gossiping with the best . . . I stifled a giggle and buried my nose in my bilious liqueur.

Just then our boys came trailing in from the dining-room where they'd been playing some table game.

"Where are the others?" asked George.

Niels said, "They've gone to bed."

George looked at Daniel and Daniel looked at George. Then they both looked at us and burst into derisive laughter.

"*So early!*" Daniel guffawed.

The otherness which I had been relishing a moment before evaporated and I was right back to the bedrock of motherhood. For one or two rather lengthy seconds I found myself entertaining the shameful wish that we had dispatched the boys on some kind of well-supervised adventure holiday and come to Hilversum *by ourselves*.

I looked at Cal meaningfully and he said, "What's wrong with an early night, boys?" but so mildly (the advocaat?) that the best-trained child on earth wouldn't have taken it seriously.

"How can they go to sleep at nine o'clock?" jeered Daniel. "They must be babies!"

Mariolain, who had just come into the room from the kitchen, said in her sweetest tone, "Well, that is what time they go to bed at holidays. In the term they go at half-past eight."

This intelligence was greeted with incredulous, almost awed silence. George recovered first, and lost no time in betraying to the utmost our failure to run a tight ship.

32

"*We* don't *ever* go to bed before eleven," he said.

This was an outrageous lie and I said so in tones I would have thought conveyed unmistakable displeasure. But our boys have an unfailing instinct for the occasions when we will not be able to lean on them because of the presence of those before whom we don't wish to make ugly scenes.

"At weekends, half-past," asserted Daniel smugly, pushing his luck.

Cal unexpectedly set down his schooner and stood up.

"When in Rome," he said portentously, and bore down on them.

They gaped at him. "Rome? I thought we were in Holland," said George blankly.

"Say goodnight, boys," said Cal firmly, shepherding them to the door.

For a moment I forgot all the pain of our estrangement and remembered that I had once adored him. In no time at all the boys had gone and the status quo ante had been restored. I sank back in my peppermint chair and sipped my peppermint liqueur and felt peace and unadulterated adulthood steal over my travel-weary being like balm.

Mariolain sat in the hanging chair, put on some granny-glasses and took up a large sewing basket. Niels brought her a drink – apricot brandy I think. Putting out feelers again, I was surprised by all this liquor. Expensive stuff, and in apparently endless variety. Perhaps I'd been wrong about their finances. It was only later I discovered that pretty-coloured liqueurs were one of Niels's little weaknesses. He found them irresistible in duty-free shops and never left an airport or arrived at one without buying a new kind. He also had other little weaknesses, for old books, for instance. And there Mariolain sat, darning endless socks, something that, at our most straitened, I would never have bothered with. (With my mother, it had been washing handkerchiefs. "I wouldn't wash handkerchiefs," she once said to me, "for God.")

Niels had a drink that looked exactly like methylated spirit.

"It is really nice that you are here," he said in his expansive way. "I must say Cal is charming."

I blinked. Charming? Cal, charming? Cal is sturdy, practical, strong-minded, intelligent, witty in a dry Bostonian way, and (I seemed to recall) a wonderful lover. Instant, turn-on-able charm such as would appeal to the likes of Niels, however – that, not. I wouldn't have thought.

I had hesitated a moment too long while I considered all this. Niels was smiling at me in a know-it-all way. "Well, isn't he? Surely *you* think so!"

"No," I said. "No. Not charming." And heard myself add: "Which is okay by me because to be honest I don't trust charming men."

Niels looked very taken aback. If there was one thing he was quite sure he had, it was charm, and he knew I knew that, and he interpreted my remark, correctly, as an oblique put-down. Why I wanted to put down my kind host I can't exactly explain. It had something to do with Mariolain and the socks.

"Well," he said, rallying, "I don't know him as well as you do, of course. But I stick to my first opinion. And when he comes downstairs I am going to test him."

"How?"

"I am going to take him into my study and show him some nice things. The test will be his reaction. Does he like . . . " He leant towards me with such a gleam in his eyes that I thought for a moment he was going to say "dirty pictures" but instead he whispered with exaggerated relish, " . . . sword-sticks?"

"Sword-sticks?" I blinked. "I doubt if he's ever seen one."

"Good. First impressions. And I expect," he added, as Cal came down into the hall, "that you women would like to catch up."

I glanced at Mariolain and she gave me one of her warm, wonderful smiles which – like her unaltered and unaged voice – carried me straight back to our young time. And the minute the men were out of the room, like something switched on, she began to talk.

Chapter 5

———— ⌁ ————

We had to talk first, she said, about what we remembered of each other from our youth. We had to 'certify our memories'. That was how she put it. But it was her own she meant, because she at once began to recall, not Venice and the motoscarfia, the parties in the squares, the guitar music and all that, but the only other time we'd been together, not twenty-four years ago but nineteen – on my first and only previous visit to Holland. From her recollections, mine were revived.

I was in my middle twenties, and unwisely but too well in love with a ghastly man called Gordon. Gordon Forster. He actually had a twin brother called Norman. My mother, who loathed Gordon for making me so unhappy, referred to them with thinly-veiled contempt as *Naw*man and *Gaw*don. "And how are dear Nawman'n'Gawdon?" she would enquire acidly, as if they were joined at the waist. As they might as well have been, for they were all but inseparable. Interestingly, I hated Norman as much as I doted on Gordon, which, as they were 'identical', should have warned me.

Gordon was one of nature's takers. I squirm now when I remember my aberrant passion for him. I think I must have been very lonely and scared at the time. This was long before women were imbued with the conviction that they ought to be able to live without men, so when I met Gordon and felt the mesmeric pull of his 'need' – for everything from a bed partner to someone to iron his damned shirts – I succumbed to a primitive servile instinct which I hope the modern era has bred out of young able-bodied self-respecting women.

Gordon's excuse was that his life had been blighted by tragedy. A previous girlfriend had done herself in, bequeathing to her lover (according to him) a trauma of such depth that he was emotionally crippled for life. Of course this revelation – which I later discovered was a tissue of lies, or at least distortions – had the effect of driving me into a frenzy of devotion and desire to heal his wounds, by giving all and demanding nothing, which suited Gordon to a tee. For months on end he sat back and took, and took, and took, periodically allowing me to happen upon him in a fit of despairing yet manly tears to signal that his trauma was not yet sufficiently healed for him to be able to take me out to dinner, let alone to begin actually to love me back. It's shaming that I didn't notice how little effect his grief had had upon his appetites.

While in the throes of this unequal passion, it occurred to my saner self that a little jealousy might achieve something. So I pretended to Gordon that I was off to Paris to spend a weekend with a former lover (who unhappily had no existence outside my own imagination). Since Gordon made such insubstantial objections, I had to take myself off *somewhere*. So I thought of Mariolain – the only foreign acquaintance living close enough for me to afford the fare – and, after a desperate hunt through the detritus of my student days, I turned up her home address. Without much hope – after all, it was five years since I'd seen her – I wrote her a letter asking if I could visit her for a weekend. Then I made contingency plans (a kindly aunt in Petersfield) but they were not needed. Mariolain phoned me and said: come, come, you *must come*. Such enthusiasm, even from another girl, was golden balm at the time.

I set off on a beautiful bright day, in the nearest to high spirits I had experienced since Gordon. Through the train and boat trip (all interesting and even exciting, much more

so than flying) I dredged my memory for details of Mariolain. Her face and persona had not faded much, surprisingly,
as I hardly remembered anyone else from that holiday. Her
small, slight figure in its broderie-anglaise ruffled blouses,
scarcely whiter than her skin nor more strongly contrasted
with the primary colours of her skirts than with her bright
red hair and blue eyes, was still vivid in memory. But more
memorable than her appearance was her talent, her personality and her behaviour, and their effect on the rest of the
party.

I sat on deck staring at the sea and England's receding
coastline, seeing instead the multiple waters of Venice.
Although the youngest, Mariolain had been the centrepiece
of our group. Where she was, there was life and surge;
where she was absent, there was a lack, a filletedness, or
rather, a dull sobriety when what we wanted was to be
happily drunk. We never thought how we must have
exhausted her. We just sucked life and energy and music
from her heedlessly.

Sitting at the ship's rail, I remembered an occasion when
we were standing around her at an outdoor café, listening
and clapping while she sang, seeing her suddenly sink to the
ground as if she had been unplugged from her own energy
source. After a moment of shocked stillness, we converged
on her with cries of anxiety: "Mariolain, what's wrong? Get
up, please, get up!" – like children whose mother has
unbearably shown some sudden weakness. She gazed up at
us from her seat on the flagstones, her eyes as unseeing as
pebbles, until we laid hands on her. Then her white face
broke into a smile. "I am all right!" she said brightly. "I just
can't sing any more tonight, that's all." And she let herself
be helped up and fussed over.

It was not the only time this happened. Were these 'turns'
real or faked, or were they a little of both – a cry for
cosseting, petting and a show of our affection for her?
Whatever, she would be quickly cured, restored to herself
and ready to 'give out' to us again. Her need for this mass
demonstration was genuine, that I was sure of. And another
oddity came back to me as I thought about her. She caused
some speculation among the rest of us, because she avoided

being alone with anyone. Several of the boys fell in love with her and tried to cut her out of the crowd, but she would never go. She would let them sit near her as an adoring group, would walk between two of them arm in arm, would tease and flatter them gently, but more to hold them off than to attract them, so it seemed. When we crowded round to fuss over her, she would look at us gratefully, put out her hands to let them be held and stroked, moving like a little cat under our pats or caresses, even letting herself be hugged and kissed . . . But always by the mass, not by any particular person, and never alone.

Her father came to the station to meet me. Expecting Mariolain, I was startled when this short, slight, thickly bespectacled, grey-haired man appeared at my side and introduced himself. "Willem Dykstra." Dykstra? But Mariolain's name was Jansen. Yet I knew it must be her father because he had a faint look of her, mainly his pale skin and rather delicate bones. He was not a very male-looking man, yet he emanated a surprising toughness. He insisted on carrying my heavy suitcase to the car, which embarrassed me because he had a bad limp.

I enquired after Mariolain.

"She has not been too well. She must keep indoors. It's good you come, you will make her lively." Make *her* lively? Me? The other way round, more likely! "What's been the matter with her?" "Oh, nothing serious," answered her father, adding almost whimsically, "Sometimes young girls get their little illnesses from their heads."

Of course this struck a chill, but when I actually saw Mariolain, waiting for me in the doorway of their house with her lit-up face, when she embraced me and led me in, beginning instantly to chatter in the old way, I dismissed her father's odd and rather patronising remark.

But it was soon clear that she had changed. There was a new feyness. No, that's not the word. It's hard to describe it. Her voice, always light in timbre, had taken on a floating quality. Her gestures were girlish and at the same time a little eldritch – fingers bent and slightly apart, elbows away from her sides. Her eyes and mouth would open wide and her head would weave from side to side on her long, slim neck for emphasis. It looked affected, yet I knew that, despite her willingness to perform as a singer, she hadn't the ego or extrovertion of an actor.

With all this, she seemed curiously self-conscious and insecure. Sometimes, while we were talking, she would break off suddenly in the middle of a sentence and stare at me.

"I am boring you. You would rather do something else."

I was startled – how could I have given such a false impression? "No, Mariolain! Of course not. Do go on. You were telling me about your sister – "

She shook her head, which was flowerlike, a russet chrysanthemum. "You can't want to hear about my sister, you don't know her."

"Then tell me about yourself."

"There is nothing to tell about me. I stay at home and sometimes I am a little bit ill, and then I am better and go out shopping." She smiled brilliantly. "There, isn't that a wonderful story? No wonder you are not bored! Now I will stop talking utterly and you will tell me about you."

This was disconcerting. I had been listening with interest to the troubles of her sister, who, though only twenty four, two years older than Mariolain, was in the throes of a painful divorce, while still in the midst of her studies. But I felt compelled to follow Mariolain's lead in everything. That was part of the strangeness I sensed. I couldn't treat her quite as I treated other friends. I felt she wasn't robust enough for the ordinary rough and tumble of girl-talk. So I obeyed her, and began to tell her about my troubles.

To my chagrin, Mariolain seemed to find it impossible to take my passion for Gordon seriously. His name, for a start, struck her as irresistibly funny. She immediately pulled the same long-jawed, pop-eyed face Mother pulled, and echoed, in almost exactly my mother's mocking tones, "*Gaw*don *Faw*ster! Such a name! What does he look like?"

I took out a snap and reverently handed it to her. She took one look and burst into renewed giggles.

39

"Oh, Suky! Can you love a man with such a coat and such eyebrows?"

I snatched the photo back to have a look. I had never particularly noticed Gordon's eyebrows (though I had had to overcome an aversion to his yachting club blazer). I now saw that his brows took off from his high-bridged nose in an arched, supercilious line, echoed some inches lower by his mouth. He was handsome enough, but looking at the photo now, I suddenly saw what Mariolain saw. He looked what he was: sensual, greedy, slightly pompous and rather cruel. All that I had endured at his hands came abruptly into focus and I began to cry.

At once Mariolain was overcome with shame at her crassness in laughing at my beloved. She jumped up, made a little rush at me, stopped short as if coming into sight of a street accident, wrung her hands in agitation and began to circle my chair uttering distraught sounds. Her distress was so patent that it penetrated my own mood of misery and yanked me out of it. (That turned out to be the last time I ever cried over Gordon.)

This display of feminine feebleness on my part over, our friendship stood at a crossroads. I was very hurt by Mariolain's mirth. She had always given off kindness and tact like the scent of baking; I felt let down, disillusioned with her. Yet as the incident slipped behind us, it settled into a revised pattern of friendship. Mariolain was flawed like the rest of us, like the rest of us capable of the occasional gross insensitivity. Perversely, stung though I was, I ended up liking her the better for it.

Of course we ate with Mariolain's father. Then conversation became polite and general. There was a formality about the man, about his household, which was basically bourgeois, well-to-do, a touch complacent. At table we discussed such safe topics as the recent British general election, and then the less safe one of the royal families of our respective countries. Mr Dykstra – or rather, Professor Dykstra as Mariolain reminded me to style him – was a staunch loyalist to the House of Oranje.

"You don't remember the importance of the royal family during the war," he said. "It is in times of crisis that the rallying and inspiriting power of royalty shows itself, when a good king – or, as in our case, a queen – proves his worth to his people. I can never forget Queen Wilhelmina's broadcasts, or how we felt when she returned to us at the war's end, a visible sign that our terrible sufferings were over."

"Returned – ? So she wasn't here during the war?"

He glanced at Mariolain and pursed his mouth into a reproachful moue, as if to say: Who is this ignorant friend of yours?

"You know nothing of recent Netherlands history, then?"

"Or much of any other sort, I'm afraid," I admitted.

"That is a sad lack," he said gravely. "One cannot understand anything that happens, without some knowledge of what *has* happened."

"Please tell me about the queen," I said, to break a brief, uncomfortable silence. "Why did she leave? Our royals didn't."

Professor Dykstra laid down his linen napkin and regarded me through his thick glasses. Mariolain had also stopped eating. I felt an unaccustomed frisson. I knew I had been tactless – I think half deliberately: he had made me feel my lack of education rather sharply. But there was no reason to feel, for just a second, scared of him.

"Your royal family," he said slowly and heavily, "did not leave, because their country was not conquered. They did not have to endure occupation by a brutal and barbarous enemy, who would have killed them to stop them from doing what they were, fortunately for England, able to do throughout the war: fulfil their duty to keep their people proud and undespairing. That we can still hold up our heads in Holland is due to a relative few, who . . . "

He stopped. The atmosphere was crackling like damp air in a sudden frost, but then it thawed again, as he leant forward, picked up his wineglass and smiled.

"Well well, let us not go into that. History has great importance, but one should not be always talking about the past, especially when it is so tragic. Nevertheless, please join me in a toast."

My strange nervous alertness (I shouldn't call it fear) dissolved into the onset of embarrassment as he raised his glass. "To our Queen and her Prince," he said with deep intensity. We drank. And suddenly I heard myself say, a little awkwardly, "And to ours." And we drank again. It was a very odd moment.

After that we talked, I think, about my job, which at that time was behind glass in the out-patients' department of a large London hospital – hardly a vital role in the nation's life, but Professor Dykstra seemed to find it both interesting and laudable. He dropped his patronising manner and became sympathetic and – almost – charming.

After dinner he retired to his study, leaving Mariolain and me to wash the dishes. He kept a servant – a scurrying, mouselike little woman whom he treated, I thought, rather disdainfully, but he didn't overwork her. She cleaned and cooked the main meals, while Mariolain laid the table, made beds and washed up. The professor himself rather surprisingly did all the shopping. Mariolain explained seriously that this was because he didn't trust anyone else to take all the trouble necessary to find the right quality at the lowest prices.

It was clear that the professor, though not hard up, was the soul of thrift and prudence. He wouldn't tolerate waste of electricity, for instance, and before retiring to bed (which he did rather early) would go round the large living-room where Mariolain and I sat, and turn off every light except the one next to Mariolain. He did this in a whimsical, diffident way, as much as to say that if I thought him eccentric, or even a tightwad, he was sorry for it, but that he could not change his ways for any casual visitor.

This nightly ritual left me in semi-darkness and Mariolain in a soft little pool of light. The effect was to make us both subtly aware of her as the focus of attention. It was after her father's retirement to bed that the chief of our talking was done.

At first I thought that the fact that she had been unwell was the main reason why she seemed muted, compared to the bright lively fun-exuding creature I remembered. Later I began to wonder whether the girl I saw now was not the real Mariolain, and the Venice one some souped-up version, overlaid, falsified even, due to some artificial or at any rate temporary stimulus. Perhaps, freedom? Being away from this house, from school, from her father . . . ? I was guessing, speculating. It was impossible not to. Her father's presence applied pressures even on me. He was alien to me in a way that I couldn't have explained. The thought of being related to him or living for years in the same house with him made me uneasy. As I observed it over those few days, his relationship with his daughter made me uneasy too.

Of course I asked questions. "Why is your father's surname different from yours?"

"Oh, that is because I decided to take my mother's name. It is not official. He would never let me change it properly. I use the name Jansen when I do something of my own, like when I travel abroad, or when I write songs. Did you know I have had two songs on the radio? Perhaps one will be made to a record."

"How exciting, Mariolain! Will you play and sing it yourself?"

She grinned and tilted her head to one side, a mannerism she had. She always looked a little bit mad when she did it, what I call her fey look, but it was stranger than that.

"If I am well enough, I might."

"You haven't told me what's wrong with you."

"Oh, there are several things. I have asthma. I am annoyingly allergic to things that no-one can find out just what they are. I get headaches . . . Oh, don't let's talk about my health, it is too shaming and boring. My father talks all the time about my health and takes me to specialists. No, that's not true. Part of the time he does this. The other part, he tells me with some impatience that no-one finds anything really wrong with me and that all my small, tiresome troubles are sitting up here." She tapped her smooth white forehead under the petal-like red curls.

"That must be very upsetting," I ventured.

She shrugged. "I wish I were healthy and my own mistress – is that the English expression? Like you. I always envied you in Italy. You were so strong and certain of yourself." I gaped at her in comic astonishment. "Oh yes! All the best suggestions for exciting things to do came from you. For this I noticed you among all the others. You never followed, you

43

were always the leader. You were as brave as a boy, and yet you were a girl. I wished and wished to be in your head." After a moment's silence she added in her most floating voice, "I hate my head and I even more hate my body."

I was shocked.

"Mariolain, why? You're beautiful. And you're talented. *I* envied *you*. I'd give anything to be able to sing and play like you."

She looked thoughtful. "Yes," she acknowledged at last. "My music is something wonderful. I love it more than anything . . . It makes me, just sometimes, able to come out of my head and body and be somewhere else. It makes me happy."

"Aren't you happy at other times?"

She smiled her gently crazy smile again and said, "Oh yes, sometimes! Like now, I am happy now. I don't mean to sound sorry for myself. It's just that one can't help what one's body feels or what one's head remembers. Or even the other way round!"

While I was still trying to work this out, she changed the subject and began to talk animatedly about two of the boys who'd been in Italy with us. But her manner suggested to me that she was merely deflecting attention from herself. I felt myself worrying about her, about her inner state, her . . . *status*, here in her father's house. I can't say why, as he treated her perfectly well, but I couldn't avoid the feeling that she was not a free agent. At some point we talked about her coming to visit me in London. The idea excited her. She wanted to know all about my flat, what part of town it was in, whether it was near any interesting shops, how often I went to concerts and theatres. But there was an air of fantasy about the project. It was as if she knew it would never really happen.

I asked next about her mother, and knew immediately that I had trespassed somehow. It was not a subject she welcomed, but I pressed it a little because in Italy I had had the impression that she didn't have a mother.

"It's not something I talk about," she said.

"Are your parents divorced?"

"More than that."

"How can you be more than divorced?"

"They are – " She stopped, stared at me with a frown for a moment, and then got up and consulted a dictionary.

"They are sundered," she reported.

I decided not to pursue the distinction, intriguing though it was.

"When did that happen?"

"In the war."

"Strange," I digressed, "how your father talks about the war, as if it were still going on."

"Isn't it still going on, in England?" she asked seriously.

I laughed. "What do you mean? – Oh, there are quite a few men around who still haven't adjusted to civilian life – air force people chiefly. I saw a play recently about a man who – But in fact, no, I think ten years have been enough to heal our wounds more or less."

"That's because they were clean ones. The jagged, pusy-ones take longer."

"But you can't remember a lot about the war, surely, you were only a child."

" 'Only a child – !' Oh, Suky, you are funny. Children don't have wars and war-wounds, you think? Besides, even if I had not even been born for the war, I would know all about it because of my father's book."

"Oh! Has he written a book about it?"

"He has written *the* book about the war, at least, the war in Holland. It is very famous. Didn't you hear about it when it came out?"

"When was that?"

"Two years ago, in September 1954."

"He took his time then – writing it."

"Yes. It took fourteen years. He began it in notebooks as soon as the Nazis came. He hid them in the roof of our house."

"Here?"

"No. We lived in another town then, nearer to Amsterdam."

"What did he do in the war?" This was still a question one sometimes heard asked at home, the answer almost invariably being something in the forces. But, I realised before she answered, that in Holland it had to be different.

"He was in the Resistance."

"Really!"

She nodded. "He ran an underground printing press. And he kept a diver in his attic."

"A what?"

"A diver. That was what they called people who had to hide."

"Jews, I suppose."

"Not only. In the end the divers were nearly all just Dutchmen who didn't want to be sent to Germany to work."

"Your father must be a very brave man," I said.

Mariolain gave me an odd look. "Oh yes, he was a hero. You can know it from his book."

We talked a lot more than this, but these are the parts I remember.

On Sunday we actually went out. We visited Mariolain's sister, Irene.

Mariolain had told me that Irene and their father were not on speaking terms, though she didn't say why. We had to pretend we were going somewhere else. This bore out my suspicions about Mariolain's semi-subservient position in the house. The whispering, signals and code-words enjoined on me by the need for subterfuge embarrassed me, but Mariolain almost seemed to enjoy it all.

We went into the city centre by bus, allegedly on a sight-seeing trip for my benefit. The professor offered to drive me, but I said I always enjoyed bus-trips in strange cities. He gave orders that Mariolain was not to tire herself and that we were to be back before dark.

We sat at the front of the bus to give me a good view of Amsterdam. Mariolain seemed tense and avid, drinking in all the sights through eyes long deprived of change. Sometimes she would nudge me and exclaim, "Oh, look! Look, Suky, what a strange-dressed man . . . Look at that beautiful house, isn't it like a fairy-tale?" I was made to feel that by simply coming out with her I was giving her an extraordinary treat. And sure enough, just as we reached Irene's block of flats, she turned to me and said, "Thanks for bringing me out. He would never have let me come but for you."

"You sound as if he were your jailer."

"Oh, no! More my protector. It is for my sake, he says. And it's true I sometimes have attacks if I get tired. Then *he* has all the trouble to nurse me and take care of me, and that takes him away from his work."

We went up in a slow, creaky lift.

"What is his work?"

"He lectures at the university. And he travels, to give talks about his book."

"All that's still going on, after two years?"

"What do you mean, all that?" she asked, startled, it seemed.

"There's still such a lot of interest in it."

"Oh . . . Yes. The good part of the interest is going on longer than the bad part."

"There were people who didn't like it, were there?"

"There were people," she said, "who tried to kill him for it."

I'm pretty sure she said that, and said it then, because I was dying to ask more but we had reached Irene's door and after that we never got back to the subject.

Irene's flat was in chaos. She had a small son, aged about three, called Jan, who seemed to be hyperactive, and they were getting sorely on each other's nerves. The continual uproar, muddle and nervous tension didn't make it easy to get acquainted with Irene or form much of an opinion of her. But one thing was plain. She was nothing like Mariolain. She was tall and raw-boned, with the dark hair and wide, flat facial and body lines of some Dutch countryfolk.

Jan came by his vitality honestly: Irene was not just a bundle of nerves but a one-woman-band of activities. She had a study-area near the window, a desk heaped with books and papers, loose-leaves, jars of pens and pencils, a portable typewriter, a small filing-cabinet. The reading lamp was on, and even as she thrust a tray of coffee at us she was dashing to the desk to make notes and look things up, so that I felt uncomfortably that we were keeping her from her work.

"What are you studying for?" I asked after one of these forays.

"I'm trying to be a psychotherapist," said Irene briefly in the same breath shouting at Jan who, in charging across the room, had tripped over a flex, nearly braining himself with a falling iron.

Temperamentally, too, the sisters were at odds. At one point, when conversation was being rendered impossible by Jan racing back and forth across the room like a demented bluebottle, Irene took an infuriated swipe at him. He dodged. Mariolain caught him as he zoomed past her and scooped him into her lap. He struggled for a moment like a little wild thing, and then, reacting to a sense of warmth and firmness, visibly relaxed, snuggling against Mariolain and tucking his little blunt nose under her arm.

The sisters had been talking English for my sake, but Mariolain now said something in Dutch which I recognised as a mild remonstration. Irene answered her sharply and flounced out of the room. Mariolain gave me a sad little smile.

"Poor Irene," she whispered. "She is so upset just now. She is so afraid to be left alone with Jan, when her husband separates from her. This little boy is not easy anyway."

"So why did you tell her off?"

"I can't bear to see her hit him. It doesn't hurt him half as much as it harms her. But it's not much use me saying anything. I can't affect things, I am not with her enough."

Later, when we had left and were walking by a different route back to the bus, she suddenly said, "You mustn't think Irene and I don't love each other. When things are wrong for one of us – like her, now, with the divorce – it is as if the other one had stomachache all the time. I feel bruised for her. And I miss her, I miss seeing her. But still when I am with her we sometimes quarrel. It was always, always like it, when we were children too, even in the worst times."

We walked in silence under an overcast sky. I was still enjoying the buildings, admiring their beautiful gables; Mariolain however now had eyes only for shop windows. Suddenly she stopped.

"Oh, I am so sorry!" she cried out, quite angrily for her.

"Sorry? What for?"

"That it's Sunday and the shops are all closed! It would be so nice to go in and buy you something. I want to buy you a lovely present to take back to your flat, to remember me until I come! I know, I'll give you a warmer. You know, what you admired, that little white china thing with the nightlight inside, to stand the teapot on. You'll use it at home and keep a little light burning for me."

On impulse I took her arm. "Then perhaps you'll tell me. About the war, about your parents – "

She turned and stared at me, stopping in the street. I could see the whites of her eyes around the blue irises.

"One day," she said intensely, "when I visit England, I'll tell you everything. I promise. Not you – I promise it to myself."

And yet it never came about. Why not? God knows. It just didn't. I wrote a long thank-you letter, and I think I wrote again some time after my breakup with Gordon. Mariolain didn't reply. And instead of phoning to see what was going on, somehow I let her slip. Friendship nearly always needs a minimum of propinquity to sustain it. The distance between us was just too great, and my life, at least, too full. I didn't even think about her much, after the first few months, only when I took out the little white 'warmer' to keep my coffee hot.

And in fact there had been nothing overtly to tickle my imagination – the visit had passed off almost without incident. Yet I must subconsciously have realised that there were profound mysteries in Mariolain's life. The writer, more, alas, than the friend in me, must have been engaged, in however low a gear; because it was all there, recorded and waiting for me – all the clues, the small oddnesses, the nuances so subtle I didn't know I had registered them.

But now, when Mariolain and I, nearly twenty years later, sat beside the lily-fire talking, back it all came, and slowly the gaps began to be filled.

Chapter 6

———— ∿ ————

Willem Dykstra was the only son of a prosperous and landed family in Friesland, in the north of Holland. He did brilliantly at the Municipal University of Amsterdam and returned there, following some mandatory travel to broaden his horizons, to take up a fellowship. This was in the late 1920s. He seemed set for an outstanding career. Then he married beneath him.

It was not for love. Mariolain wouldn't ever agree that her father had married her mother for love. He married the daughter of one of his father's tenant farmers, in other words a peasant girl. So, at any rate, his people called her, at the time and afterwards. The reasons may not have been as simple as Mariolain believed, but I have only her version. She said her father married to have someone he could command.

He was, as the world measures and perhaps even by kinder criteria, her superior. She had no education. She had little native wit. She was not a beauty. She had no charms or graces. She had nothing more, it seems, than a strong healthy body, and her simplicity. Even these assets were to prove to some extent delusory.

Mariolain showed me several pre-war photos of her. She had Irene's build, of course, but without the intelligence in Irene's features. She looked like a bland, well-meaning, baffled Friesian cow, right down to her dark hair and white skin (Mariolain's skin) and black country dress with white collar and cuffs. Handing me the photos slowly one by one, Mariolain wept.

"She was so stupid," she said. "She was such a poor stupid woman. She thought my father was a god. He looked down on her as his servant. No, before you ask – he didn't discover her shortcomings after they were married. He chose her because of them. He married her for them. For her lack of beauty because my father was short and wore glasses and he had the limp then, though it was made worse in his accident, after the war. He didn't want a beautiful wife who would despise him and make a fool of him with other men. He didn't want an intelligent wife who he would have to talk to, who might be in any way his rival. He wanted sons, and he had some stories in his head about peasant women making the best breeders. What an irony! Serve him right! She had miscarriages with three boys. Then she had Irene and me. Then a stillborn boy. Then he had her sterilised. Not to save her from more pain and trouble. Because *he* couldn't bear any more to see what a mistake he made, how he had picked the wrong cow."

The families on both sides withdrew from the couple. Willem Dykstra's for obvious reasons: they felt his choice degraded them by association, so they didn't associate. His wife's family were dismayed in a different way. They had the sense to realise that there was something basically wrong. Why did this man want their Griet? His wooing had been cold and calculated. They saw no way to protect her, though her father went to Willem's and told him bluntly that he opposed the match.

Once the marriage was a fact, though, there was no more to be done. The couple found themselves cut off from their roots. They came to live in the city, where he became a lecturer at the university and later got a professorship, while she settled down to housekeeping and a routine of pregnancies.

Then the war came.

It's so important, how old one was, as well as where one was, when one's country went to war. I never quite realised

51

that until I learnt Mariolain's story. I was nine, and living in Richmond, Surrey, England. Cal was twelve, in Boston, Massachusetts. Mariolain was five and Irene seven. Niels was one and a half. He was living in Java with his parents; his father owned a factory in Surabaya.

What does a one-year-old know about war? He can die, of course, but if he doesn't, how can his psyche be wounded? Later I was to think: if only Niels had had Cal's years! – the extra years Cal, in his happy situation, didn't need.

Cal, in tranquil, dignified, civilised Boston, went to high school and played softball and got off with the bobby-soxers and did holiday jobs as even rich men's sons do in the States. He learnt about the war at a very far remove, mainly from the radio and newspapers, though he once confessed to me he scarcely read anything but the funnies till he was eighteen. The war quite literally left him untouched.

As for me: at the first hint of danger my mother hung my gas-mask round my neck, put me in our baby Austin with its tank full of the petrol she was entitled to as a member of the WVS, and drove me into the wilds of Wales. There she quite ruthlessly thrust me into the household of an old school friend whom she hadn't seen for years and who was too astounded (and well-bred) to protest effectively. Then home went my mother to look after my father, who was in a reserved occupation and had an early hernia.

I thought myself very hard done by. I hated my foster father, who occasionally drank too much, and my foster mother, who paid my mother out by turning my rations into the kinds of untemptingly nourishing meals I loathed most, and my foster brother Greville, who spoke Welsh and teased me out of jealousy for my intrusion. I saw my mother and my two much older sisters regularly and never heard a shot fired in anger. As soon as the immediate danger was past I was swiftly collected and re-entered my home to be welcomed like the prodigal son.

So much for Cal's and my sufferings.

The Nazis conquered the Dutch army (which hadn't fought a

war since the Battle of Waterloo in 1815) in five days, and marched into Holland in May, 1940.

It's astonishing how ignorant I was. Willem Dykstra did right to reproach me. I was amazed when Mariolain told me that the jack-booting and deportations and firing squads didn't start right away. The Nazis, it seems, weren't interested in rousing the Dutch to rebellion; they needed Holland as a base and to prevent its coasts being used by the Allies as an invasion route, but they also had their eyes on its food production and its manpower. So they put on velvet gloves, and a honeymoon period ensued.

It didn't last long – about six months – and in fact not everyone fell for the German blandishments. Professor Dykstra, for one, didn't. He had good if personal reasons to be aware of the rottenness of fascism, and of the stupidity, corruption and brutishness of the NSB – the Netherlands National Socialist party – under its plump, strutting version of Mussolini, one Anton Mussert.

When the Nazis began to dismantle other groupings under the pretence of rationalising the diverse and chaotic Dutch political system, and to establish Mussert and his NSB Nazis as the only valid Dutch political party, Mariolain's father's last shred of hope, that the Occupation might turn out to be less than disastrous, vanished. From that time on, he entered the lists of the Resistance, which, as he'd hinted to me at his dinner-table, were not precisely over-subscribed, especially in the early days.

It was some time before even he committed himself fully. At first, his resistance, within the framework of the university, had a small 'r'. Unlike a lot of his fellow academics, he foresaw that the Occupation would last for years, and that any rash or open opposition would sooner or later be ruthlessly crushed. He also knew himself. He recognised that he had in his character a streak of reckless courage and patriotism which could easily lead him into self-defeating and self-destructive gestures, and he didn't intend to be defeated or destroyed. He meant to survive the war.

Mariolain said that he already carried in his mind the seeds of the book he would one day write about the times he was living through. He kept a journal of day-to-day events both as they touched him personally and as they affected Holland and the war in Europe. He kept this journal, in school notebooks, carefully hidden under the eaves of his house, long before there was any question of the benign and brotherly Germans claiming the right to search Dutch property. By the time the iron fist emerged fully from the velvet glove, the professor's hiding-place had had to be changed and enlarged to hold more than a growing manuscript.

The behaviour of the faculty of the Municipal University of Amsterdam was not the most heroic of any in the Netherlands. In Leiden, for instance, the enforced removal of a certain Jewish professor of law in November, 1940, resulted in an electrifying address by the Dean of the Law School, a Professor Cleveringa, to virtually the whole student body, in which he said plainly what no-one in Holland seems to have said plainly till then: that the actions of the Nazis against the Jews were an affront to international law. He also spoke very highly of his deposed Jewish colleague. His speech was swiftly printed by the Resistance on leaflets which were distributed all over the country. Mariolain's father pinned his copy into his journal and then tried his best to persuade his colleagues in Amsterdam to respond with equal courage and outspokenness.

By and large, they refused. Professor Cleveringa had been arrested and Leiden University closed down. If the other three public universities in Holland – that's all there were – brought the same fate on themselves, where would the scholars come from who would be needed to restore Holland after the war? Besides, students were so far exempt from the early 'call-ups' to serve Germany which were affecting many young Dutchmen. Better to keep classes going to save as many as possible from the draft. Those, at any rate, were the excuses.

Professor Dykstra with difficulty suppressed his fury and sense of shame even when, a short time later, he had to watch one of his favourite colleagues (not a Jew) being frogmarched out of his classroom under arrest for some infringement of the new teaching regulations, and two days later found his friend had been replaced by a man whose chief qualification for the place was his membership of the NSB.

Dykstra took a week's 'sick' leave and argued out his position with himself in his journal. He never acted until he had carried his course to its logical outcome in his rather circumscribed imagination. Then he offered his resignation to his Dean, who, no doubt spotting a potential trouble-maker, accepted it. Dykstra longed to make a public statement about the impossibility of teaching philosophy and history under restrictions which made a mockery of both, but he saw no ultimate benefit in getting himself interned or imprisoned. Instead, he sold his house in the city and moved out to the suburban town of Hilversum, where he bought a smaller house, carefully chosen because it had both a cellar and a lot of roof-space and was, in this respect only, unlike its neighbours. One has to admire the man for having foresight. He also changed his name.

His wife's name, before her marriage, had been Griet Jansen, a common one in the main part of Holland, though rather uncommon in Friesland (Dykstra is a typically Fries-landic surname). Jansen was ideal for his purposes, more especially since it meant he didn't have to worry so much about whether his wife would remember that she was now Mevrouw Jansen and not Mevrouw Dykstra. He applied to a local primary school for a humble job as a history teacher, and, since they had just lost several of their staff to the labour draft, they gladly gave it to him. Professor Dykstra-now-Mijnheer Jansen reckoned that the Germans would not interfere unduly with the running of elementary schools, nor scrutinise them too closely, at least not until the rule of National Socialism really began to bite, and that would not happen until the tide of the war turned. He was right. For several years he was able to live his life quietly and earn a modest living, while being covertly active in the Resistance, now with a capital 'R'.

After school when he had had his dinner and done his preparation for the following day, he would slip along to a local club which was a cover for a secret printing-press. Ever since the swift and efficient dissemination of Professor Cle-veringa's speech, Willem (as I'd better call him to avoid confusion, though it's rather hard to imagine being on first-name terms with him) had been sure that the underground press was the branch of the Resistance that he wanted to be part of. Touch-typing was one of the useful skills he had taught himself in his student days, because his wordy essays otherwise took too long to write out. He soon came to wish that instead (or as well) he had put himself through an intensive course in forgery, but he had to be content with learning the rudiments of journalism and stencil-printing. That was all the underground press amounted to in the early days. Willem's production, a couple of sheets of stencilled news, was run off at irregular intervals in the cellar of the club, while upstairs the ordinary members drank and chatted and laughed as if the Germans had never ventured across the border. The cover of noise was useful; but its bovine obtuse cheerfulness sometimes made Willem's blood simmer. He had already begun to despise the majority of his countrymen who managed to carry on their normal lives regardless of the fact that their nation was under the heel of barbarism, just because that heel was not yet grinding them into the dirt.

Willem didn't consult his wife in any of this. All these radical and potentially ruinous decisions, which affected his family so closely, were just added to the long list of aspects of his life from which he excluded Griet. His regard for her intelligence had not increased over the years. (Mariolain told me that one of her earliest memories was of her father coming into a room where her mother was reading the two little girls a story. He listened for a few moments to her rather faltering reading – made worse, no doubt, by his presence – and then, as she stumbled over a word, walked across the room, removed the book from her hands, read the sentence impeccably and gave it back – upside down. "You might just as well read it that way for all the sense you're making of it," he remarked, and walked away.)

He had never bothered to tell Griet where he was going or when he intended to be back. So of course, when he joined the Resistance, he left her completely in the dark. He had not even consulted her about the move to the suburbs, ignoring her distress at leaving the home she had got used to, and expecting his domestic arrangements to continue almost uninterrupted in the new place. Griet was a passable plain cook and had learnt to run her first household quite adequately with the help of a servant, with whom she was on terms of friendship and equality (something Willem, and his innate snobbery, hated). Of course when they left Amsterdam to go into 'retreat', he had let this woman go, and Griet had to manage alone without her old friend, something that upset her very much.

Now she was without companionship. Despite her phlegmatic temperament, her nerves, already worn down by repeated pregnancies, were beginning to fray. The war and the Occupation had not touched her directly so far, but the atmosphere in the big half-known world outside her home, together with the persistent lovelessness and lack of esteem inside it, began to tell on her. Her home and her children were all she had, and anything which threatened them filled her with unspecified and unspeakable terrors. Mariolain said her mother used to come up to their room after they were supposed to be asleep, and stand at the foot of their beds gazing at them in a kind of palpitating, yearning silence. If one of them stirred or spoke to her, she would drop on her knees beside the bed, gather the child into her arms and clutch it close, rocking it back and forth, moaning softly as if bursting with unutterable feelings. This disturbed the girls, perhaps because it was so out of keeping with their mother's daytime attitude, which was plodding and practical and undemonstrative. Inevitably they had absorbed some of their father's unconcealed low opinion of their mother's intelligence. He hardly spoke to her except to give her instructions (often very curtly) and offer sarcastic criticism. Sometimes, in those brief conflicts which happen in every family, Mariolain and Irene would shout at their mother, "You're stupid!" They felt they had their father's mandate for this behaviour. That was why Mariolain invariably cried whenever she spoke to me about her mother's lack of intelligence. She couldn't deny it, because of what happened later, but it always stabbed her with guilt.

One day, which Mariolain remembered clearly, or thought

she did, she and Irene came home from school to find a strange man sitting at their table. Their mother introduced him with an unaccustomed note of pride in her voice.

"Girls, this is Dirk van Sluis. He has come to stay with us."

Dirk van Sluis was tall and thin and bony, with a long narrow head and prominent cheekbones and a shock of stiff dark hair. He had small wide-apart eyes and a flat nose without much bridge – Mariolain particularly noticed this because he wore glasses to read and there was nothing to keep them up. She used to muffle sniggers as the specs slipped to the tip of his nose. To the girls he looked old, but he was probably about thirty.

At first the girls automatically resented his presence. He occupied a spare bedroom and ate many of his meals with them. They felt him as an interloper. Their mother said he had been billeted on them by the Germans, who were moving men about the country to fit some complex design of their own, and that it was not for them to question this; but the girls were surprised their father had not something to say.

Willem had, in fact, a good deal to say, but he was forced to swallow it. Outraged and alarmed though he was at this intrusion, he was helpless. He became more taciturn and withdrawn than ever. He seldom seemed to be at home, and when he was it was to bolt a meal and then retreat to his tiny study, the door of which he locked noisily after him. Effectively he was less a participant in the daily doings of the family than, in a short time after his arrival, 'Uncle' Dirk became.

Griet treated their lodger as an honoured guest. She fussed over him, and not only put up with his whims and fancies about food and other arrangements (he liked his bathwater very hot, and two clean sheets every week) but even indulged them. Several times she actually took 'Uncle' Dirk's part against the girls when he was being cross with them for some petty infringement of his self-made rules. He was fanatical about his personal possessions, especially his linen: if the girls carelessly wiped their hands on 'his' towel, or moved or even touched anything belonging to him, he would bark at them, though later he usually gave them sweets 'to make up'. Their mother's strange possessiveness and tolerance toward their lodger annoyed both girls and did nothing to endear him to them, though he often tried to ingratiate himself.

As time went on, Griet persuaded them into accepting 'Uncle' Dirk's pressing invitations to take them on little outings. Admittedly these would provide a pleasant enough break from their rather dull routine; he would take them to the places they wanted to go, and even buy them small presents.

"Here you are! Pretty little babies for pretty little mamies," he once said winningly, pressing a miniature pair of bright pink celluloid 'dollies' into their hands. "See? You can take their clothes off. I'll show you." Mariolain watched as his big knob-knuckled hands fumbled with the tiny ill-sewn dress and knickers. "There, see? She's a little girl, isn't she, like you." He turned the doll over. "When she's naughty you can spank her botty."

Mariolain snatched the doll from him. "But she's not naughty. I'll never spank her," she said. She began hurriedly dressing the doll, bending low over it, in an undefined impulse to hide its nakedness from him.

Then 'Uncle' Dirk said something odd. "Don't tell your Papi."

Both girls looked up at him enquiringly.

"About me giving you the dollies. He might not like it."

"Why?"

He shrugged. "Your Papi doesn't think much of me, you know. I don't know why. I've got a lot of respect for *him*." There was a self-pitying note in his voice. "But you like me, don't you?" he added jovially, and put an arm round each of the girls, squeezed their shoulders and smiled at them in turn. Dolls in hand and full of herring fillets, they smiled back and nodded in unison, with children's unconscious hypocrisy.

Chapter 7

———— ᨓ ————

If the two girls had been older, or a little more wordly wise, as children are today, they might have had suspicions about their mother's relationship with their lodger. But, as Mariolain was to discover years later, there was nothing untoward about it, at least not in the usual sense. The warmth, the deference, the pride that Griet showed toward Dirk van Sluis stemmed from something even more basic to her needs than sex or romance.

Her hunger was for approval, for a sense of worth. It was not even van Sluis himself who gave her this. But he was connected with something that did. It was called *Winterhulp* – the Winter Aid.

The Germans started this early in the Occupation, modelling it on something similar in Germany. It was supposed to be a charitable organisation to help the underprivileged. Griet had been recruited one day when she was out shopping. A woman she didn't know got chatting to her in a queue, and told her about this new organisation which 'did a lot of good' and needed helpers. She persuaded Griet that it was her duty to volunteer, and arranged to call for her next morning when the children had gone to school.

"But what will I have to do?" asked Griet, ever anxious that she would be out of her depth.

"There's a fund-day. You'll stand in the street and collect money in a tin."

Griet was relieved. She could do that, all right. She had seen people doing it for other causes such as the Red Cross, and had sometimes thought that for something so important they ought not to stand there so unobtrusively, merely showing their collecting tins to passers-by, but should rattle them compellingly under their noses, especially if they looked rich.

She mentioned the encounter to Willem that night at supper, but he wasn't listening. "Good," he said. "Fine." And went on correcting some papers at the table.

Next morning, as promised, the woman came. She had a car, and drove Griet to the town centre, where they collected their tins and placards at a place she called 'our headquarters', a converted shop in a back street. It was very simply furnished so far, but workmen were in, painting and putting in new wiring. There were a number of other women there. Some of them looked as nervous and unsure of themselves as Griet. This made her feel better. Obscurely elated by the car-ride and the general atmosphere of bustle and purpose, she was emboldened to start a chat with one of these women, who looked like 'her sort'.

After exchanging a few words, this woman murmured, "I don't really know if I should be here. I don't think we ought to help the Germans."

Griet felt a slight shiver of unease. "But it's for the poor," she said in the rather pushed-out voice she occasionally heard herself use when she felt defensive.

The woman who had recruited her chipped in briskly. "We ought to be thankful that these Germans are helping us to organise our welfare services better. It's pathetic how little we do for people worse off than ourselves."

Griet spent three hours in the main shopping street, shaking her tin. A number of people dropped in coins. In return, they received little tin badges to pin on their coats, luminous ones decorated with a windmill. Griet thought they were sweet. She wanted one for herself, so she conscientiously popped some coins into her own tin, and took a badge, pinning it to the collar of her coat.

61

Mid morning, a man stopped, looked at the placard dangling from the tin, and said, "What's all this, then? Some Nazi racket?"

Griet felt affronted.

"It's for the unemployed, and the sick," she said. "And for the silent poor." It was a phrase she'd pick up at 'our headquarters', and she liked it – it suggested patient, undemanding people who would be surprised and grateful for any help. "It's good of the Germans to help us organise a charity," she added defiantly.

The man stared at her for a moment. Then, quite unexpectedly, he spat on the pavement.

"You won't get so much as a button off my flies for your stinking tin," he said loudly, and turned on his heel.

Griet felt upset, but only because he'd been so crude. She couldn't imagine there could be any harm in collecting money for a good cause, and she rattled her tin under the noses of passers-by with even greater boldness because of it. She didn't want to doubt she was doing something useful and good. She felt very pleased when coins tinkled into the box, rather hurt, even indignant, when people passed without contributing. When she got back to 'our headquarters' at the appointed time, and discovered that she had collected more money than any of the others, a most unaccustomed warm glow of pride suffused her.

"I'll come back and do it again tomorrow," she offered eagerly.

The organiser laughed.

"We can't have a fund-day every day," she said. Then, seeing how crestfallen Griet looked, she relented. "If you're really keen, you could come and help around here. We could always use an extra pair of hands."

Griet walked all the way home in a haze of satisfaction. When she got there of course she took her coat off, forgetting to transfer the luminous button to her jacket. That night, Irene noticed something like a cat's eye shining in the dark hall cupboard when she opened the door to it. She asked her mother what it was, and Griet, in her newfound benignity and happiness at being needed and appreciated, took the button off her coat and showed Irene how to hold it

62

under the light to 'charge' it and then told her to take it into the dark. Irene was enchanted.

"Do you really like it?" Griet asked, delighted, as if the child had paid her some compliment. "Then have it."

She began to work regularly at the headquarters, now quite a smart and proud-making place to be in. Then someone new appeared. A German. Germans were seldom seen there; their arrival always caused a little frisson among the Dutch workers. But this man was not in uniform. He seemed very nice and polite. He told the women that a number of Dutchmen from down south had been moved to the Amsterdam area 'in the national interest' and needed accommodation. They were all young men, bachelors. It was hard for them to be away from their homes. They needed to be taken in, fed and looked after. It would be a kind as well as a patriotic act to give them lodgings. Furthermore, no-one would be out of pocket.

There was no lack of volunteers. In fact, there weren't enough young men from the south to go round, which caused quite some ill feeling.

Griet's hand had been the first to go up. She got Dirk van Sluis.

So she didn't quite tell Willem the truth. She said Dirk had been billeted on them, whereas actually she had offered to take him. It seems from this, and a few other indications – for instance, after that first, failed attempt, she never made a serious effort to tell Willem anything about her welfare work – that Griet had some dim idea that he would not approve.

If I'm right about this, I would guess that the reason was less to do with a correct assessment of his probable reaction to a charity founded and backed by the occupiers, than with a vague idea that anything which gave her so much personal gratification could not seem right to Willem. That he might try to interfere with it in some way, to reduce her again to her 'proper' condition, that of undervalued and unpaid servant.

It's easy to understand why she couldn't have borne that.

The odd thing is why Willem didn't notice the change in her. Both the girls did. Their mother became, for a time, quite different, almost a strong personality. She ordered them about briskly and did unexpected things such as changing the arrangement of furniture in the house, overseeing their homework and taking them on improving outings.

Once, when they had a day off school when she was pledged to work, she took them to 'our headquarters'. She sat them down on some shiny hard chairs and invited them to notice how nice everything was, how clean and orderly, and how full of kind, busy, unselfish people. She herself was very busy, and she was not averse to their seeing this, hoping, I'm sure, that they would observe her good relations with her fellow workers, how she was respected. Mariolain remembers her saying something like, "Look how Mami has to do the filing! Did you know your Mami knew how to file papers and letters? It's not such an easy thing!" And she showed them the big metal cabinet with all its drawers and folders and strange words written on sticking-up bits of card.

But probably what fixed the day in their memories was that afterwards, because they'd been so good and patient, their mother took them off for an icecream at a café and, while they were eating, leaned across the table and said, "Don't tell Papi about our headquarters, will you?" Mariolain, intent on her ice, simply nodded, but Irene was getting curious about this insistence on keeping Papi in ignorance and asked, "Why?"

Their mother leaned back in her chair, frowning. She seemed to have to think out why. Then she said, "Papi keeps lots of secrets from us. Do you know what work he does, shut up in his room?" They shook their heads. "No. And no more do I! So it's only fair that *we* have some secrets, too."

The girls accepted this. They, or at least Mariolain, enjoyed the feeling of complicity with their mother. Mariolain liked her mother's new self-confidence. It gave *her* added security. In retrospect she knew that she had hated feeling that her mother was stupid and despised.

The thing which made Mariolain a war casualty must have

happened in the spring of 1941. The iron hand was emerging from the velvet glove by then, but only stealthily and occasionally, here and there. The promise that no Dutchman would be sent to Germany to work or fight unless he volunteered had gone by the board quite early on, as the Reich's need for manpower grew. There were no *razzias* – forced round-ups – yet; but certain categories of men were being drafted. There had been actions against the Jews in certain urban centres, and reactions against the actions, including a damaging dock-strike. Dutch people were beginning to discover – by personal experience or report – what prison camps were like.

But there had not been many deaths. People still had their radios, and many of them listened to Radio Oranje, the Free Dutch broadcasts from England, which mingled remote hope with immediate inspiration. The Resistance was small and patchy, but active when it dared to be, or saw good cause. Yet there was still a determined reluctance, among the mass of the Dutch people, to face the implications of occupation – an overriding inclination to pretend nothing was deeply, dangerously wrong, that normal life could continue.

In Hilversum, as in most other outlying places, it actually could, and did. The iron hand had not touched this place. Not directly.

Spring was early and very sweet that year. It crept in to Hilversum in late March. The country was poised on an edge it could not see – with hindsight, Willem in his book was to describe Holland at this critical point in the war as

"a fledgling which creeps to the brink of its nest and stares blearily at the spring leaves and the sky, unaware of the deep lethal drop beneath. Pitifully few (the present writer is proud to have been among them) understood our vulnerability, felt the underdevelopment of our pinions, knew there was a yellow line round our national beak . . . *We* alone felt the shadow of the hawk which hung above us in the deceptive blue sky of that first spring of our occupation. We apprehended how its talons would grasp us and crush our fragile bones before we could taste flight in the summer sun. But many of our fellow-countrymen simply scented the spring air and allowed delusory hopes to distract them from reality."

It sounds less pretentious in Dutch, I believe. I can't help wondering, in view of what he knew when he wrote this years later, how much of the imagery was Freudian.

For the two little girls it was a time to assert themselves by refusing to wear their winter coats to school, a time to see what bulbs the previous owner had left in their small garden, to scratch gardens of their own; to beg (in vain) for a puppy to take for walks on 't Gooi, the local heath, with its heather and birch trees coming into bud; to look forward to Easter.

Easter was an important festival in the Dykstra family. There were eggs, dyed and decorated, which Willem – the jolly father for once – took in a basket and hid on the wooded heath, setting a trail for the children with arrows marked on the soft, damp ground or drawn on treetrunks or formed of twigs. Here and there would be little printed notes, telling the searchers to hop five times on one foot or recite a poem or stand on their heads before proceeding.

Excitement ran high as the girls dashed from arrow to arrow. For Mariolain, it was better this year than ever before. She had been slow to learn to read; in previous years, Irene would rush ahead, reading the notes to herself, performing the 'task', dropping the note on the ground and running on, leaving Mariolain flummoxed and often in tears, for it was a rule that you could not go on till you had obeyed the note. This year she could read, and the hard words 'Uncle' Dirk read to her. 'Uncle' Dirk was doing the egg-trail, too, hops, headstands and all. Griet was not there. She had stayed at home to prepare the celebratory lunch.

There was always, in the trail, a point about half-way along when Willem invariably left an instruction to: "Sit down and rest while you count to 200." This served a double purpose. It enabled him, as trail-setter, to be sure the girls would not catch him up before he could hide the eggs at the trail's end. It also gave the little runners a breather. Mariolain and Dirk came upon Irene, obediently sitting in a hollow, the note at her side. The heather, stretching itself in its spring growth, curled over her legs. As they started down the slope into the hollow, which was wooded in on all sides, Irene waved at them and then, puffed out, threw herself on her back. Mariolain took a mental photograph of her as the heather and scrub yielded to the pressure of her small body. Her dark hair, springy as the growth she lay on, framed her flushed face. She was wearing a blue woollen skirt and a paler blue jersey. The sleeves were pushed up. She must have taken off her coat and hidden it somewhere as she got hot from running, to be picked up on the way back – they often did that. As she rolled back, she kicked her legs in the air for fun, and her skirt fell back, showing her white knickers and suspenders, holding up flesh-coloured hand-knitted stockings. Mariolain remembered thinking primly: *She shouldn't show her knickers like that*, and: *It must be scratchy, lying on the heather*.

Suddenly 'Uncle' Dirk stopped and said, "You run and hide."

Mariolain, who loved hiding, said, "But she's seen us."

"You hide," he said. "And we'll come and find you."

Mariolain obeyed without thinking. It seemed all part of the fun of the occasion, an extra thrill. She turned, ran up the slope again, ran a little way into the wood, and then crouched behind some small rhododendrons. Knowing without having to read it what the note had said, she thought she would carry out this 'task' now, so that after they found her she would be able to finish the trail with the others. Irene would say, in that rather snooty way she had sometimes, "You can't come until you've sat and counted to 200," and Mariolain would retort, "I already have." She crouched, steadily counting under her breath. A bird was in full spring voice in a still transparent tree-top. Mariolain looked up, located the source of the song, and forgot to count, watching the thrush open its throat on the thin trembling branch bent under its slight weight.

Afterwards, she obsessively tried to remember the number she had reached when she stopped counting. Because later she told Irene a lie about it.

Chapter 8

———— ✎ ————

Mariolain and I were alone in the house, I think on about
the second or third day of our visit. It was a cold bright day.
The four children had gone out on bicycles to explore the
wide, quiet avenues of the suburb, and weren't expected
home till lunchtime. The men were out too. To my astonishment, Cal had allowed Niels to sweep him off to see the
studios where his commercials were generally made. Though
Cal and I had not permitted ourselves one sideways look
since we'd arrived, even when alone in our attic, I couldn't
help wondering if he had gone on this unlikely jaunt as much
out of a desire to be shot of me for a while as out of
politeness. He couldn't have *wanted* to see the source of the
hated spurs-to-consumerism, I was sure of that, though he
seemed surprisingly to have taken a liking to Niels. He'd
even smiled upon the sword-sticks, apparently, he who
hated weapons and wouldn't let the boys play with pop-
guns.

So that left Mariolain and me to get on with the housework, which included sweeping the polished floors in hall
and living-room, shaking out the rugs (a heavy job, even for
two of us) and making the beds, which, unlike ours, were
not blessed with labour-saving duvets. It wasn't till we were
getting lunch that Mariolain started up a serious strand of
conversation.

"What do you and Cal talk about when you are alone?" she

asked. She was shredding carrots on the draining-board.

I didn't feel like talking about Cal, naturally. We were putting on such a good front, I didn't want to spoil it, so I just bluffed. "Oh, everything, just about."

She gave a little sigh. "How you're lucky! I don't talk much to Niels at all, except little things, and about the children."

I was slicing holey cheese with a marvellous gadget which had a little sharp-edged slit in it. The flat slivers of cheese came away uniform and paper-thin with an ease that was going to my head. In a semi-suppressed echo of my own problems, I asked: "Was it always like that, or is it just lately?"

"I can't remember how we talked in the beginning. I remember a lot of things about our beginning days, but not that. Perhaps we talked . . . The physical side was so loud that it drowned out our voices."

I glanced at her appreciatively. It was an almost writerly image.

"Well, they say marriages are made or marred in bed," I remarked. "I don't think I quite agree with that, but that's what most of the experts profess to believe."

"I believe it. I know it," she said fervently.

Something in her voice made me think she wanted me to ask. "Was yours . . . which? Made, or marred?"

"Is marred, broken?" she asked after a moment. "I don't know that word."

"Well – spoilt, more than broken."

"I thought. Yes, well . . . our marriage was very marred. It was marred so that I thought that the end of our honeymoon would be a court of divorce."

I stared at her. She went on mechanically rubbing the carrot up and down on the grater, smiling at me over her shoulder. The same brilliant, strange smile, so at odds with the sadness of her words and her tone. Somehow to see that child-like smile on her forty-year-old face was more discomforting than ever.

"What went wrong?"

"Oh, I did. I went wrong. I was wrong for Niels. He needed a very, very sexy woman, you see, a sort of – sexy motherly woman, like Simone Signoret or Jeanne Moreau. But I was not like that."

"You weren't old enough to be. How old were you?"

"I was old enough. To him I was 'the older woman'. I was twenty-six . . . A twenty-six-year-old older woman of no experience at all. Except the one experience which didn't help us very much, that I was raped by a man when I was seven." And she put down the grater, shook the carrot-flecks off her fingers and moved to the sink to rinse them.

My own hands had come to a stop with a tongue of cheese half-way through the silver mouth of the slicer. I remember gazing at it and not thinking of anything for quite a few seconds and then hearing Mariolain at my shoulder saying, "Oh Suky, you have done enough cheese for the army! Now I must do fondue for supper, Pieter will be very happy, he loves fondue." And she briskly finished my stalled slice and removed the cheese from my reach.

I don't know if she was aware of my shock. One would think she had said something perfectly ordinary. Yet she avoided my eyes as she moved about, getting the salad and cheese-plate ready, and I sensed her waiting for my reaction.

"Mariolain," I said after a while, when I felt able to. "How did this – at *seven* – do you mean, actually raped, not just – ?"

"I suppose it was actual. Perhaps not, how shall I say? – all the way, or I would have been more injured. It's hard to know now. For years I didn't know what had happened to me. Almost I didn't believe anything had. That it was some sort of mad bad dream I had. You see, it was only once, and then nobody spoke about it, and the sky didn't fall down, and I suppose I just – as the psychiatrists say – you know – "

"Suppressed it."

"Yes. Except that I didn't, because I remember it perfectly. Shall we have some coffee or will it spoil our appetite?"

"If you want some," I mumbled. I was feeling stunned and rather sick.

She made us each a mug of instant and then said, "You know, it's so nice, let's sit out in the conservatory."

The conservatory was an extension to the kitchen. It

didn't have many plants, just a few pots of variegated ivy and some herbs. The floor tiles were broken and dusty and the glass roof was so dirty that half the possible sunshine was kept out. It was an oddly neglected corner of the place, a contrast to the beautiful cherished living-room. But its very left-outness made it peaceful. We sat out there on folding canvas chairs and rested our mugs on the slatted shelves and stared out into the back garden, not yet brazen with daffodils but underembellished and looking rather secretive.

Mariolain didn't seem to want to talk for the moment and neither did I. I was remembering my own deflowerment, so unspeakably different from my friend's. It had happened when I was twenty – a good age for it, I think – and working in that hospital. It was actually rather like one of my novels. I fell in love with an older man, not a doctor, an administrator, about twice my age and, naturally, married. I felt terribly guilty about this but made my hypocritical quietus by ruling that I would only spend time with him that he would not, otherwise, be spending with his wife and family. Thus, when he had to stay overnight at the hospital, as happened occasionally, we would seize a couple of hours at the end of his duty, and repair to his office and lock the door.

The first few times I was so riven with doubt and compounding terrors that if he had tried to go (in Mariolain's now forever tainted phrase) 'all the way' it would probably have put me off sex for years. But being sensitive and sweet and self-controlled, he didn't. What he did was, now I thought about it, the exact antithesis of rape. He worked me up to it so gradually that I hardly knew where it was all leading. I remember lying on the couch with him kneeling beside me, very gently and slowly exposing bits of me to the touch of his lips and fingers which were as delicate as butterflies at first. There was such a feeling of there being no hurry, nothing to fear, no demands, nothing in view but my pleasure, endless time, endless affection, endless delight . . . In the times between our intimate meetings, ordinary working days, nights at home alone in my flat, I lived and relived every caress and sweet word, and thrills brushed over the surface of my skin and my memory. Thus even our times apart were imbued with sensuality and formed a part of the continuum of our lovemaking. By the time he actually made love to me fully I was so ready, so happy with my own body, and with him as my lover, that it couldn't have been simpler or more beautiful. Or a better preparation for the rest of my life.

Perhaps my inbuilt conventionality suggests to my subconscious that thoughts of this infinitely positive if illicit and brief love-affair are somehow seditious to my marriage. Cal always said he didn't care what I'd got up to before I met him, provided he didn't have to hear about it. Being himself a very robust lover – something I was well able to adjust to when the right time came – there were few points of comparison; it was hardly like the same act as the one I performed with my gentle first gentleman. But now I suddenly and for the first time knew how much I owed to him. And the contrast formed in my mind as I sat with Mariolain staring out into her pre-spring garden was between her initiation and mine.

"I can't say what I feel," I said abruptly. "It's the most terrible thing I've ever heard of."

"Of course it's not," said Mariolain rather sharply, as if to check any exaggeration of sympathy. "There are many, many worse things. Did you hear about the German commandant who shut seventy-five women prisoners into a little cell, just pushed them all in there on top of each other and left them there overnight, and when they opened the doors in the morning –"

"Mariolain – don't!" I cried suddenly. Usually I can hear horrors, one has to be tough and stand it, but I was still raw from thinking about this helpless little girl being raped by some bloody Nazi and I couldn't bear anything more just then.

"I am just showing you that what happened to me was not so *very* terrible. I should have been able to get over it. I gave myself plenty of time to. I didn't go with any man until Niels. Not just because I didn't want to, but because I on purpose gave myself a long time to be healed."

"And did Niels – did you tell him?"

"Of course. He had to know. I was telling quite a few

72

people by then. The first person I told was my sister Irene. I told her when I was sixteen. And what do you think she told me? That it happened to her, too. The same man. The same day."

"I suppose he was some German soldier," I said with a shudder of hatred.

She smiled. "I'm afraid I have to tell you he was Dutch."

"*Dutch*!"

"A Dutch collaborator who was billeted in our house."

"He raped – you, and your sister, in your own house?"

"No. Out on 't Gooi. The heath. On Sunday, when we go there for Easter morning, I will show you where exactly it happened."

I was lost for words. I just looked at her. She sipped her coffee, her cornflower eyes gazing into mine over the rim of her mug.

"You can bear to go there?"

"Oh yes. It's a beautiful place. We often go. One should not blame places for the things that happen in them. One has to go to them and be happy in them, to sort of clean them of the awful thing. Besides . . . " She stopped, frowned, put down her mug. "If I am to be honest, I never had bad feelings about the place. With Irene it's different. She never goes to 't Gooi. I think pehaps she had more trauma from what happened than me."

"Why do you say that?"

"Well, if you can judge by marriages, you remember, hers broke up. And mine, though it's – marred – it is still here. And then there is our different feelings about our father."

We sat for a time in the dancing dust-motes of the conservatory. At last I said, "Did your parents – didn't they guess? After all – there must have been some signs, you and Irene can't have been exactly the same after a thing like that."

Mariolain became perfectly still. Her eyes opened wide and seemed almost to glaze as she stared out of the dirt-streaked panels of glass into the spring garden. I looked at her hands. They were balled into fists and clenched in her lap, the top part of her lap, she was pressing herself unconsciously the way a child does who needs to go to the lavatory.

"My mother knew," she said. "She must have known. She saw the blood marks. She knew."

Knew, and did nothing. Knew, and said nothing. Knew, and let the situation of Dirk living in the house continue. Because she was stupid. Because she was repressed. Because she was frightened. Perhaps even, a little, because if it all came out and Dirk was unmasked as a sordid child-molester, a villain, *her* mask – the mask she was just beginning to believe was her true face – would also be torn away and she would be left as she had been before, only worse, much worse.

So she must have taken the poor little stained bits of underwear and burnt them or washed them clean and pretended that what had clearly happened had not happened. Perhaps she honestly couldn't face the results of her importation of Dirk into the house. Adults, too, can suppress knowledge. Perhaps she meant to tell her husband, to confront Dirk, to question the girls, to complain to 'our headquarters'. Perhaps she even tried to. But it was evidently beyond her. Things went on from day to day, as before. She probably watched the girls for signs. But she didn't want to find any. So any that there were, she failed to notice.

Mariolain doesn't remember the end of the Easter egg-trail. But I can imagine how the girls, alone now (for it's impossible to think of Dirk staying with them) wandered from arrow to arrow, from note to note through the woods, silent, numbed. Laughterless now, like automata. Perhaps they paused and perhaps they even did the 'tasks' because not to have done them would have been to acknowledge that something cataclysmic and irrevocable had taken place. And then they must have come up with Willem at the trail's end. And he would have been full of his twice-a-year bonhomie and so disappointed and irritated by their pale faces and their lack

74

of excitement and response. I can imagine him clapping his hands and urging them to hunt for the coloured eggs, and later complaining to Griet that her silly little daughters had no fun in them and got fagged out after a run that wouldn't have tired a three-year-old, that Irene had found only two eggs and Mariolain, who was normally the quicker because the greedier, none at all. Then he would have lapsed into a paternal sulk.

And Griet would have bent over them querulously and asked them why they'd spoilt the game and got into a bad mood, meaning got their father into a bad mood, and later at lunch (which they couldn't eat), got cross on her own behalf. Then there'd be questions about where 'Uncle' Dirk had got to, had they played a trick and run away from him or what, *that* wasn't nice . . . And before long it would be the children who were feeling obscurely guilty because pain and scolding only come to bad children.

Perhaps both the girls secretly supposed they had seen the last of Dirk, instinctively expecting the protection that is every child's right. They were probably put to bed early and at that point one might have expected them to speak to each other about what had happened, but they didn't; the moment – the only moment – passed. They fell into an exhausted, escapist sleep, and woke the next morning to find – Dirk. At the breakfast table. As if nothing at all had happened. So perhaps . . . perhaps . . . perhaps . . . nothing had.

The only change that occurred in the pattern of their lives was an ironic one. For entirely self-interested reasons, Willem began to show his resentment at Dirk's presence in the house, and Griet's frequent absences from it. He had held himself in until now because he knew that Dirk was a collaborator, a veritable 'mole' in his own vulnerable patch, and he dared not endanger himself or his work for the Resistance by antagonising him. But, without clearly understanding the link between Dirk and his wife's welfare work, Willem's patience began to be tried sorely.

The truth was, he wanted the house to himself. However careful he was, he didn't see how even a dolt like van Sluis could fail to guess that Willem was up to something if he stayed long enough and just kept his eyes open. After all, why should a primary school teacher have to go out two or three nights a week and stay out until ten or eleven o'clock? Why should he carry a small suitcase about with him, empty when he left the house and heavy when he returned? The contents of this case – source of poignant anxiety to Willem – was the clandestine newspaper that his Resistance cell was printing, and which it was part of his job to distribute.

Willem was not the sort of man who puts himself into danger in a great cause while striving to keep his family out of it. To Willem, the German Occupation was a national tragedy which had to be met, as far as possible, by a national response. And nations are made up of women and children, old and young, as well as able-bodied men. The time had come when Irene, who was now getting on for ten, could be useful.

Willem rationalised it in his journal.

"If I had had sons, they, or at least those over the age of, say, nine, would have been valid participants in our struggle, beneficiaries of our eventual victory. Females are as capable of courage and subterfuge as males. Little girls are as invisible to the watchful enemy as boys. More so. Why should they be shielded from moderate and calculated risks, such as, in proportion to our age and capabilities, we must all take, or cheated indeed of that sense of triumph and personal satisfaction we shall all feel when the enemy is destroyed?

"My children shall not ask me, when it is all over, what my contribution was. They will know, because they will have played their part and shared in the national achievement. I want to be proud of them, as I hope they will be proud of me."

So Irene – already, though her father in his blindness had no notion of it, a war victim – was recruited.

76

Mariolain was not recruited, yet. And nor was Griet. Willem's high-minded and progressive views about female equality did not extend to his own wife. He didn't even tell her how he planned to employ their daughter. He was entirely certain he was doing the right thing. He had no time or energy to waste convincing Griet, or overcoming any pusillanimous maternal objections.

Irene's allotted task was explained to her, with due solemnity, behind the locked door of her father's study one evening after supper. She was to disseminate the Underground newspaper – more of a magazine now, the early single-page effort having been steadily enlarged into a publication of some dozen stapled, cyclostyled pages with its own letter-head and logo, an orange with two spear-like leaves. She was given a short list of addresses to memorise and Willem ceremonially introduced a secret compartment into her schoolbag. She never carried more than a few copies at a time. She delivered them two or three per day, before and after school, usually calling at the houses of neighbours and acquaintances on some ordinary errand and secretly slipping them into a prearranged hiding-place in the house. 'Her' people did not change unless something happened, which it didn't for some time, so after the first few weeks her deliveries became almost routine. The chief difficulty was that she was, of course, forbidden to say a single word about it to anyone.

Irene was by nature a chatty little girl, outgoing and demonstrative, an extrovert. But since the events of Easter Sunday she had changed. Her father had observed this, but, with his usual obtuseness about his family, complacently regarded the change as one for the better. Irene's previous boisterousness had often got on his nerves. He decided his older child had become more mature, more serious. In fact her newly subdued manner was what initially encouraged him to entrust her with her very grown-up mission.

So Irene now had something more to keep bottled-up. Not surprisingly she became very wary and close-mouthed, given to sitting in corners or retreating to her bedroom. Mariolain remembers this time as a period when they didn't fight or squabble, when she became the more assertive one.

Often her mother would have to check her if she became obstreperous and noisy. It was probably the mindless noise disturbed children make to drown out inner tumult.

Meanwhile Irene did her war-work and her father was proud of her. He records this in his book.

Chapter 9

———— ✑ ————

While Mariolain and I were still in the conservatory, her two came bursting in, spouting Dutch so excitedly that I feared for a moment that one of mine had come a cropper off his borrowed bike. But it turned out to be only complaints. Mariolain replied pacifyingly, and with that warning note which alerted me that her children were saying unflattering things about mine. Of course, shortly afterwards *my* lot appeared, and their side of the story couldn't be veiled from bilingual Mariolain, who tactfully moved out of earshot.

Not that it was anything terrible, just the usual maddening child-muddle. Daniel had refused to ride on the right, and finally Pieter had cycled off in a rage, with Anna trailing him out of loyalty. George, infuriated by Daniel, belted him one and gave chase to the others, leaving Daniel howling and abandoned. By the time the others, belatedly overtaken by conscience, came back to look for him, he'd vanished . . . Oh, why go on? It all took time just to listen to, and by then the men were back and it all calmed down over lunch, but we decided some outing was in order, so we spent the afternoon at a local museum. There, Pieter and Anna showed themselves dauntingly *au fait* with matters historical, military and costumical, while George and Daniel showed themselves bored out of their minds. So I got home in a bad temper, while Cal, who chooses to regard his sons as next to perfect and never, ever compares them with other children, seeing my mood and interpreting it quite correctly, was giving me evil looks which boded no good for our unspoken mutual resolve to hold our antipathy in check for the duration of our visit.

Quite suddenly, when we got back, Niels invited us out for dinner. All of us – the four children as well. I saw Mariolain blench, especially when he mentioned the restaurant (a famous Indonesian one) and jovially asked 'the girls' to eschew trousers and 'the boys' to wear ties. Ties! I admit I paled, myself. None of my three males had brought a tie. The only ties the kids owned were school ones – Cal wouldn't have been seen dead in one at that time, it was a sacred item of non-conformity with him. He took it upon himself to lay this before Niels, who immediately relented, but said his ladies must dress up enough to make up for the sartorial deficiencies of the men.

Half an hour later Cal and I went upstairs to get changed. The temperature had dropped sharply (the outdoor one I mean). There was a lace edging of frost round our skylight, and the room was deeply cold. Cal switched on the electric fire and we found ourselves standing rather closer together than we had been for some time as we shiveringly began to change.

"I don't think this is a very good idea," I said. "I think he's just playing the bonhomous host, and it's silly."

Cal didn't say anything at once. The fire was burning my shins while the rest of me froze. In clambering into a pair of thermal salopette liners, Cal bumped against me with his forearm, and I moved away, but the small area in front of the fire drew me back. I slipped my dress – last year's, unfashionably short and tight – over my shoulders. It felt like a cold douche. My remoteness from Cal felt like a cold douche, too. Funny how you can long for the sheer warmth of someone's body even when you're estranged from them.

"I dunno why you're so suspicious of Niels's motives. He's not showing off, he's just being very generous."

"I'd much rather eat at home," I said. "We're costing them enough as it is."

"We'll pay half, then."

"Even half will be a fortune if it's such a posh place. It's

80

nonsense, taking the kids. Ours won't appreciate Indonesian food."

Cal threw me an angry look over the top of his polo-neck as it descended.

"What ever happened to the rose-tinted specs of uncritical motherlove?"

"I left them in the labour ward."

"Evidently. More's the pity." He paused to let this rankle and then added, "I want my boys to try everything. I love seeing how they react to new things and new tastes. All you ever seem to want to do is offload them."

"Well," I said shortly, "we evidently aren't offloading them tonight. I suggest you don your rosy glasses and go down and see if their appearance matches the occasion."

Cal laid down his comb with deliberation.

"I won't care a damn if it doesn't."

"Niels will."

The festive evening had an ominous beginning. We discovered on reaching the restaurant that something had gone wrong with the booking and we had an hour to wait. At this point we all voted to call if off, except Niels. Seven to one.

"We won't go home," he said. "Instead, we'll go for a walk."

The four children's mouths dropped open in unison. So did mine.

"A walk!"

"A *walk*?"

He gazed round at his party with a steely gleam of determination in his eyes. He really was very good-looking. His tousled dark hair fell on to his forehead, and his jaw stuck out. His tall figure was poised, as if ready to be launched against all of us if we pitted our wills against his. I glanced sideways at Mariolain. Her lips were parted too, but she was not, like us, aghast at the unearthly prospect of an hour's walk in the dark and cold. She looked like Jane Eyre gazing at Mr Rochester. How often have I tried to capture that look in words, the look of an adoring uncritical woman at the

81

domineering man she loves. Seeing it in reality made me feel faintly nauseated.

"We will walk," he decreed, "for one hour and get appetites." He dropped the car-keys meanfully into his pocket and turned on his heel. We had no option but to follow.

The four children straggled along together, the boys grumbling loudly, Anna mute but mutinous. Cal left me and moved to walk with Niels, and they were soon well ahead, walking briskly and deep in conversation. Mariolain and I brought up the rear. She took my arm for warmth.

"Are you cross?"

"Not yet," I said. I was still more or less warm, but only to my skirt-hem. Nylons and low-cut pumps are not much protection against piercing cold.

"I love him when he is like that," she said.

We walked on, from lamp to lamp. It was an elegant district, the houses well set back, redolent of secure wealth. I wondered how all this had looked during the war.

"Did you live anywhere near here when you were little?"

"In the war, you mean?" She must have realised that our conversation of the morning was still resonating. "Well, this is Hilversum and we lived in Hilversum. But a poorer part of it, near the centre."

"Was that because your father wanted to blend in with his surroundings?"

"Perhaps. But if so it was silly. A professional man always stands out in a streetful of working people. My mother fitted in all right. But we didn't. Even in bad times, we dressed differently, and talked differently from the other children in the street. I remember Mami urging us to play out with them, but I don't think we ever did. We sensed they wouldn't accept us, and to say the truth we looked down on them."

We walked along in silence for a few moments. She was clinging to my arm now like a little girl with both her gloved hands. I wondered if – super-sensitive as she was – just talking about her childhood threw her back into it so vividly that she entered again into its insecurities and fears, and needed something more than the companionship which had led her to put her arm through mine to begin with.

82

"I'd like to see the house," I remarked.

She jerked her head round to look at me.

"Which house?"

"The one your father bought at the beginning of the war, the one you used to live in."

She kept staring at me for a while, her white skin and dark mouth and eyes a recurring chiaroscuro as we passed the lamps. Then she faced front.

"I will give you the address," she said in a remote voice.

Suddenly one of the kids – Pieter, I think – let out a cry. He was out of sight somewhere, and there was something in the sound that made us all stop. It was not a frightened sound but a joyful one. After a second he raced into the nearest pool of lamplight, and at the same instant we all saw that it had begun to snow.

"Oh God," groaned Cal, who is like a cat about the weather. "That's all we need!"

But my spirits swooped upward. The flakes were huge. As the first few descended on our heads and on the bleak pavement at our feet, I saw they would settle, and realised that before we could return from our purgatorial walk the world would be white. Bad news for my daintily-shod feet of course, but suddenly I no longer cared.

Nor did the children. In an instant they were transformed from foot-dragging mutineers into leaping dervishes, swirling in and out of the lamplight in unconscious imitation of the snowflakes, shouting with pure happiness as they reached up their gloved hands toward this glorious visitation. I felt like joining them. Instead I stared up into the snow-speckled darkness, and opened my mouth to let the prickly flakes float in.

"Don't eat it!" exclaimed Mariolain. "Don't you know how much filth and pollution it catches as it falls?"

"It purifies the world," I said exultantly. "I adore snow!"

We strolled on. The men were about ten yards ahead, the kids everywhere and nowhere. The falling snow broke down the last barriers between our two and their two. They'd begun a wild extempore game of hide and seek, pouncing out at each other from behind trees and fences. By tomorrow the snow would have welded them into a four-headed unit. My easily-distracted thoughts had swung away from the war and its horrors into unreasoning delight, but Mariolain pulled me back.

"You adore it and I hate it," she said.

"Oh, why? It's so beautiful!"

"It's beautiful *now*, because any time we choose, we can be warm and in the light and eating hot food."

"You're thinking of the 'hunger winter'," I said soberly. Obviously she could not shake off her memories so easily.

"Yes, that is part of it. But not only. Long before we reached real hunger and no fuel and all that, the snow was a horror to us. You see, that first spring, when Irene was doing the deliveries, she – " Mariolain paused. "You don't want to hear," she said in a flat voice.

"I do."

"And I want so much to tell you," she said.

"Why?"

"I feel I need to. I can't explain. But it will spoil your mood, and you are here to have a holiday."

We walked in silence. What she said was partly true. I felt how deeply this afternoon's 'episode' in her story had penetrated, how it had taken the advent of snow to lift me out of a depression, and how, in a way, unwilling I was to let her draw me down again into her past, and the past of this comfortable-seeming place, simmering with secrets. Yet at the same time I was very willing to let her talk. A strange sort of need of my own met her need. I couldn't explain it then, nor did I try to; I simply said, with complete seriousness, "I do want to hear, Mariolain."

Chapter 10

———— 〰 ————

There was a late snowfall in 1942, just about the same time as our visit so many years later. It's nothing unusual. Nor was the reaction of the children, then, any different from that of our children when the first fat flakes began to fall. They forgot the war (insofar as they were thinking about it as yet), they forgot all their troubles, and, as the wonderful whiteness obliterated the ground, they revelled. Even Irene, the 'little postman' as her father had proudly and privately dubbed her, forgot her responsibilities and left her regular beat to join friends who had made an ice-slide on what had been a long spring puddle.

Hanging her satchel across her back, she took her first run at the slide. The weight unbalanced her. She fell, her legs pawing. The boy next in line came shooting along the slide behind her and hit her in the back. They tumbled on the ground together, the boy on top.

Suddenly Irene began to scream as if she'd broken a bone. The boy, disconcerted, leapt up and others gathered round. Irene was lying on her back, her eyes glazed, shrieking and shrieking like something demented. Her satchel had burst open at the bottom, and a number of papers had slid out and lay scattered on the snowy ground. The children stood around her, scared and helpless.

Soon the screams attracted several adults. The first to

reach her was a neighbour. Without hesitation he attended to the most vital thing first. He gathered up the pamphlets with a swift two-handed movement which grazed his knuckles, and stuffed them under his own coat. Then and only then, he bent over Irene and began trying to calm her.

People crowded round. Before anyone could begin to question her, the man scooped her into his arms, first twisting the burst satchel round her body so it lay across her stomach. She had stopped screaming and lay limp with her eyes closed. The man ran with her to her house several streets away. Willem was at home alone, and answered the door. As he was later to write in his book:

"I have often thought since of that moment when I saw her, lying there apparently unconscious, for all I knew dead or badly hurt, in the arms of my neighbour – a man I knew was not one of us. His eyes were fixed upon mine in an obvious effort to convey some intelligence – whether warning or reproach. I looked down, and the first thing I registered was the torn schoolbag with five or six corners of the newssheet sticking out.

"If I am to be truthful, it is necessary to confess that my first thoughts were for the fate of the newssheets my daughter had been charged with delivering. It was them I reached for first, the schoolbag I carefully detached and removed to a safe place before I returned and took Irene in my arms and laid her on our living-room sofa. Only then could my alarmed thoughts concentrate upon reviving her.

"Were my priorities wrong? They were not consciously formed in my brain. Perhaps my reaction was, for a father, unnatural. But calculating it all later, I could not but decide that though Irene was my daughter, she was, after all, only one child. If those sheets had fallen into the wrong hands, our work would have been aborted and many grown men and women with more power than she to further our efforts, arrested. Throbbing through my brain as I attended her was the fear that the man who had brought her constituted just such a deadly threat. As he tersely explained what had happened, I had to suppress anger with the child for taking such a risk, for falling where this particular man would be the one to pick her up . . . "

Irene was not injured or dead. She had merely been reliving her recent rape. She soon opened her eyes and some colour came back to her face.

Willem left her briefly to see the other man into the hall, where they held a brief, tense exchange.

"I won't pretend that I don't know what you're up to," said the neighbour. "I'm astonished, a man of your intelligence, how can you take such a mad risk? And involving a child like that, you ought to be ashamed."

Willem met his eyes steadily. He had suspicions of his own, which were abruptly confirmed when the other, apparently driven to some definitive act by the situation and those penetrating eyes, suddenly made an almost spastic movement of one hand, turning back his lapel. On the underside Willem was horrified to see the NSB badge.

He held himself rigid so as not to show the fear that flooded him.

"It's not I who should be ashamed," he muttered, staring at the hated emblem with his breath sticking in his chest.

"We must agree to differ," said his neighbour coldly. "But you had better call a halt to these illegal activities from today."

Then he left.

Later, in his journal, Willem was to write:

"Uncannily, I had a strong feeling that he would not betray us. He was pro-German by temperament, NSB by conviction, having fallen for their lying pre-war propaganda about being 'all one family'. But there was a certain safety for us in that. All was not quite black and white even now. I had a bad few days before me, but I consoled myself with the thought: If nothing has happened by then I will know that that gullible wrongheaded idiot is before everything a Dutchman and our neighbour."

Incredibly, that was all he wrote about the episode, or

about that day. He did not write about what came next, nor was he, apparently, aware of the irony in the words: "All is not black and white even now."

The front door closed, and Irene's father came back into the room. He stood over her. His face was severe, not tender.

"Are you feeling better?" he asked her.

She nodded. She felt, not for the first time, afraid of him. He crouched down beside her.

"You must never, never do anything like that again when you have the papers with you," he said almost in a whisper, as if even their own home was not safe from the hostile listeners he had warned her were everywhere.

"I'm sorry, Papi. I forgot."

"You must not forget." His low voice spoke with piercing intensity. "You must never forget. You could have brought men to prison – good men, who are working to save our country."

What could a child make of such a statement? For her, there was no perceptible threat; nothing was visible to her from which they needed to be saved.

"Why did you scream? You weren't hurt."

She stared at him wordlessly. At that moment she remembered nothing about it.

"Cry-babies can't be 'postmen'," he said slowly and meaningly.

She would have been so happy and relieved not to be a 'postman'! But she couldn't disappoint him. Tears of confusion came to her eyes. Even his heart softened at the sight of them, and for once he had an impulse of physical affection. He put his arms round her and gave her a brief forgiving kiss on the forehead.

"Come," he said, "your Papi will carry you to bed."

And so he did, and she was feeling a good deal better when the worst thing of all happened.

He had deposited her on her bed and covered her with her quilt, removing her coat as he did so, and her outdoor shoes. He picked the coat up and opened the door of her little wooden wardrobe to hang it away. Then he stopped.

Something in his utter stillness froze her flesh. She raised herself on one elbow and stared at that straight, narrow back, the head slightly sunk between the shoulders, gazing into the dark interior of the cupboard, his hand poised to take down a hanger.

"Papi! What's the matter?"

He moved his hand in front of him where she couldn't see it, and then turned. His face was pinched.

"Where did you get this?" he asked in a strange, sing-song tone.

She looked. In his hand was the little luminous windmill-button.

"Mami gave it to me," she whispered.

"Your *mother*," he said slowly, "gave you this?" Irene nodded, fearfully. "And where did she get it?"

"At – at 'our headquarters'," Irene answered.

"What is that?"

Irene swallowed.

"*What do you mean by 'our headquarters'?*" her father suddenly roared.

"I – I don't know!" Irene cried, the tears starting to her eyes again.

"Tell me the truth! Have you been there?"

Irene was now so frightened, she couldn't think straight. Had she been there? Her mind was a blank for a moment and then she remembered. "Yes! Yes! It's a nice place, there are red chairs there, and filing-boxes, and Mami does the filing, she knows just where everything goes!"

After an interminable moment of absolute silence, her father, now dark with the oncoming of an ungovernable rage, asked, "Are you telling me your mother works for these people?" He thrust the innocent little button nearly into Irene's face.

Irene nodded. Then she saw the unprecedented menace in her father's eyes and she changed the nod into a frantic shaking of the head.

For a moment she thought he would lay hands on her. He clenched his teeth and between them drew in a long shuddering breath. Then he turned on his heel and walked out of the bedroom.

Irene (who told all this to Mariolain when they were

89

grown women) stayed exactly where he had left her until the arm she was leaning on went numb and she had to lie down. She could hardly breathe for fear.

When she woke up, many hours had passed. It was the middle of the night. Mariolain had come to bed unheard by Irene and was fast asleep. It took Irene a few moments to notice that their mother was in the room.

She wasn't frightened. It had happened this way before. Usually she pretended to be asleep, knowing that if she stirred, her mother might come and cradle her and moan over her (though she hadn't done this for a long time). But tonight was different. Tonight Irene wanted the comfort of her mother's arms. She turned on her back and reached out in the semi-darkness.

"Mami . . . !"

Her mother came between the beds. She sat on Irene's bed and bent over her, gathering her close, rocking her. She didn't moan, or say anything. She just held her and stroked her hair. Irene could feel something unusual. Her mother was trembling all over. It was a deep, deep trembling, not like a shiver of cold. Her hands, though, when they caressed Irene's face, were like the hands of a stone statue that she had once touched in a museum.

Then Griet stood up. She turned her back on Irene and stood looking down at Mariolain for a moment. She bent swiftly over her. Then she walked silently out of the room.

Her daughters slept through the rest of the night. They woke in the morning to an empty house. They dressed and went down to breakfast, but there was no breakfast. They looked for their parents, but they were nowhere about the place. This was unheard of. Uncle Dirk was not in, either. But it was not until Mariolain peeped into his room that she saw it was deserted. All his things were gone, but the bed had not been stripped and there were signs of a hasty and disorganised departure. She didn't go into their parents' room because, most oddly, it was locked.

Bewildered and fearful, Irene made some hot chocolate

90

and they drank it in silence and then by mutual consent put their things on and went out to play in the snow. But Irene didn't feel like playing. A heaviness lay on her; the idea of playing now made her feel guilty. Her mother's visitation in the night, coming after her father's strange and threatening behaviour, had unnerved her. She kept running back to the empty house in the hope of finding that her mother had come back, that everything was restored to normal.

At last on one of these forays she met her father coming up the path in his hat and overcoat. He looked very strange.

"Papi! Where have you been? Where's Mami? Why did you all go out?"

"Call your sister and come indoors. I want to speak to you."

Irene fetched Mariolain and they went indoors. Their father was in the dining-room, sitting at the table with his head in his hands. He straightened himself as they came in, and pointed to the chairs opposite him which were their normal places. They sat down, still in their outdoor clothes, their woolly hats and scarves. Their mittened hands clutched each other out of sight of their father, under the table.

"Your mother has gone."

They exchanged puzzled looks.

"She has left our house," he went on in a toneless voice. "She will not be coming back."

They couldn't take this in, of course. If they thought anything coherent, they thought he meant, 'today'. But he at once disabused them.

"She is *never* coming back."

At this, Mariolain felt the beginnings of a deep frightened desolation (it was a completely physical feeling at first, a pain of emptiness like hunger in her stomach) which was never completely ;o leave her while her childhood lasted. It forced tears out of her eyes. Irene sat motionless, staring at her father, waiting.

"I don't want to discuss this matter," Willem went on in the same hollow voice, the voice of someone who has recently been violently sick. "You are never to mention your mother again. She has made herself unfit to live with us."

"But where is she?" cried Irene suddenly in a piercingly

loud voice which made her father jerk backwards.

"Be quiet! Don't shout like that, we don't need any more hysterics from you!" He spoke with such icy command that she shrank down in her hard chair. "I've told you all I'm going to. Don't speak about her. Don't think about her. She is gone, as much gone as if – " He didn't speak the words, but Irene at least understood them. "Now it is just the three of us."

No mention was made, then or ever, of Dirk van Sluis. It was to be years before the girls consciously thought of him again, or wondered how their father, during that cataclysmic night through which they had slept, had got rid of him, as one of the calculated moves in his design to rid his household of every tainted member, to start again, cleansed of his all-but fatal error in taking for a wife not merely a cow which could not breed as he wished, not merely a stupid, plain, uncultivated inferior, but something far worse, something, to his rigid, obsessive mind, altogether intolerable.

A traitor.

Chapter 11

———— ⌇ ————

Mariolain and I walked through the snowy streets arm in arm in silence after she had finished this part of her story. My legs were now numb to the knees with cold, and my shoes were as good as ruined, but I'd stopped noticing. I'd even forgotten to be hungry, though our decreed hour was up and Niels had brought us round almost back to the restaurant. Glancing ahead, I could see at the end of the street its low lines and the inviting glow of its windows making orange parallelograms on the new snow.

"Did your father," I asked at last, "put *that* into his bloody definitive book?"

Mariolain stirred as she walked, straightening her back as if the story had made her feel old, and gave a deep sigh.

"It is a bloody book," she said without a smile. "It is supposed to be a most brilliant and honest personal account of the Occupation, but in reality it is a book about doctoring."

"Doctoring?"

"Isn't that the right word? To doctor the truth?"

The children had reached the restaurant well ahead of us, and were to be seen dancing up and down in the patches of light, both from eagerness and cold feet, impatient for us to catch up. We quickened our pace.

She said, "Of course he didn't put in that he threw his wife away, banished her from his life and from ours because he had been too busy with his own concerns to protect her from being involved with the Nazis. He chose her because she was stupid and then he destroyed her because she was stupid."

We climbed the brick steps, slippery with snow, into the Indonesian restaurant. Little candle-lamps on each table, low beamed ceilings, delicious smells and, best of all just then, blissful warmth. I felt as if I were being held back – my mind aching to go on to the next part of the story. That poor mother, where had he sent or taken her? And what would happen to the now reduced family in the house in Hilversum? I felt an actual, physical anxiety, however silly that sounds when here was my friend beside me, eating herself bloated.

Niels had been right, of course. The walk had sharpened our eagerness for his meal. He waved away the menu and ordered a vast *rijsttafel*, which shortly spread itself over every inch of our large round table until you couldn't see the cloth. The children, including ours, tucked in and ate and ate until it seemed they must roll under the table like blown-up beachballs. Daniel kept saying, with his mouth full, that he had never tasted anything so good in his life. George simply ate his way methodically through all the exotic little dishes which Niels, afire with delight at the evening's success, put before him in relays. We were all as hungry as each other. Mariolain ate as much as anybody. She leant back in her chair occasionally with an expression of untrammelled bliss on her little-girl's face. It relieved me to look at her. Oh, she was a survivor, all right! I got a strange, deep pleasure out of watching her eat that meal.

Late at night, in bed in the attic, I lay awake looking up through the skylight – or rather, at it, because it was now opaque with snow. Cal had really tried to grab the huge bill but Niels had acted absolutely outraged at the mere idea . . . It had taken quite a lot of energy for me not to be friendly and chatty with Cal as we got ready for bed. I had such a lot to talk to him about and share with him (though not Mariolain's story – at the best of times I wouldn't have felt free to talk about that, yet).

After a while Cal broke our self-imposed silence.

"Nice evening, in the end," he said gruffly.

"Yes."

"What do you and Mariolain find to talk about so much?"

"I've been wondering that about you and Niels. Hardly your sort, I would have said."

"Oh, I don't know. He's surprisingly interesting."

"But do you like him?"

He didn't reply. We lay there separated, on our backs, both looking up at the faint grey square of glass above our heads, carefully not touching. I had one of those moments when I wondered what the hell we were enemies *about*. I couldn't remember or make it all seem important, compared to the delights of cuddling up in the dark.

"I tell you one thing," Cal said abruptly. "I'm sorry for the poor bastard."

"Who, Niels?" I said, startled. "Why?"

"Lot of problems."

"Like what?"

"Well, your friend, for one."

I took this in.

"Has he actually been complaining to you about Mariolain? I don't think that's on. He hardly knows you."

" 'Bad form', eh?" Even in good times, Cal was inclined to tease me about his notions of middle-class Englishness. Naturally, he nowadays gave his taunts a more cutting edge.

"Yes," I said. "If you must put it like that."

We seemed to have concluded our conversation, and after some ten minutes during which I suppose each of us was waiting for the other to break down and say something, we turned, with ironically mutual accord, on our sides, back to back, and went to sleep.

On the day after the snowfall, just as I'd foreseen, all alienation between the children vanished. All became sweetness and light and soaking wet clothes. Luckily Mariolain was the kind of mother who never throws anything away, so spare ratting trousers and sweaters outgrown by Pieter were dug out for Daniel and George while relays of their own things were hung up to dry on an old-fashioned pulley over the Dutch equivalent of a Raeburn. The grown-ups had a pleasant morning lying about in the glorious sunshine which flooded all the delights of the long living-room while the kids disported themselves in the snowy garden. I wondered at Niels's apparent freedom from work, and asked him what he was 'making' at the moment, but he was very off-hand and said that as a freelance he could more or less follow his own inclinations. Mariolain flashed me a look and I let the matter drop.

In the afternoon we went to 't Gooi.

I personally had some dread of the place. I felt we were going to visit the site of an awful happening, a haunted place, something like the Tower of London which I loathe, or the Coliseum (in Rome, not St Martin's Lane) which made Cal's hair bristle on his neck. Mariolain seemed to understand. When we'd driven there in our two cars – the men in ours, Mariolain and me in theirs – and the others had flung themselves out into the beautiful sunny snowy landscape, and rushed away up and down the gentle birch-scattered slopes with whoops of joy, Mariolain and I sat motionless for a while.

I eventually said, "I don't really want to get out."

She patted me soothingly. "Don't be silly, Suky."

We got out and began to stroll. The others, even Cal, could be seen flinging handfuls of snow in all directions. Cal is not usually given to outbreaks of uninhibited physical activity, he seems to be too busy inside his head most of the time, but he was showing a different side of himself here. I wondered if he was feeling he had to keep up or compete with Niels, who was romping zanily with the kids, rolling about like a ten-year-old. If so, Cal was giving a very good imitation of a man who is thoroughly enjoying being a boy again.

Mariolain and I were rather staid by comparison. We stood on a little rise watching them playing and shouting below us, and suddenly Mariolain broke into my silence by saying, "Cal is very masculine, isn't he? Does he need lots and lots of women to satisfy him?"

I had been about to respond to her first sentence when the second hit me. I stared at her.

"Well," I said, trying to keep the surprise out of my voice, "if he does, he keeps it very well under control."

She stared back, an unreadable look.

"Do you mean he is completely faithful to you?"

That hardly reflected the current situation. Nevertheless I said, "I believe so," which was technically true.

"Yet he is so virile looking."

"He is virile," I said, feeling awkward with the word, having had so little recent proof of it.

Mariolain turned her head away and gazed at the carefree group below us.

"Niels has never been faithful to me since our honeymoon," she said in her floating voice.

"How do you mean – never?"

"He has so many women I don't bother counting any more. I stand only on that he won't bring them any more to our home. I feel very strong and fierce about that." I said nothing. I was looking at Niels with new eyes as he raced up a hill in pursuit of Pieter and George. Mariolain went on, "That's one reason why I hardly ever go out any more. I used to, a lot. I used to teach guitar and singing in local schools, and do things connected with our church. Now I have given them up, all those things, and I stay at home nearly always. Because I can't really trust him, you see. I got very tired of finding people's underclothes in my bed and their hairs in my comb and other things which make me sick so I won't say them."

"Haven't you talked to Niels about all this?" I asked after a few moments.

Unexpectedly and startlingly, she laughed, her gay, as-if-untrammelled laugh.

"Talked to him! You can't imagine! Only it was not talking, it was shouting and screaming. We have been married for fifteen years and I seemed to spend the first twelve of them in hysterics. Once I took everything of his that I could lay my hands on and threw them all out of the window of our bedroom. I have done worse things. I have spat at him and clawed his face with my nails. I have locked him out of our house so he had to break in like a burglar. Once I ran away and stayed with Irene, but she was so unhappy and I couldn't bear to be away from the children, so I crawled home and after that I just went back to screaming. I made us both so miserable with my jealousy that it is a big miracle he didn't kill me or run away from me."

"But it didn't stop him from having other women?"

"Sometimes he said he would stop, he promised and swore he would stop, but the moment he was away from me, or I was out of the house, it would start again. He is an alcoholic, only with him it's women. He *can't* stop. When I began to understand that, I began to stop screaming. Out loud, anyway."

We were walking now, away from the cars and the others, just strolling through the snow-covered heather.

"And does he still do it?"

"Oh yes, I'm sure. I told you. He is an addict. But now he is more hidden about it. At least he doesn't do it as if he had every right. And yet do you know, I think he resents that I have made him hide it, that I am at home so much he can't bring them any more to our bed. How was he in London?"

I was silent, remembering the make-up on his shirt.

She sighed. "But at least he could not bring them to *your* house. Perhaps it's unkind of me but I don't see why he should be able to do it in ease and comfort. The funny thing is, he is such a home-person. He'd rather be at home than anywhere. Do you know what I think, Suky? What he would like best is if he could bring his girls back and I would have supper ready and we'd all eat together and then we'd all go to bed together. Then he would feel quite happy and comfortable, me lying there beside him watching – not like a voyeur, I don't mean that, but like a nice mother watching her little child playing with his toys, nodding and saying, yes darling, that's nice, enjoy yourself, everything is fine. I sometimes think his greatest anger with me, in his deep heart, is that I won't give him that sort of acceptance."

We walked on in silence. I was hating Niels. After a while she took her arm out of mine and stopped. The sun was quite hot now and the snow was beginning to melt. She pointed to a beautiful spot just ahead of us, a little dell surrounded by birch, and said quite casually, "That's where Irene was sitting that time."

I didn't understand what she meant at first. Then she walked to a single tree, standing apart from its fellows, and put her fingers to the flaking silver trunk.

"The note Papi wrote, telling us to rest and count to 200, was pinned just here with a drawing-pin. He always carried them in a little box in his pocket."

"It must have been lower down," I said stupidly. I knew, I felt certain, that now she was going to tell me the details, and the detail about the note and the tree was a safe digression to hold off the rest for a few moments.

She looked at me whimsically, cocking her bright head.

"You're right! How clever, that's your writer's eye. We were so much littler then. Well, about here then." And she drew her finger tips down the bark with a rustling sound. The sun and wind made the bare tree throw spindly dancing shadows on the snow and she told me about the thrush and took me to the other place, where she had hidden, and the bird above her had suddenly stopped singing.

It crouched down on its twig for a moment, then leapt upward and flew away. There was a momentary stillness. Then Mariolain felt a hand on her shoulder and jumped with fright. The hand pressed down so that she couldn't get up. Off balance, she lost her crouching position and rolled on her back. She was still fuzzy-headed from her fright when she saw it was Uncle Dirk.

She grinned up at him, but he didn't grin back. His bony, flat-nosed face, which they had got so used to they didn't notice its ugliness any more, was drawn into lines of utter seriousness, just as when the girls had moved his matches or dried their hands on his towel. Mariolain had time to wonder what had annoyed him. Then she felt his hand slide up her thigh and clasp her bottom inside her knickers.

It felt cold and surprising. She gaped at him. His other

hand was on her chest, pressing her so that she couldn't sit up. His face came down on hers. His loose wet mouth suddenly fastened itself on to her own. She felt two simultaneous invasions, his tongue in her mouth, fat and hot and slippery, and his thumb jabbing into her body between her legs.

There was a bursting sudden pain down there. Instinctively she clenched herself – lips, teeth, thigh muscles, buttock muscles, like a little limpet trying to hold itself to its rock. The wet fat tongue was snatched away, leaving a salt taste, and instantly the pressure on her chest was relieved, but the big hard hand clamped down across the lower part of her face so that she could hardly breathe.

Suffocating, she struggled frantically. She could see his face just above her. His mouth moved grotesquely, trying to whisper to her, but the blood pounding in her ears drowned him. The horrible feeling between her legs stopped. She became still from sheer relief. Cautiously he lifted his hand off her face. Now she could hear him.

"Don't," he hissed at her. "Be quiet. I won't hurt you."

She lay perfectly still as if stillness would make her bodyless and invisible to his goat's eyes. The air felt so wonderfully good in her lungs that she forgot everything else for the moment, forgot the nonsense in "I won't hurt you" when he already had. He was still talking. *Irene was nice to me. She likes me better than you do. Don't you want to make me happy? Irene liked having me inside her. All little girls like it. I'll show you. Don't talk. I won't kiss you if you don't like it. Just be quiet because it's a secret.*

His face was hypnotically awful. His eyes were bulging, and his flat forehead with the taut yellowish skin over it was shiny. He was moving swiftly and yet furtively, doing things to her. Somehow he had got her knickers right off. She felt the sudden chill where she had been warm before, like sitting down in cold water. And now he was kneeling astride her, one hand still hovering over her face ready to clamp down again if she should offer to cry out. The palm of his hand with its strange pattern of grooves and wrinkles blotted out the trees against the sky. She felt something between her legs like a big hot sausage, only much harder, pushing and pushing at her – his other hand was down there too, fumbling, trying to hold her legs apart while she was struggling to press them together with the sausage in the way. And then there was that pain again and it wasn't a sausage any more, it was a treetrunk, being forced in where she did peepee. Who could think of such strangeness and fear and pain? But she couldn't scream or help herself. She stared at the great hand with the panting wild-eyed face above it and she knew the tree-sausage was going to kill her and that the worst thing in the whole wide world was happening and that it couldn't not happen and happen and happen and then suddenly – blackness.

. . . And then a scrubbing of rough grass between her legs. And she was warm again. And the pain was not a blaze but only a raw throbbing soreness that she didn't feel as pain after the other. The tree-sausage was gone and Dirk was lifting her to her feet and brushing off the bits of last year's dead leaves with hands that shook and saying clumsy things to her about a nice girl and secret like the dolly and now she must go and finish the egg-trail. And he took her to the edge of the little clearing where Irene was sitting under the single birch tree and gave her a little sharp push and walked away.

And Mariolain thought: I've had a bad dream and I wet myself. And walked in pain down the slope to Irene, who didn't look at her. And Mariolain said: "I counted 200. I finished counting."

And that was the first of the lies.

After a while I said, trying to keep my voice steady, "Can I ask you something? – How did Niels behave to you – I mean, when you were first married? On your honeymoon?"

"He behaved like any eager husband."

Incredulous, I said, "You *told* him what you've just told me – and he wasn't – careful? Kind and gentle and – I mean – surely he let you set the pace?"

She laughed again and shook her head. "He made two big jumps. One into our bed and one on top of me."

I was too surprised to speak.

101

"He was madly in love with me. He said, 'I'm going to show you how wonderful it can be. I'm going to chase all that happened to you away.' And he jumped on me and when I started to struggle and cry he was absolutely shocked and broken."

I said, thinking of the children, "But it came better later, presumably."

"Oh yes," she said. "Nothing could have been as bad as that first time. He left me alone altogether and had a lot of other girls and then he came back to me and tried again. Maybe one of them had told him that wasn't quite the way with someone like me. So he – what's that funny word – vood me."

"Wooed?"

"Yes! Everything. Flowers, nice words, gentleness . . . Oh, Suky, he can be so very sweet and tender! And we *were* married, and for me marriage is – I mean, I believed it would be my only chance. It was Niels or no-one. And I wanted babies. So when he began to voo, I set my teeth and I thought, I will do it, I will do it, I will do it. And I had a lot to drink which I never do, and I think I was almost unconscious when he finally – popped in his little sausage!" I went cold all over at the word, but she laughed. "And do you know what?"

"I'll believe anything! Even that you liked it."

She seemed delighted with what she took for my astuteness. "*Yes*! I did! It was quite nice! After that I gradually stopped being so horribly afraid. I would get drunk and say 'Now!' and he would do it very gently. And that way I got pregnant. And Suky, after you have had a huge baby coming down that little tunnel, a sausage going up it can't seem so bad any more, so for Anna I didn't even have to get drunk!"

I don't think I have ever been so impressed with the resilience of the human female in my life. We walked back to the car in the most outrageous fit of uncontrollable giggles. It was only later that I began to reflect again on all the pain that lay behind her victory over herself, and on the fact that that randy swine Niels was apparently still laying women all over Hilversum, not to mention London. I could hardly speak civilly to him for the rest of the day.

I could see Cal getting puzzled and then angry. After dinner during which he had had to make most of the conversational running, much against the grain as he's no great small-talker, he signalled me very brusquely to come upstairs.

"What the hell's eating you? You're always going on about the boys having no manners, what about you?"

I didn't bother to ask what he meant.

"I don't like him," I said shortly.

"What's he done to you, except be damn generous?"

I knew Cal so well. I knew exactly what he'd say if I mentioned that his new buddy was shagging away like a lunatic and making his wife desperate. He'd say it was none of ours, and he was technically right. The rest I couldn't tell him. It was too private to share with someone you can't feel you love. I was far fonder of Mariolain just now, and closer to her, than I was of and to Cal. My loyalty veered to her. This made me feel so deeply unhappy that I wouldn't even recognise it.

"Could it be," Cal was asking sarcastically, "that a bit of bad-form bitching has been going on between the *women* of this party?"

"You don't know anything about it," I said, and began brushing my hair.

"Nobody knows what goes on inside a marriage," he said "But I think I know more about this one than you do. Troubles like theirs go right back to childhood."

I stopped brushing and looked at him in the mirror on the flower-painted chest of drawers.

"And what," I heard myself asking quietly, "about troubles like ours?"

His eyes shifted.

"I'm going down," he said. "Shall I say you've gone to bed early, or do you think you could manage to pin a smile on your chops?"

Chapter 12

———— ∿ ————

Next day most of the snow had melted, but Pieter had a plan for something even more exciting which he announced eagerly at breakfast. Could we all go to Madurodam? What was Madurodam, we asked. The two Dutch children stared at us as if we had showed unfamiliarity with the word 'heaven'.

"It is the most wonderful thing in the Netherlands," said Anna solemnly.

Niels explained that it was a miniature town in a park near The Hague. The children had only ever been twice because it was far away and very expensive. Cal and I instantly saw a way to pay our debt for the holiday, or part of it.

"Let's go to it," we cried in unwonted unison. "Our treat!"

Eventually it was agreed that the men would drive down there in our car with all the kids while Mariolain and I stayed behind. It was two days to Easter and Mariolain insisted that she had to go into Amsterdam to shop for the festival.

Mariolain seemed rather quiet. We passed the first signpost to the city but to my surprise she turned the car in a different direction.

"Aren't we going to Amsterdam?" I asked.

"Yes, but we're going somewhere else first. It was your idea, but I have thought about it and now I want to, too."

I noticed that we were driving now through a humbler district, where the houses were built in rows not unlike our bit of Wembley, and suddenly I knew where she was taking me. I didn't say anything. After a short drive she pulled up outside an end-of-terrace house just a little larger than those alongside it, and we sat in the car staring at it.

"That was my father's house. That was where we lived until my mother . . . left."

I stared at the house. It was so ordinary. The garden was neat and trim, the tips of bulb-leaves standing bravely above the remnants of the snow, at attention for the coming of spring. The door set back into its protective porch was shinily painted, the door furniture polished. In the front windows were trailing plants and a smug little mobile of silver fish. Some very houseproud people evidently had it now.

"Where – what had happened to her?"

Mariolain didn't answer at once. Then she said, "Slowly I am telling you everything, as I promised to, years ago. It's doing me good, I think. But it must be in the proper order. I will tell you what happened to my mother in its right place, when I found out myself, after the war."

"Well, what happened to you, then? After she left."

"This was not our home for long. About two weeks after my mother disappeared, we went to live somewhere else."

"You moved?"

"*We* moved. Irene and me. My father went on living here."

"What do you mean? He sent you away, too?"

"He moved us. He had to. When you think about it, he had to."

Of course. Because if she had known where they were, she would have tried to come back to them.

"So tell me what happened to you and Irene."

"I'm going to show you. This is my day to revisit all my haunted houses."

We drove into Amsterdam along the autobahn.

"You see, my father had a brother, Oom Adriaan – my

uncle. He lived in the city, in a big old house. My father had had his thoughts on this house for a long time as a possible hiding-place in case we needed one, and now he moved Irene and me into it. Into the cellar."

"Cellar?"

"Oh, I don't mean shut up with black beetles and rats. It was quite a nice cellar, with rooms. He took our beds there and other furniture and our Tante Miep helped to make it as nice as she could for us. She was very special. She didn't say much but she did a lot. She treated us like her own children that she didn't have."

"Did she know – about your mother?"

"I don't know. She never said. If my father had convinced her Mami was a Nazi . . . In any case she would not dare stand against my uncle and my father. She was very obedient. But she was not – what can I say? – not tame."

"But what was it like for you?"

"Uncle Adriaan, though he had no children, had very strong ideas about them. He talked a lot about discipline and duty. He was very religious, almost a puritan. I don't think he wanted to have us. He used to say love was not a matter of feeling, it was a matter of the will. He said what most people meant by love was the lowest form of it, something between what animals have and a kind of fancy which is frivolous and doesn't last. He was always trying to make us understand his kind of love, the kind that made him adopt us when he didn't feel like it. Since we were first with him he belittled the *feeling* kind of love. I think now because he never knew it. Tante Miep had other ideas, though she never argued with him.

"But there were other kinds of discipline she saw the sense of, and so did we. We were in hiding. We had to keep very quiet and not let my uncle's neighbours and friends know we were there."

"You don't mean you had to stay in there all the time, like Anne Frank?"

She smiled. "Oh, no. We came out every day to go to school." She glanced sideways at me as she drove, seeing my surprise. "We were not Jews. We were hiding as much from my mother as from the Germans, at first. These things are not always as simple and dramatic as you think. We went in and out by the back gate, which was not overlooked. In our old place it would have been impossible to prevent people knowing there were children in the house. But somehow we got through the whole war without being discovered, even after we were joined by the divers, even after we moved upstairs."

When we reached the house, we found it boarded up. It was a big detached house of the kind I would call Victorian, in its own walled garden. The front gate was padlocked; the drive and path were thick with weeds. Mariolain parked the car in the wide, tree-lined, quiet street and led me round the back by an alley. She was remarkably calm.

"We wouldn't get away with it now," she said when we reached the crumbling back wall with its rotting door. "Look." She pointed. Looming over the back of the house was a big block of new flats.

It appeared that the house was due for redevelopment too. It was obviously years since it had been lived in. The gate gave at a touch and Mariolain led the way through a back garden made all but impassable by self-seeded trees and untrimmed bushes.

Halfway along the overgrown path leading to the back door, she paused uneasily. I thought she meant to turn back, but she turned only at a right angle and began pushing through the undergrowth towards the side wall of the garden. When she was nearly touching its brick face she stooped and began to shift some brambles aside with a stick. A shallow depression, overgrown with rank grasses, was revealed.

Mariolain crouched beside it and I crouched too, puzzled.

"What is it?"

"My aunt's grave."

A goose passed over mine. "Your aunt's buried – here? In the garden?"

"Not now. You can see there's a sort of hole. That's where they dug her up after the war. She's buried properly now."

She stood up and let the brambles fall back, and we

struggled back to the path. I felt inhibited from asking questions. But now the deserted old house amid its cold leafless trees seemed truly haunted.

When we reached the back of the house, Mariolain stooped and showed me a kind of window at ground level. The glass had long ago been smashed, but there were still rusted bars in place. One couldn't help thinking of a dungeon. I tried to peer in, but the subterranean darkness was impenetrable.

"There were eight of us living down there by 1943," Mariolain said. "In three rooms. Well, four really, when Uncle Adriaan had cleared out the little storeroom for the Jews. We didn't see them much. They never dared to come out at all, while the rest of us – even the men who had dived to escape the *razzias*, the manpower raids – could all go outside sometimes. Irene and I were quite free compared to the rest. Uncle used to say, 'Children are invisible when grown men are the target.' "

We were skirting the building through the undergrowth, and came to a peeling green door. It was padlocked, but the wood was rotten. Mariolain looked at me.

"Shall we – ?"

"It's up to you."

She put out her hand and grasped the bar of the lock and pulled. The screws slid out and the door sagged. It was just a matter of a good heave. But Mariolain stood there with the rusty lock in her hand for a long moment. I waited. The wilderness around us hadn't yet started to show signs of spring. There was no birdsong and the sound of traffic was very faint. It was an eerie, dismal place, and what with the filthy windows, the crumbling brickwork and the faint smell of decay, I wasn't altogether sorry when she said abruptly:

"No. I don't think so."

She let the lock bar go and struck out through the long grass and brambles toward the front. I followed. The thorns seemed to cling to her cords as she strode through them, as if to detain her. And suddenly, in one abrupt impulsive movement, she turned, nearly bumping into me.

"Sorry," she said shortly. "I've changed my mind."

We went back to the green door and I helped her half

push, half lift it open. Then she did an odd and touching thing. She took hold of my hand, and like two children we moved forward into the dank dark of the old abandoned house.

"One must not be a coward," she whispered. "I must look at it."

"Why are we whispering?"

"There are ghosts. There are, Suky."

"Is your uncle dead too?"

"Yes. In America. But I don't mean only that."

She paused and opened a door on our right. A large, square kitchen was revealed. She glanced round it for only a moment and then we moved on, still hand in hand. Next we passed through another large empty room, which must once have been a handsome living-room. Mariolain paused in front of the open fireplace and said, "This is where my uncle used to sit in the evenings."

"He must have been a very good man," I ventured. "To have hidden all those people. What a risk!"

"He wasn't good. He had principles and he was a patriot and he was very very religious, so he did some good things out of duty. I know people think doing is the same as being good, but it's not. My aunt was good, she was a really good woman, she had no big principles, she did everything from love."

She tugged my hand and we moved through into a hallway in the front of the house. A heavy front door with a fanlight, still miraculously intact, stood with its back to us. It was chained and bolted as if still protecting occupants. Mariolain hesitated between the stairs leading up and a door under them which must lead to the cellar. Then she sighed deeply and opened the cellar door.

"This was camouflaged then, to look like part of the panelling."

It was pitch dark. She flicked a light switch but nothing happened, of course.

"We can't," she said, with relief in her tone.

But now I wanted to more than she did.

"Yes, we can. There'll be some daylight from those little windows once we're down."

Now I led the way, groping down the creaking wooden stairs holding a handrail I couldn't see with both hands, wondering if the stairs were rotten and might give way. Mariolain whimpered softly once or twice as she followed me. As soon as we reached the bottom, we could discern the outline of a square area and several doors leading off it. I stopped and Mariolain moved past.

"It seems almost small now," she said. "This was our playroom when we first came. It seemed so enormous to us, we felt lost in it – we'd never had such a big room to play in, and nothing to fill it. Just the big table in the middle, some old cupboards and crates and shelves . . . My uncle laid this floor himself and my aunt put old rugs down so we wouldn't be too cold . . . And here, in this corner, below the windows, we had the big paraffin stove. Tante used to come in the morning and light it before we got up, and move it into our little bedroom an hour before we went to bed at night. She would never let it burn while we were asleep, she was afraid the fumes might poison us. Oh, my God!" she exclaimed suddenly. "Look, Suky! It's still here!"

She ran into a dark corner and crouched beside an ancient stove, almost caressing its rusty sides. After a moment she looked up at me.

"She would bring us a saucepan full of oatmeal or some-times hot chocolate – that was in the beginning before chocolate became a dream. The saucepan would stand here, on top of the stove, so that if she couldn't come to us for a few hours – you can't imagine how long it took to go to the shops then – we could always help ourselves to something warm. Later in the war we could not ration ourselves and would swallow everything the minute she had gone, and then scrape and scrape at the saucepan with spoons till the next meal came. That was at weekends and on holidays when we didn't go out to school."

She straightened up and began to explore the room prop-erly. Our eyes were used to the dark by now. There was little enough to see. The floor was worn lino over concrete. The walls were plastered brick, now overlaid with mould. Apart from the old stove, there was almost nothing. Yet

Mariolain moved about, pausing now and then as if at a special spot. I felt shivery.

"Suky," she said in a strange voice after a while, "I didn't know it till now, but it was for this I begged you to come and visit me."

She broke off to open one of the three doors.

"This was our bedroom," she said.

I went to look. Small, empty – one little slit of a window high up – a cell. "My bed – " she pointed to one corner. "Irene's bed – there. A little table with our washing bowl on it. A bucket with a lid to empty our pot into. That was another thing Tante Miep did every morning, was carry up the – all that. For us children, that was one thing. Later she did it for four grown men, one woman and a boy as well. Later still, I am glad to say, Irene and I helped her. It was not a nice job. I'd forgotten till now. Phew. It was a stinking job. I always, every day, tried to get out of it, when we were living upstairs."

The next door led into another, similar room.

"Here slept one of our three divers. The other two had mattresses in the big room. They put the mattresses in here during the day so the big room could be for us all. Their names were Henk, Tonnie and Robert. Henk and Tonnie were my aunt's nephews. I don't know who Robert was. This was Robert's room because he was the oldest. He was crazy about dogs . . . "

She stopped speaking for a long time, looking into space as if she were watching a film.

"Bert," she said at last, in a whisper. "Bert nineteen-oh-one nineteen-thirteen."

I waited. She woke up and looked at me with a little smile.

"I just remembered it," she said. "Bert. He was a dog, but a stuffed one. A little short-legged smooth dog, white with black bits on him, and glass eyes. He lived in a glass case and it had a brass thing on the base of it with those words: Bert, and the dates of his life, 1901–1913. We found him, and a lot of other things, stored in this little room here."

She showed me a room, if you could call it that. It was doorless and windowless. Its only light came down a sloping small opening which went up to the garden. Probably a chute for coal – the room was just about large enough to have been a biggish coal-cellar. The mouth of the chute was covered by a metal lid with a few perforations in it in a flower pattern. This had rusted till the divisions had fallen in, making jagged, larger holes.

"My uncle had packed a lot of old junk from his antique business in here when we came. Of course we found it. There were some treasures besides Bert 1901–1913." She paused. I felt her hand touch my elbow very lightly as if to focus my attention, though it hadn't wavered. "It was here we found Julie," she said.

"What was Julie?" I asked. "A doll?"

There was a long silence, and then she said, in an altered, an artificially light tone, "Robert used to take Bert into his room and talk to it. We laughed at him because he used to pretend to take Bert for walks and tell us where they had been and which were Bert's favourite trees . . . I could tell you so many stories about those three men! – "

Her fingers were still touching my elbow, which made me say, "Tell me about Julie."

She walked a few steps from me into the darker dark of the coal-cellar room.

"We found her with some other dolls in a chest, right here. She was an old doll with a head made from papier-mâché and real hair but a soft body. She wore a long white petticoat to her feet. She was supposed to be a baby doll but she had a very grown-up face with eyes that opened and shut."

I could only just see Mariolain. She stood in the corner with her back to me.

"I think she was our mother," she said.

The aunt and uncle had been instructed by Willem that Griet's name was forbidden and that no question or mention of her was to be tolerated. Even Aunt Miep fell in with this. So the girls almost unconsciously evolved a secret language in which they could talk to each other about their mother, though they never even whispered about her directly.

Her code name was Julie. Of the fierce quarrels which were an inseparable part of their relationship, the most frequent concerned whose turn it was to hold Julie, the doll – play with her or sleep with her. Sometimes they fought over her until their uncle would come down the cellar steps to silence them with threats or even real punishment. Several times he whipped them with a slipper for making a noise. But the importance of Julie was always hidden from him. They would unite instinctively in pretending they had been quarrelling about some other toy.

They had a particular game they played when they were sure they were alone. It was called "Where's Julie?" One of the girls would hide the doll, and the other one, instead of hunting for it, would ask questions. The peculiar part of the game was that the one who had hidden the doll had to pretend, even to herself, that she didn't know where it was.

"Where's Julie?"

"I don't know."

"Let's try to guess."

"Maybe she's living in lodgings in the city."

"That's silly. She'd find us."

"She might not be able to."

"Why not?"

"She's a prisoner."

They arrived at this point by different routes over and over again. But they also examined other possibilities.

"Maybe she's on the farm." Griet had told them a lot about her farmland home and her father and brothers, whom, due to the schism in the family, they had never met. These legendary people figured large in the girls' imaginings about where 'Julie' might be.

"She'd like it there. She'd milk cows and walk in the fields by the canal and play checkers with 'the boys' and have cream for supper every day."

They'd brood in silence over these projections. But neither got any but fleeting pleasure or relief from thinking that their mother might be happy somewhere without them.

They each secretly preferred to think of her as a prisoner. Not that they wanted her to suffer. They simply wanted her to want them so badly that only some form of physical restraint would keep her from returning to them.

After a while the girl who had hidden the doll would go quietly and fetch it. They would play silently with it after the manner of little girls with dolls, unconscious of the strange reversal of roles as they dressed and undressed it, wiped its face, combed its skimpy hair, kissed and cuddled it and, between them, laid it tenderly into bed. The fact that the doll's face gradually lost its features was a strong, ironic reflection of the truth. Within a year Mariolain at least could hardly remember what her mother looked like.

When Mariolain had finished telling me this, we were still in the coal-cellar room, both shivering with cold and she, also, with remembered emotion. I put my arms round her and tried to bring her out but she hadn't finished in there. Giving herself a little shake (which also shook off my hands) she turned round and said, as if something had interrupted the main part of her story:

" – And then later, this was the Blumenfeldts' room."

"Who were the Blumenfeldts?"

"The Jews. They were a Jewish family. Mother, father and son – Adam. He was two years older than Irene."

I gazed round in astonishment.

"*Three* people lived in this tiny place?"

"Yes, they did. And they lived in it not as we lived, coming out now and then, but all the time, for years. Because they were Jews, and from 1943, when my uncle cleared out this room for them, they knew, and we too, that if they were found they would be killed. Not like the other divers. For them, the worst would be forced labour or a prison camp. So my uncle and Mr Blumenfeldt made three bunkbeds, one above the other like shelves, and the bottom one they used for a table, with low stools which could go underneath – it was all very well thought out. They took in many, many books, and a few things to eat with, and their clothes in a box, and a primitive toilet, and then my uncle bricked them in there."

"*Bricked them in?*"

114

"Yes, of course. See? Here are the marks of the mortar. There were a few little holes left for air. Irene and I would push rolled-up notes through the holes to Adam. That was how we knew him, not by seeing."

"How did your aunt feed them and take out their slops?"

"See up there? That little hole in the corner? – no, not their 'window'. Up there, in the ceiling. There was a little lift. It went up and down on a rope, to the kitchen upstairs. They never needed to come out at all. And do you know, we never even felt specially sorry for them . . . I remember saying to Irene, isn't Adam lucky he doesn't have to go to school? The wonder is that sitting in there, three of them, listening to us 'one-degree' divers out in the big room talking and laughing and not being afraid of our lives, they didn't go completely mad."

I kept taking the measure of the room. It was hard to believe.

"How did they get exercise?"

"How do you call it? – daily dozen? One at a time, of course. Never did they miss. Adam wrote us he could do one hundred crouch-and-stands. There was no room for press-ups. Look – see that bar up near the ceiling? That was for a curtain so they could do their toilet in some sort of decency. Adam used to pull up on that to strengthen his arms."

I couldn't stay in the room any longer. It gave me claustrophobia. I came out into the big room, and Mariolain followed.

"I told you we used to think of our mother as a prisoner. And we were prisoners too, or so we felt, at first. Alone in that cellar, coming out just to go to school, having not to talk to or be too friendly with any other children, so many rules of silence and behaviour to keep . . . Our father used to come every Sunday to visit us. He would bring us little presents of food and books and ask us about our schoolwork and impress on us how important certain efforts were, the effort of self-discipline, of politeness to our aunt, obedience to our uncle, of hard work and discretion at school . . . He kept saying, 'You are the future' and 'You must be strong'. To Irene, at first, he apologised because she couldn't be his postman any more. She made a face behind his back . . .

That was the one good thing! But he apologised for nothing else, nothing at all, ever. And sometimes we thought, at least I did, that *he* had shut our mother up somewhere. I remember I dreamt once or twice that he had killed her. I really couldn't believe that anything less could keep her away . . .

"Of course, as we grew up a little, we both secretly thought she must be dead. We stopped playing at 'Where's Julie?' We stopped talking about her. Thinking about her . . . because there was anger in it too. Why hadn't she come? You see . . . When the others began to join us in our cellar-life, it didn't feel like being prisoners any more. It got more and more like a family, because of the company, the long table with benches where we all ate together, the laughter and jokes that happened alongside the anxiousness and fear and anger about what was going on outside. Even the stories each person told about why he'd 'dived' were exciting. We weren't lonely any more. We weren't two little motherless orphans."

We had left the cellar and gone back through the dim hall and climbed the wide wooden stairs to the upper floor.

"Tante Miep felt it was wrong for us to be alone down there with the men after my sister stopped being a child. So then we were taken out of the cellar. We lived for a year up here with Tante and Oom. Look. This was our bedroom then. What an improvement, you'll say! A nice room with a proper window looking out over the garden and curtains and wallpaper on the wall . . . " She found a loose edge of paper and tugged at it. Two or three layers came away and as she ripped a piece off she cried: "Yes, look! Here was ours, violets and rosebuds, with little bumps . . . But apart from the comforts we were not comfortable. We missed the cellar. We missed Henk and Robert and even poor Adam. We felt we had deserted them. And as things in the country got more and more bad, Uncle got stricter and stricter. Our father came less often because transport broke down. It was as if Uncle Adriaan was our father, and he treated us as he thought a father should. And Tante Miep could not help us so well because he would not let her be 'soft' with us."

She took me into the bedroom next door.

"This was their room. Here was the bed. It was a big boxy one with no space under it. You know at a certain point the Germans got very tired of all Dutch people getting hope and news from Radio Oranje and the BBC so they called in all the private radios. No-one could own one without a permit. To listen to a radio could mean prison or worse. Of course our father had a secret radio, and so did Uncle. Father kept his in a telephone directory! Uncle kept his in the boxy part of his bed. After we were in bed at night we used to hear it talking softly through the wall. My father tried to teach us English so we could understand the BBC. He still believed we should be part of the war, especially now I was ten and Irene was thirteen."

We walked round the rest of the house in silence, ending up in the first room we had looked at – the kitchen. Mariolain stood in the doorway for a few moments and then said, "If there is any ghost in this house, it is here. Here is the room where my aunt died. If you had known her, you would have guessed it – not in her bed, but here, in the kitchen, at the table, cutting up sugarbeet."

And then she did something she hadn't done yet. She let herself cry. I tried to comfort her, but what she needed to do was stand on the bare tiles where the table had been and let her tears fall for her aunt in the proper place. I stood near her without touching her and she hugged her body with her arms and shook with silent sobs for long minutes. Then she came out of it. She went to the sink where there was still running water, washed her face and said, "We must go. I've got all the shopping to do."

Chapter 13

There is one uncharacteristic section of Willem's book, in which he very humbly pays tribute to the role of women in Holland at that time. The men, he says, might be the breadwinners, as long as there was any bread, and the fighters or resisters, and they were still nominally the dominant figures in their families and communities. But as things got more desperate – as foodstocks got lower and privations more extreme, as what he called the deep, deathly apathy caused by hunger and cold laid its iron hand on the population – it was the women who kept life, and a faint survivors' will, going at the grassroots.

Though Willem did not credit his sister-in-law personally, Mariolain filled in the details. It was Tante Miep who stood in endless queues and cooked whatever she could buy, wangle or grow in the garden for her flock of secret dependants. It was her small untidy figure which gladdened the hearts of the 'trolls' (as the cellar-dwellers nicknamed themselves) when she appeared at the top of the stairs carrying laden trays. Upon her depended the many minor and major necessities apart from food: the cigarettes called 'beks' which stood for 'certified first class garbage'; for clothes, made, adapted and scrounged, for medicines while they were obtainable at any price; for reading matter and games to ward off that most deadly enemy, boredom. It was she who sneaked notes and messages in and out.

It was also Miep who took it on herself to sift the news, emphasising the positive and reducing the impact of the negative. But Adriaan – who shared Willem's belief in 'facing up to the truth' – would often vitiate her tact by hastening down to stun the divers with bad news of an Allied setback, the latest rumours of mass round-ups, internments or executions, and the lesser horrors (which Miep's various womanly skills might have hidden from them for a time) of growing shortages.

It was also Adriaan who almost fell down the stairs one day in his eagerness to bring, for once, good news – wonderful news. The Allies were coming! Part of the south was already free! The British and Canadians would soon overrun the whole country, driving the *Moffen* out. He had heard it on the radio, from England, it was certain, it was definite, the war was over, liberation was at hand! They could stand by to come out, to join the dancing in the streets, to wreak vengeance on those who had collaborated.

There were hysterical rejoicings in the cellar. Every hand was laid on the bricks and boards that walled-in the Jewish family, and soon they, too – poor pale spectres whose faces no-one had seen for many, many months – were moving incredulously about the wider world of the cellar, the woman stretching out her hands as if she might fall over a precipice with so much space before her, the man fighting tears, the boy Adam, remarkably sturdy-looking despite his pallor, shouting and dancing and embracing everyone, including Irene and Mariolain.

But as they began to ascend the stairs, Miep stood at the top, barring their way.

"No!" she cried in her thin little voice which none of them had ever heard raised. "You're not to! You're not to! It's not over yet. Don't go out there yet! Wait till the Allied soldiers are really here!"

Her fervour checked them, and they stayed put, though trembling with thwarted hope. All but one. Adam, the boy, now sixteen, couldn't bear it. Adriaan had said that the Germans were withdrawing, retreating in confusion, that the Canadians were nearly here! This quiet, controlled, patient boy who had borne so much now erupted with an uncontroll-

119

able passion to witness the flight of the Germans, to spit perhaps upon just one of their retreating backs . . .

Miep tried to stop him physically. She wrestled with him all the way to the front door. It was Adriaan who pulled her off, saying, "Leave the boy alone, woman! Do you want to cheat him of his moment? This is the day he'll describe to his grandchildren!" And he held her back while Adam ran from the house.

He came back once, twice, full of excitement, his eyes madly brilliant, carrying a branch of leaves to his mother, a newspaper he'd found in the street, tiny tokens of the bliss of his new freedom. Then, while he was away for third time, the rumours reached them. It had all gone wrong. The assault had failed, the Allies were not pushing forward, the Germans were not leaving, they were coming back! It all happened so quickly, the plunge from ecstasy to despair and alarm. The Jews, the mother and father, were urged back into their hidey-hole, crying and protesting. The bricks, the boards were replaced, leaving just room at the top for Adam to be thrust in the moment he should return.

But the night passed, and so did the following day – a day of the most absolute disappointment and dismay throughout northern Holland, where the vengeance the Dutch had planned for their traitors on 'Axe Day' was turned upon themselves by the furious Germans. And Adriaan came dragging down the cellar stairs to tell the Jews, with a terseness born of his own unendurable guilt, that they must give up hope, that Adam had been taken.

After that, Mariolain and Irene lay in bed for many nights, listening – not to the radio, which Adriaan swore he would never trust again, but to their uncle justifying himself, cursing the Allies who had aborted their announced advance, calling on God to help them. Miep lay at his side, perfectly silent. Though none of them knew it, she was already mortally ill.

She probably had cancer, but it was never diagnosed or

treated because after the disaster at Arnhem the country descended into such chaos that there simply never seemed to be time. The unwillingness of many people even under ordinary circumstances to find out that they have something seriously wrong with them was exacerbated in Miep's case. Without conceit, she had a realistic understanding of how vital her role was in the lives of her extended household. Irene, coming upon her one day slumped at the kitchen table, told her she should see a doctor. Miep smiled, pushing back her wispy hair, and said: "And what if he put me in hospital? You'd be the only woman in the house then! Don't be a silly girl, I'm all right. I'll last the war."

And now the nightmare of the Hunger Winter began.

Ill though she was, Miep kept going. The regular queues which had been for butter, eggs and skim-milk were now for bread and firewood. Miep stood in them patiently hour after hour in pouring rain – it was the wettest autumn on record. When things got worse, it was she who suggested to her brother-in-law that he get one of his 'friends' to 'find' them extra ration cards. Willem, who had strong scruples about nepotism, needed some persuasion, but when it came down to his daughters eating grated tulip bulbs and some black-market meat masquerading under the euphemistic name of 'roof-rabbits', as an alternative to public soup-kitchens, he gave way. Miep got three beautifully forged ration-cards to add to her legitimate ones. It wasn't nearly enough to keep nine people fed, but it helped.

Miep learnt, and taught the girls, how to cook sugarbeet (previously considered inedible); how to make soap-substitute which was like stinking grey clay; how to use a billhook on trees in the park; and how to scour deserted gardens for leftover root vegetables. But she left the girls behind when she crept to the black market to exchange gilt clocks for eggs, her wedding ring for a chicken, a winter coat for a quarter-sack of wheat. They all took turns keeping warm in the long, curfew'd evenings by grinding the grains in a stiff old hand-cranked coffee mill, which yielded arm-ache and blisters and the makings of little hard breads like dog-biscuits. Mariolain became an expert at unpicking old woollen garments, washing the strands to straighten them out, and then rolling them into balls. These they sent down in the Jews' lift. Mrs Blumenfeldt, emerging slowly from her agonising haze of grief, had sent up a note with her half-empty plate: "Please give me something to do or I shall go mad."

Keeping warm was, next to eating, the biggest problem. Before long every tree in the vicinity had been chopped down and spirited away. Even the wooden blocks between the tramlines were prised up. At first the Germans tried to stop this, but the wood-raids got bolder, more people took part in them, and soon all attempts to control them were given up.

One day Adriaan was passing through the Jewish district, now deserted, and saw that many of the doors which their owners had left locked or boarded up were open, and downstairs windows broken. He had an impression that the buildings were somehow alive – not with legitimate occupants, but with intruders, as a cockroach-infested kitchen might appear alive if a torch were suddenly turned on it at night. He paused. After a few moments a couple of young boys darted out of one of the gaping doorways and scurried away. They had sacks, bulging angularly on their backs. Loot . . . ? Surely not, thought Adriaan. The houses were already stripped of any portable valuables. Then the obvious solution occurred to him.

That night he went down to the cellar.

"Listen," he said to Henk, Tonnie and Robert. "We might as well be shot for looting as freeze to death. There's an empty house four doors away. We could creep down there in the dark after curfew – across the back gardens, of course – and break in, and get some of the floorboards. Good, seasoned wood, it'll burn much better than that green stuff from the trees. What do you say?"

The men were more than willing. Their young bodies were aching for any kind of action; after being so long immured, even the possibility of capture had lost some of its terror. In any case, the *razzias* were getting more frequent. Sooner or later their house would be raided and, despite the efforts to conceal their hiding-place, there was a better-than-even chance they'd be caught.

"We might as well warm up before we get taken," they agreed.

The expedition was a grand success, and enormously enjoyable. Irene went to help. "There is a looter in all of us," said Robert cheerfully as he prised up the boards with satisfying screeching sounds and sawed them into carriable lengths. The younger men set about the doors with hatchets. Adriaan ripped an antique pine fire-surround away from its moorings, scarcely sparing a regretful thought for the days when he could have got good money for it in his shop. That night they had a wonderful midnight blaze in the living-room fireplace, and Miep opened a precious jar of preserves.

They made several trips to the empty house on successive nights. The fuel pile in the cellar was growing; it seemed they would soon have enough to last the winter. Then one night as they approached the back of 'their' house, they froze . . . Muffled sounds of chopping and sawing could be heard. After exchanging looks of mute outrage, they were obliged to creep home empty-handed, furious that other neighbours should have trespassed on their established wooding territory.

Two weeks later they heard some incredible news. Part of the empty house had collapsed, killing two people who happened to be in it. Adriaan related these tragic tidings to the trolls in solemn tones. After a few seconds' silence, Henk and Tonnie fell on each other's necks in gales of hysterical laughter.

"Serve 'em right! House-wreckers! They must've got greedy and started on the joists and staircase!"

A few days after this, Miep and Irene were in the kitchen preparing a meal of sorts when they heard the sound they dreaded most: heavy vehicles rumbling along their street, the squeal of brakes, the slamming of doors and the loathsome shouting of German voices.

They looked at each other, petrified.

"A *razzia*!"

"Quick!"

They'd practised the drill, of course. The cellar windows were already partly blocked up and covered from outside with ivy and bushes which had been trained over them. The door in the hall leading down to the cellar, however, though partly disguised as panelling, had to be covered. Adriaan was out, so it was Irene and Miep who had to run and shift a heavy, cumbersome hall-stand from its usual place into position across the door. The grating sound this made was the arranged warning signal which sent the trolls, below, into action. Their role was to scatter or hide the signs of occupancy, in case the 'Greens' should penetrate their fastness, and to bolt themselves into Robert's room – not that that would save them if the raiders got that far.

As soon as the hall-stand was in position, Irene rushed upstairs to make sure the radio was well concealed, and that Mariolain was prepared. Mariolain was already hanging out of her window, gazing at the scene below. Men in and out of uniform were spreading out from the trucks, banging on doors up and down the street. The shouts, distant and getting closer, pierced the air like shots:

"*Aufmachen! Aufmachen!* – Open up!"

Irene tried to pull her sister away from the window, but the scene caught her and she stopped, her hand hooked round Mariolain's arm. Men were now being dragged or frogmarched out to the trucks. Some were coming out unforced. The trucks – two of them, one close by and one at the far end of the street – were filling up.

Across the street a couple stood on their doorstep. The man had his coat and hat on. The woman was holding him tight, her face buried in his shoulder. A 'Green' pulled him away, leaving the woman sobbing.

Suddenly Mariolain felt a tremor through her arm from Irene's hand, and Irene began to scream out of the window:

"You hateful pigs! You dirty pigs! I hate you! I spit on you! I sick-up on you! I hope you die and go to hell, you beasts! You beasts! You beasts! Leave them alone!"

It was Mariolain who dragged Irene from the window and slammed it down in the middle of this tirade, luckily before any of the raiders could locate the source of the abuse. Miep came flying up the stairs in a panic. She took charge at once, shaking Irene and slapping her face and then clutching her in her arms, where she rocked her back and forth desperately.

"Enough, child! Enough, my poor! They are swine, but we must hold ourselves in, or we're lost – sh – sh – !"

She had to muffle Irene's screams for several minutes before she dared release her. Mariolain was stunned. She stood close to the other two, stroking bits of Irene, her back, her arm, trying to soothe her. She hadn't seen her give way like that since she stopped being a child.

By the time the dreaded knock came on their own door, they were all in such a state that it seemed impossible that they could carry off their prepared act. But Miep, after one desperate look about her, as if for help, pushed Irene towards her bed – "Get into bed quick, I'll say you're ill!" – and ran down the stairs at once. They heard her open the front door.

While Irene got into bed, dazed and obedient now, Mariolain crept to the head of the stairs and listened in astonishment to her aunt's extraordinary performance.

"There are no men here," she was saying earnestly. "Yes, I have a husband, Adriaan Dykstra, he is in the city searching for food . . . He is fifty-five years old, I can show you his birth-certificate . . . No, the only others here are my two nieces, they are visiting us. Of course you may look if you wish. While you're searching the house, shall I make you some coffee? You must be cold. Not real coffee I'm afraid, it's only that stuff that tastes like burnt shavings, but it will warm you up!" (Laughter! – Yes, they were laughing . . .) "Come through this way, I might even find you a little something to eat . . . " And she lured them into the kitchen. Shooing them gently ahead of her, she glanced up and spotted Mariolain crouched at the top of the stairs. Mariolain was startled by the gleam in her eyes. Despite her painful thinness and the ageing lines on her face, her aunt looked momentarily quite young.

"Ah, there you are, Mariolain!" she called cheerfully. "Fetch Oom's birth-certificate from his collar-box, will you, dear? Some gentlemen want to see it."

Mariolain fetched the document at once. Although her uncle was only forty-seven, well within the age-limit of recruitable males, the birth-certificate gave his date of birth, sure enough, as 1889. It was a very fine forgery indeed, made by a contact of Willem's in the more skilled reaches of the Underground press. The same man had made the forged ration cards, which lived in one of the kitchen dresser drawers. Mariolain, running downstairs with the certificate, wondered whether her aunt had remembered to hide them. If the 'Greens', now standing by the table rather awkwardly waiting for their 'coffee' while Miep fawned on them, were to make even a cursory search of the room, they could hardly help discovering more ration cards than admitted eaters.

Mariolain was to do far braver things later, but she now did the thing that, by the time she told her story to me, she was the most proud of.

Without drawing attention to herself, she laid the certificate on the table, and went to the pantry to get a shopping basket which hung there. To her horror she noticed that the little door at the top of the Jews' lift-shaft was ajar. She shut it stealthily. With so little in the pantry it was hard to conceal it, but she shifted a big bread-bin fractionally along the shelf so that at least the handle of the lift door was masked. Then she picked up a jar of apple preserve – one of the last, hoarded by her aunt like a miser's gold against some special festival or dire emergency – and, leaving the door of the pantry open as if there were nothing to hide, re-entered the kitchen and set the jar on the table.

The men fastened their eyes on it instantly. So did Miep. For a second her face tightened. This was not what she had had in mind. But a quick look which flashed between aunt and niece was enough for her.

"Ah, just the thing! A little apple jelly with your coffee . . . "

While she was bustling at the stove, Mariolain walked to the dresser, opened the drawer, took out the ration books and dropped them casually into her basket.

"Could I have some money, Tante? I'm going to the shops," she said.

Miep swung round in surprise.

"To get the *rations*," added Mariolain.

Luckily the raiders had their eyes on the jar of jelly, for her aunt's face paled visibly as realisation came. Without a word she took her purse from her handbag and gave it to Mariolain, who slipped out of the back door.

As she went round the house to reach the street, she passed the entrance to the coal-chute. She stopped dead. A faint blue vapour hung above the innocent flower-perforations in the metal lid . . . the smoke from the Blumenfeldts' 'miracle-stove'!

Mariolain was appalled. Had the other divers been able to let the Jews know that there was a *razzia*? Would they have heard the sounds, understood . . . ? What if they sent their lift up? It made a distinct bump as it got to the top . . . Mariolain, after a quick look round, crouched above the metal lid.

"Mr B! Put out your fire, they're here!" she whispered.

For answer she heard a muffled outburst of coughing. Both the Blumenfeldts had dreadful coughs . . . A flush of fear like icewater washed over Mariolain. Before she could prevent herself she had jumped up and was running.

She remembers a dream-like sensation of running down the street, dodging the 'Greens' and their flushed-out captives, past one of the big open trucks with its cargo of men standing passive as cattle, and on, and on, clutching the handles of the straw basket as if she were sinking in a flood . . . She doesn't remember any more about that day, not even coming home and finding everything all right. How was it the 'Greens' did not hear that terrible tell-tale barking cough from under their very feet? Who knows . . . Thorough as the *razzias* were, or were intended to be, hundreds and thousands of Dutchmen slipped through the net.

Henk, Tonnie and Robert re-emerged into their little world, gay with relief, almost triumphant. Robert extracted Bert from his glass case and stroked and patted him, saying jubilantly that he was their mascot, their good-luck piece. Nobody thanked Miep especially, though the Blumenfeldts sent up a grateful note to Mariolain.

Chapter 14

———— ⌒ ————

Christmas that year was a travesty of a celebration. There were next to no presents, of course. Tonnie drew pictures for everyone. Henk whittled some funny little shapes, vaguely recognisable as dolls, for the girls, and dressed them in straw skirts and birds' feathers. Irene hemmed a strip of cloth into a ribbon for Bert's neck and gave it to Robert, who solemnly tied it on. In exchange he wrote her a witty verse. Mariolain made up a song about the glories of sugarbeet which she sang to the assembled company in the cellar, and was rewarded with her first performer's applause.

They all wanted to do something for the Blumenfeldts, even though presumably they didn't celebrate Christmas, and indeed how could they feel like celebrating anything now, without Adam? Miep knew that the Jews had a feast falling at about the same time which involved candles. So she collected some candle-ends and the girls melted them down and added some drops of food-colouring and made a strange stripey candle in an antique mould supplied by Adriaan. The colours didn't come out very well, and the wick was crooked, but it was something. They arranged it on a little tray with some ivy leaves and some tea in a pretty pot, together with the meagre 'festal fare' they were all having – rye pancakes with a trace of sugarbeet jam. They lit the candle and sent the lot down in the lift.

After a long time it came up again. To their astonishment

there was a parcel, and a note. The parcel contained a narrow scarf, knitted from multiple scraps of wool, as patchy and odd-looking as the striped candle. The note said: "Thank you. It is a miracle you knew we wanted a mourning candle. Bless you all for ever."

The highlight of the day was Queen Wilhelmina's broadcast. All the household, including Willem who had joined them for once (he came very seldom now due to lack of transport) gathered in the main bedroom to listen. The girls were allowed to stay up late. Adriaan had overcome his aversion to Radio Oranje. There was, after all, no source of hope other than these voices coming to them from that other world where people were still free to fight – and to eat 2,500 calories a day.

The Queen's voice stole into the room, the strength of her expressions conquering the volume-knob which was turned down low. As she told them that Christmas was a feast of promise, every man in the room had tears in his eyes. The girls, for whom the Queen's voice was just a voice, stared in embarrassment and unbelief at their father and uncle crying. Tante Miep didn't cry. She didn't seem to be listening to the radio. Perhaps she was listening to her cancer growing inside her.

Bicycles of course had long ago been confiscated. But very old ones, stripped of their tyres, were sometimes passed over. Willem had foreseen this, and had buried one of the family cycles while dutifully handing the others in.

In February he dug this bike up one night, removed its tyres (which he later sold for a handsome sum, enough to buy 400 grams of some unidentified meat,) and seeing it was rusty and decrepit enough to stand a chance of escaping notice, rode and pushed it on its wheel-rims all the way from Hilversum to his brother's house.

In his book he records how, as he ground painfully along through the snow-heaped streets of Amsterdam, his spirits rose, despite the decayed, poverty-stricken, deathly atmosphere. He had thought of a new way in which his daughter could be drafted in to the national struggle before it ended – and end it must, this year, whether in victory over the loathed oppressor or in the total destruction of Holland by flooding, hunger and decimation. By this time people were dropping dead in the streets. He passed two of them on his way, crumpled bundles like the destitute dead of India.

When Irene was informed by her father that she was to undertake weekly journeys into the country to find food – to join the hordes of 'hunger-trippers' whom she had seen, trailing exhaustedly through the streets with their hand-carts, prams and wheelbarrows, she rebelled openly for the first time in her life.

"I won't go," she said. That was all. She wouldn't argue. She sat staring into space, refusing to look at her father or say another word.

Had she been older, she might have asked him why he didn't go himself. He gave the answer in his book, though naturally not the full one. He didn't reveal, for instance, that he had made his way – long before Christmas – up to Friesland, taking a week, and had actually approached Griet's family for food, and had had the door of their farm slammed in his face for his pains. His official excuse was that by that time his work for the Underground press had become so demanding that he could not spare time or energy for hunger-trips, and this was true.

However, Irene didn't ask. She sat, while Willem reasoned and cajolled and eventually threatened. He was shamed by her refusal to do what he saw as her duty. Other girls of her age were doing as much, why should she refuse?

But Tante Miep, now looking like a little wraith with great panda-eyes, who moved with one transparent hand perpetually pressed to her side, answered for her. Irene was already doing her share. She emptied slops, she cleaned, she cooked, she chopped wood, she did everything her aunt asked of her and more. In her faint wheezing voice, Miep told Willem that she didn't understand how he could ask a girl of Irene's age to risk going into the countryside to barter with peasants, carrying goods both there and back which might attract all kinds of undesirables. Why, she might be *attacked*! Irene didn't move or speak, but sat under their gaze like something frozen. After a long silence, Willem said, "Then Mariolain must go."

Miep gasped.

"Yes," he went on. "You are right, Miep. Irene is too old. She has the shape of a young woman. It would be dangerous for her. But Mariolain won't attract notice. No-one will bother about her."

Irene turned her eyes on him with a look he could not read.

"She can't," she said. "I'll go."

But now Willem's mind was fixed.

"It's the obvious solution," he said. "I don't know why I didn't think of it at first. It's time *she* did her bit."

Nothing would sway him. So Mariolain, aged ten, joined the hunger trips.

At first Miep tried to go with her, but it was no use. Her frail strength was inadequate. It was more toilsome for Mariolain to ride the tyreless bike slowly enough to enable her aunt to keep up, than to ride it properly. And she wasn't alone. Half Amsterdam seemed to be trekking into the farmlands on bicycles or on foot, dragging home-made carts, weighed down with panniers and sacks and suitcases full of objects to barter.

The nearer farmers had either been cleaned out or had become fed up and unwilling to do business with the starving city folk. There were still dogs on some farms and they knew their job. Once Mariolain and a woman she was travelling with were met with an overhead blast from a shotgun through an open window. At other places they were luckier. The farmers were only human, in all senses of the word. It was hard for some of them to resist the family treasures urgently pressed on them in exchange for something to eat. It was hard for others to hold out against the hollow-cheeked, barefoot children who begged and wept at their gates, telling heartrending stories of starvation at home, of old people and young ones beginning actually to die . . .

No-one had so far died in Mariolain's household, but something almost equally terrible happened. As December came, Adriaan went down into the cellar and told the three divers they would have to go. It was simply not possible to go on feeding them. He must put his own first. Henk, the youngest, raised himself from his mattress and turned his eyes to the bricked-up room. "And the Jews?" he asked feebly. "The Jews stay," said Adriaan. "As a Christian I can't send anyone to certain death. But you three can find some other hiding-place. Or join the Underground!"

It was Willem who had persuaded Adriaan. That didn't go into the book either. Instead, Willem wrote this:

"There were patriots who risked everything, taking part in sabotage actions which could have – and in many cases, did – cost them their lives. But their numbers were shamefully small. A greater number, though still nothing to boast of, took lesser risks in sheltering fugitives from the labour drafts and even Jews, to hide whom could mean death. And there were others who performed less dangerous tasks, others still who knew much and served by keeping silent.

"But a man can come to a point where he has a higher duty even than that he owes to his country. If he sees his children starving and there is no food, or too little to keep alive both his own and others, then he must make an accounting which in retrospect may seem ruthless: One's own before the stranger. The future before the dying present.

"Let those who did nothing dare to reproach those who risked everything, and then, as that deadly cruel winter sank in its remorseless fangs, drew back from further over-extension of resources, material and spiritual, to concentrate on their fundamental and ineluctable responsibilities."

For all his grim determination to make his children share in the war effort, he could not stand by and see them starve. He told his brother he would take them back into his own home if Adriaan couldn't feed them. Adriaan was shocked. He had his own reckoning. His wife was obviously ill. Each day she could manage less, and little by little Irene was taking over from her. Mariolain was being modestly successful on the hunger trips, and was also not unhelpful in the house. Adriaan saw the future suddenly looming womanless . . .

"You landed me with your girls," he snarled at his brother. "I've been a father to them while you got on with your own life. No, don't tell me what you're up to, but whatever it is, I don't believe you risk more than I do. I've made endless sacrifices for those girls, and now, just when they're beginning to be a bit useful, you want to take them back! Well, you can't, that's all. It's too unjust. Besides, it would break Miep's heart to lose them."

Willem reflected. It really wouldn't suit him to have them at home. He was no longer teaching – his school had closed some time ago – and his whole life now revolved around his Underground work. He also had a diver living in his roof-space with whom he had to share his rations. Irene might be of use to him, but he feared she could be a burden as well, especially since had had seen that she could be stubborn and intractable . . .

"All right," he said at last. "Keep them. But I can't let you starve them to death just to earn yourself a crown in heaven. Get rid of those other three. There's so little organisation among the Nazis now, they'll probably slip through the net, and even if they don't, they're a drop in the ocean . . . It's the children we have to preserve, the next generation. You kick those fellows out and give my girls something to eat."

So the three young divers surfaced one night and by next morning the cellar looked much as it looked when Mariolain and I went into it so many years later – empty, bleak and abandoned. Adriaan rolled up the mattresses and carried them one by one on his back to the market, where he exchanged them for scraps of food and fuel. The table and benches had long ago been broken up for firewood. The old stove was shoved into a corner – there was nothing to put in it. Only the dumbwaiter creaked secretly up and down the square shaft twice a day to the Jewish couple in their under-ground cell. One of the last things Mariolain remembers her aunt saying in her life was, "The stench of grief and loneli-ness comes up to me in that little box, stronger than the stench of slops."

Miep died, as Mariolain told me, sitting at the table struggling to chop up a sugarbeet.

It happened just after what Mariolain called the dead dog episode. She'd been on one of her hunger trips, and had gone in a new direction this time, hoping to find farms whose bounty was not totally exhausted, but she had had no success. After sleeping through the curfew hours in a haybarn, she was coming home (on foot – the bike was used chiefly as a draft animal) with her sack of untraded articles across the saddle when she saw a dead dog in a ditch by the roadside. Overcoming her revulsion, she added it to the contents of her sack, balanced it somehow, and pushed on.

By the time she finally reached home she had mentally translated the carcass into a savoury stew, but when her aunt saw it she put her nose to it and at once told Mariolain to take it out and bury it. To Mariolain this was the last straw. She flew into a passion of tears.

"It was a fine idea, sweetheart," her aunt consoled her. "If you'd only found it a few days ago, I would have cooked it, believe me! But it's gone off now, it would make us ill." She stroked the thin matted flank of the dead animal briefly. "Bury it nicely, poor old thing," she said. (Mariolain couldn't contain her tears when she told me this. "It needed a person like my aunt to spare pity for a dead dog at a time like that!")

So they fell back on sugarbeet.

Sugarbeets are large, tough vegetables. To cut them while sitting down, with a blunt kitchen knife, when you are in a state of abject weariness, is an almost hopeless task. There was no-one to help. Adriaan had gone to Jordaan to find a black marketeer to buy some of his last valuables. Irene was gardening, Mariolain sleeping off her trip. So Miep sat by the table alone and dug futilely at the resistant sides of a big sugarbeet, and slowly the pain overwhelmed her like a black wave, which, in the end, may have seemed merciful. She had once told Irene that the pain was so familiar it was like a friend.

The mourning period was short. After a terse conference,

they buried the body in a far corner of the garden in the dead of night, whispered some curtailed version of the funeral service over it, and went back into the house to try to survive without Miep but with her rations. (Mariolain said: "It was hardly worth doing, but she would have wanted us to have them. For weeks whenever I put food into my mouth I fancied Tante was feeding me. It helped with the pain of missing her.")

The preparing of sugarbeet devolved, with all Miep's tasks, upon the girls. To cook the beastly stuff to anything like edibility, it first had to be grated to a mush, a wet, cold, slippery, endless task.

One day while they were struggling with a recalcitrant bone-hard beet, Mariolain had an idea.

"Let's ask Mr Blumenfeldt," she suggested.

Irene stared at her. She didn't seem to understand the suggestion. The Jews were hardly people to her by then, they were the lift, coming and going; they were a terrible burden of fear, pity and responsibility. But Mariolain took the grater, a knife, two beets, and some paper, and wrote: "Mr Blumenfeldt, please can you grate these for us?" She opened the secret door, put everything into the lift and lowered it down, hearing it bump at the bottom.

After about half an hour came the signal to pull the dumbwaiter up. And there were the beets, grated on the paper to a cookable mush. The grater had been wiped clean. They swooped on the prize, lifting it carefully by the paper corners. They were so pleased they almost missed the wavery writing under Mariolain's note:

"My wife is dead. Take her away and then give me other jobs to do."

The circumstances in which I heard all this made it even more difficult to absorb than it might have been otherwise. We were shopping for Easter: walking and driving through the busy lively streets of the city, filling our shopping bags with good food, weaving back and forth through the gaily dressed well-fed crowds between the shops and the car. The logistics of our expedition imposed maddening hiccups on the story, involved recaps and run-ins and back-tracks. The flow of Mariolain's war was interspersed with glancing inter-jections about our husbands and children, casual references to tonight's dinner menu or reflections on how 'safe' it was to park. I had to hang on to the thread with my teeth, gradually building up a picture which, while I trusted it absolutely as the truth, at the same time I found impossible fully to comprehend. Around me was normality and plenty. Behind me was my own war, which hardly qualified as one compared to Mariolain's. Ahead, home, our families, a cheerful nourishing meal. Yet these contrasts made the stark horror of the Hunger Winter stand out in acute relief.

Toward the end of the story and the shopping trip, we were standing in a delicatessen before a glass counter filled with a wealth of good food. Spectacular arrays of cheeses, sausages, smoked meats, prepared salads, fancy breads, baked hams, pickled fish, cucumbers, peppers and olives, made a riot of colour and savoury smells. Mariolain was weighing the possibilities for tonight. She'd overspent on Easter goodies. She had broken off her narrative to indulge with me in one of those friendly, womanly brawls about food and who's going to pay. We settled on salami, tongue and honey-cured ham, all in neat little trays, agreeing to make something with potatoes at home to bulk the meal out.

Just as we were leaving, Mariolain picked up a packet of pumpernikl, heavy as a black brick, and hefted it in her hand.

"You can't imagine," she said, "how I used to dream of this! I'd only had it once, with some cream cheese, before the war. But I couldn't get it out of my mind in the Hunger Winter. Irene dreamt of soft, white bread – most people did. But I longed to break my teeth on pumpernikl!"

After a moment's silence, I took it from her, handed it to the man, and paid for it. She made no protest as I slipped it into our shopping bag. "I've got the cream cheese," was all she said.

As we emerged from this final shop and carried our load back to the car, I found myself looking at Mariolain's feet. They were shod in old but good Jaguars, warm, well-made and comfortable. I made a conscious effort to imagine her feet when they were little, chilblained and filthy, held with nailed-on cotton bands to a cracked and mudlogged pair of clog soles.

"Did Mr Blumenfeldt get through the war all right?" I asked.

"No," said Mariolain.

"What? – Don't tell me he was caught!"

"No. He wasn't caught. He just didn't come through."

"What did he die of?"

Mariolain gave me a surprised look. "Hunger, of course."

"He died alone down there in his cell?"

"Yes. Please. I don't want to talk about that." But a little later she said defensively, "Thousands of Dutch people died of starvation, they were dropping dead in the streets, I told you. The old ones and the very young went first. Uncle Adriaan told us we had done very well to keep the Blumenfeldts alive as long as we did!" Abruptly she was on the verge of shouting.

Startled, I said: "I wasn't blaming *you*, love."

We stowed the last of the shopping in the boot and drove away in the direction of home. Neither of us spoke till we were nearly there.

Suddenly Mariolain swerved into a lay-by and stopped. She sat for a long moment with her forearms on the wheel and her head bent.

"Sometimes I stole their food," she said in a strangled voice.

I closed my eyes while pity spread all over me like sweat.

Chapter 15

———— ⌇ ————

That evening we made the salad (tinned green beans, fresh cucumber and walnuts), plus a huge pot of spinach-and-potato mash, and set out the tissue-thin sliced meats and cheese, bread, fruit and butter, and a big jug of milk coffee.

As we'd expected, the men and children came back ravenous, and we had the satisfaction of seeing them fall on the food, regaling us with the wonders of the miniature city between mouthfuls.

To my astonishment, Cal was ecstatic, even more than the boys. *They* had found the little city fun and full of small functional charms. But they had inevitably dashed from vantage point to vantage point, never stopping long enough in one spot really to examine and marvel at the vision, the workmanship, the miraculous detail.

Until that evening I hadn't known that Cal loved scale models. Perhaps he hadn't himself. Madurodam had really got to him. I felt abashed, somehow, at not having known or suspected this small trigger in him which the miniature city had pressed, releasing such a bolt of enthusiasm.

Between spoonsful of soup he talked in bursts, mainly, I couldn't help noticing, to me. Had things been better between us, I might have believed he was urgently trying to share his pleasure with me. I should have come, he said, and seen everything – the scale buildings, copies of real ones

138

all over Holland, none taller than one's waist; the sense of
the life of the town, with people and traffic moving about,
and music and lights, and smoke coming from the factory
chimneys; the superb craftsmanship and planning; the story
of the actual creation of the place, which had taken years.
He pushed the guidebook in my direction. It did look marvellous. I would have been sorrier to miss it if my mind
hadn't been so preoccupied with that other world-at-one-
remove that *I* had spent my day in.

We went up to bed early. As I was coming out of the
bathroom, Anna buttonholed me.

"Will you come?"

I followed her into her bedroom.

She was standing at the mirror over her dressing-table,
trying out how she would look with 'bangs', as Cal calls a
fringe. She had some of her longish back hair drawn over the
top of her head, but the ends were too wispy to give a good
effect.

"Will you cut this straight for me?"

I stood up. She handed me a very business-like pair of
scissors.

"Are you sure about this . . . ?"

"Yes, I am sure. Please cut."

I trimmed the feathery ends into a straight line just above
her eyebrows, while she pinioned the rest of the lock to her
crown. I gathered the wisps in my free hand and fluffed the
fringe out, but she contradicted this, licking the palm of *her*
free hand and slicking it down. She smiled up at me coquet-
tishly.

"Do you like?"

"Not really. It spoils the shape of your face. I like to see
people's foreheads."

She let go of the hair, which fell away into its former
position. Then she turned on me. Her sweet little face had
gone pinched with fury.

"I hate old people!" she said viciously.

I suppose my shock showed. She did an abrupt volte face.
"I'm *sorry*!" she shouted, but in exactly the same angry tone,
and, turning away from me, flung herself onto the bed.

"I'm not that old," I said. I made no move to go to her.

"I said sorry," she mumbled into the quilt.

"Why were you so angry that I didn't like your hair? You shouldn't have asked me what I thought."

She didn't reply. I softened, and went and sat on the bed.

"What's the matter?" I asked, putting my hand on her back.

"Nothing. I don't know."

"Wasn't it a nice day?"

"Yes," she said, meaning not really.

"Maybe you didn't like being the only woman."

Anna lifted her head and twisted it to look at me out of the sides of her eyes.

"After all," I went on, "there were five of them and only one of you."

"And they teased me."

"Who did? My boys?"

"Yes, too. Pieter began it, then yours helped him against me."

"What about?"

"Everything. About not liking to be so many in the car. Then at Madurodam I liked the little cafés and the shops more than the things they liked, the boats and trains and cars. I liked so much the church with the coloured windows which had inside a light, and you could make the people sing. I put money in three times and all the way home they were pretending to sing holy songs to make joke of me."

"Didn't the men stop them?"

"The fathers were in front talking all the time. *All* the *time!*"

"About Madurodam?"

"No. About the *war*. The *stupid, boring* war."

"What about it?" I asked curiously. It seemed ironic. There had we been, talking about the war, and there they had been, doing it too. Only what sort of war could Niels have had?

"*Oh* . . . Papi was on an island and the Japanese came and . . . I don't know." She shrugged crossly, but sat up on the bed and blew her nose.

"But he can only have been a baby at the time."

"He still talk about it."

"I bet it isn't boring really."

"It is to me." Then she added, grudgingly, "He lived with *tippelaarsters*. That part is a little bit interesting I suppose."

"What does it mean?"

But she didn't know the English. I sat with her for a bit longer, and we talked about the things we liked, and when I got up to go she put her arms up to me to be kissed goodnight and I had the most agonising pang of sorrow for not having a daughter. I have it in a generalised way quite often, but I don't remember ever feeling it as sharply as I did then.

"You are very nice," she whispered in my ear. "When do you must to go?"

"Back to England? On Monday."

Her face lit up. "So you will be for Easter?"

"Of course."

She snuggled down under her quilt.

"On Easter we make all-coloured eggs and Papi hide them in 't Gooi."

I sat in silence for a moment, and then swallowed and said casually, "Does he make a trail?"

"What is that?"

"How do you find the eggs?"

"He make – " she indicated an arrow – "on the ground, and we come after."

"That's a trail."

"Mami did with her Papi, when she was little."

Incredible. And will she, one day, tell you more than that?

"Do you see much of your Tante Irene?" I asked.

"No. She live in Brazil."

"*Brazil*? Really? What about Jan?"

Anna pulled a face.

"Jan is in – " She put her face down on the pillow and gave a nervous giggle.

"In Brazil?"

She gave me a funny little look, and sat up in bed. She mimed, very clearly, a little window, with bars. I thought of the divers at first; then, with a mental jolt, I understood.

"He's in prison?"

141

She nodded vigorously.

"What for?"

"I don't know. Something bad. Mami goes to see him. Tante Irene married a man and went to Brazil because she don't want to know Jan."

"But he's her son."

"I know. She is funny. I mean she is strange. Would you run to Brazil if Daniel was in prison?"

"Why not George?" I asked, trying to make light of it.

"Daniel is badder than George," she said sententiously.

I laughed. "Oh dear! But he's more fun, too, sometimes."

Anna gazed up at me in the lamplight.

"It's so very nicer with you here," she said.

"Even with Daniel?"

"Daniel would be good for me if he is a girl."

"I do know what you mean," I said, but at once felt guilty. It's surely awful to wish your sons were daughters. It was only later I wondered what she'd implied with that "So very nicer with you here."

The silence in which Cal and I got ready for bed was somehow not so charged as usual. It also didn't last as long.

One symptom of our ill-will towards each other had been that we didn't look at each other's bodies. We had, for some time, dressed and undressed back to back, or in the bathroom, to avoid intimacy – it was a sort of silent mutual insult, stressing that, even if we did have to share a bed because things had not reached a pitch where either of us was ready to suggest another arrangement, we were physically alienated.

Tonight, however, Cal glanced, as if by accident, over his shoulder at a critical moment, just as I was pulling on my pyjama bottoms, and before I had pulled on my top.

"You'd better get in bed," he said brusquely.

"Why?"

"You'll catch cold in this icebox."

My hands paused in their automatic movements. This was undoubtedly the most loving thing he had said to me for weeks. Or was it months?

I looked over my shoulder and for a second our eyes met. Then he turned away and went down the ladder to the bathroom. I had cleaned my teeth already so I got into bed. I felt a strange excitement. It must be being in an unfamiliar environment, I thought. He's half-forgotten what it was all about. Perhaps it's because I'm not spending three or four hours a day typing, his nose isn't being rubbed in it. For a mad moment, I wished we could stay forever, never go back to Wembley and our flawed situation.

Cal returned, shivering, turned out the light and dived into bed.

"Are you warm?" he asked without touching me.

"Yes. What about you?"

"I wish I had a nightcap."

For a moment I thought he meant a hot drink, but then I realised he meant literally a nightcap, to cover his bald crown. I wanted to reach over and touch it. I don't mind him being bald. I like the smooth skin over his skull and the way it turns into thick, curly hair just above his ears. I could feel in the palm of my hand the sensation of stroking him. I wanted to so badly that I forgot myself and did. He moved his head a fraction on the pillow in shock at a gesture which had become unfamiliar with long disuse.

"Leave it there," he said.

I kept my hand over the top of his head, which was cold. After a few moments it got warmer.

"Anna said you and Niels were talking about the war," I said.

"Yes," he said. And after a silence: "God!"

"What?"

"Unbelievable story, that's all. Christ. How can he have gone through all that, and be – "

"What? All through what?"

"Normal. Well. More or less."

"What did he go through?" I asked sceptically.

"Enough to justify – "

"*What*?" I asked for the fourth time.

"Don't keep saying what. I'm telling you."

I took my hand off his head and we lay again in our

separate halves of the bed, in our separate silences.

"The *sine qua non*," he said at last slowly, "for sane balanced adults, is supposed to be a good childhood. The experts keep telling us what a good childhood *is*. They contradict each other, of course. Disciplined, permissive, structured, loose . . . all that. But basically they agree. Let them be children as long as they can. Hold them, feed them, love them, don't scare them, don't nag them, let them focus on one or two people . . . Jesus! And even when you've had all that, half the time you can't make it. You grow up and you blow everything, which is to say you don't grow up. You can't cope with life. Half the alleged adults I know can't. Me included."

I said nothing. He hadn't talked like this for months, either.

"But get a load of Niels. You say he's not treating his wife right, but she looks okay to me, more or less – and the kids, they're okay – not like ours, of course – "

" – Not like ours, of course – " I chimed in.

He made a noise which might have been an aborted chuckle. Then he said tonelessly, "Okay, smartass. You know what I mean."

He moved a bit, as if restless, and his left knuckles brushed my right thigh.

"I don't think they're okay," I said after I got over this.

"I know a lot of couples in far worse shape than they are. At least they're still together."

"With difficulty. For the kids' sake." But again, I was remembering something contradictory to what I was saying – Mariolain's parted lips and adoring eyes, her romance-heroine expression, when Niels was bullying us.

"They're hanging on. That's the point. Everyone has problems." There was a charged pause, then he hurried on: "The creditable thing to do is to try to solve them, not just to walk away. I mean, that's the adult thing. And they're doing it, Niels is, anyway. And I don't see how he can, after the start he got."

He thinks *he* got a lousy start, I thought. How can a year-old baby, who survives, have a lousy start that he can remember and blame things on? But then, uneasily, I thought: But the war lasted five years.

"What happened to him?"

There was a longish silence. The house was very quiet, in a way our house never was – traffic zoomed up and down our road however intermittently all night.

"Listen!" Cal said suddenly. "That's an owl . . . " After a moment he rolled over, not towards me as some part of me had been unashamedly hoping, but away from me. "I wish I lived in the country . . . " he mumbled.

I, not we. My thigh, which would soon enough be shrivelled with age, burned for his touch. I've had no practice writing about sex. Queen of the asterisks, that's me . . . Just as well. Burned for his touch! Christ.

We were wrenched from our dreams, troubled or otherwise, at sparrowfart next morning by a noise from below which sounded like two hysterical *castrati* rending each other limb from limb. Cal and I knew that sound of old. We were out of bed and falling down the ladder before we were properly awake.

Cal made the boys' room just ahead of me. We fell on the struggling, shrieking pair, Cal on George, who was on top, me on Daniel as soon as I had him clear in my sights. With an accord we hadn't shown of late we muffled their mouths with our hands and threw them on their respective beds, just as the four heads of our host family popped round the door. It was all too clear from their shocked expressions that no such unseemly scene had ever marred the tranquillity of *their* Saturday mornings.

"What is wrong?"

"Are they all right?"

"Can we help?"

Pieter alone said nothing, but merely watched with popping eyes as we manhandled the boys into something like passivity. The brief glance I had of him made me wonder whether the look I saw in his eyes didn't contain something like envy. There was certainly something of relish in his deep sniff.

"No thanks," gritted Cal. "We can cope."

Anna moved to come into the room. Her mother yanked her back. A moment later, the door was tactfully shut.

"Now, you little bastards," grated Cal with unwonted fury. "What do you mean by fighting here? You're not in your own home now, you know!"

I'd never heard him swear at them like that. George and Daniel, pinioned on their backs on their beds, exchanged a scared and astonished look. Daniel, of the ever-ready tongue, spoke first.

"George – "

"Shut up, I don't want to know about it," said Cal, standing up. He was shaking. "It's sure to be something idiotic. You just take a hold of yourselves, or before you know what's hit you you'll be in the back of the car heading for home."

"We can't go before Easter!" said Daniel, shocked.

"Our tickets are for Monday," said practical George.

"I can always change them," said Cal.

"No you can't," said George. "You said you'd got the last car-place on the boat."

"If you're so smart, be a bit smarter and don't push me! We can spend Easter in a boring hotel in the Hook."

Daniel sat up, looking tousled and thwarted.

"You can't afford it," he said cheekily.

Cal went absolutely livid. Daniel, who had not seen that look on his face as often as I had, and certainly not directed at him, actually flinched, and not a moment too soon. To my incredulity, Cal's hand flashed out and slapped him across the chin. It would have been his cheek, and a good hard one, if he hadn't jerked back in the nick of time.

"Watch your tongue!" Cal almost spat out. Then he walked out of the room. Usually so beautifully co-ordinated, he was so upset that he stumbled and bumped his shoulder against the door, which he left open as if daring any of us to make any more commotion.

I looked at Dan, who burst into tears (but quietly, I noticed).

"He hit me!"

"So I saw."

"What did I do? I didn't do anything!"

But it was only empty words and both he and George knew it. George got off the bed and began to get dressed. "Dry up," he said shortly. And as I got up to go, seeing the worst was over, he unexpectedly added: "Sorry, Mum."

I reached for him to give him a forgiving kiss and he instinctively jerked away just as Dan had done from Cal. It's a terrible thing when your child does that. I didn't think I whacked them all that often. I crept away with my tail between my legs as if I was the one who'd been slapped.

That afternoon Mariolain asked to be left alone in the house to prepare the Easter feast. Also her cleaning woman was to make her weekly visit and needed a clear field. After the usual kerfuffle about coats, gloves and boots, Niels eventually took the four children off the premises. Mariolain gave Cal and me a meaningful look which I interpreted as "*And* you two, please". She retired to the kitchen. Cal and I glanced at each other.

"Come on," said Cal. "We better just drive around, give the poor girl a break."

We got into our car and Cal started to cruise. We didn't say much. I was prodding in my mind at this morning's episode as at an abscessed tooth, but last night's less-than-frigidly-hostile mood between Cal and me kept intruding. Something else was nudging my memory as well. When Mariolain had mentioned her cleaning lady, I had felt a little frisson – a bell had rung, reminding me of one of the taproots of my quarrel with Cal. For of course it had not *begun* with Cal Senior and his letter, it went back far further than that.

Sometimes silences generate their own dynamic desperation. Abruptly, I heard myself say: "D'you remember Betty?"

"Who?" he asked, as I knew he would.

"Betty," I repeated doggedly, though I was quaking inwardly. This was no time to start digging up taproots, but I couldn't stop myself somehow. This morning's episode seemed to have stripped away the top-layer of my control over my tongue.

"Look at that," Cal said, indicating a large house, embellished with statuary, which rose picturesquely out of a small lake. I barely glanced.

"Our first cleaning lady," I persisted.

"Yeah, I remember Betty," he said in a grim tone which indicated that he also remembered what went with her.

"It all started with her," I said.

Would he say, "What did?" No. He said nothing, just drove, facing straight ahead. Neither of us was looking at the scenery, interesting as it was with all sorts of bodies of water, yet I must have taken a mental photograph of it because I see it now. The dark rain-laden sky hung down as a backdrop to little bright houses, green meadows, early-blossoming trees, which all glowed against it as if front-lit, with the canals and lakes glittering in between. A paradigm of cosy domesticity against the ominousness of a grumbling, lowering storm which hadn't quite broken. You don't have to be a trashy writer to see the obvious symbolism.

All too aware that I was throwing thunderbolts, I pushed on helplessly. "You really punished me for employing a cleaning woman, didn't you? And for getting the kitchen done. You never forgave me for that."

"I could have done it."

"With your back? You're not sup – "

"Oh fuck my back, it wasn't that anyhow!" he burst out violently. "You never gave me a chance. The minute you had a bit of spare money you couldn't wait to get those cowboys in, and we've been paying for it ever since."

"What do you mean?"

"Doors that warped, work surfaces that turned black, grouting that rotted, floor tiles that worked loose . . . Maybe I'd have taken longer over it but *by God* I'd've done a better job in the end! – Just as I could've cleaned the house better than that dimwitted Betty, or her successors. I *did*, before she came."

"I didn't want you cleaning the house!"

"Why?" he shot back. "Do you, for all your talk about sexual equality, secretly think a man emasculates himself by doing housework? It was okay for me to reclaim the garden from a junk-yard and build-in cupboards and rewire half the house when we first got it, that's men's work by you, right? And redecorating, that's men's work, and scrambling about on roofs, and even cooking, on account of everyone knows about great chefs all being men. Boy! Stereotypical female thinking! – But when the basics got done and you meanwhile had started making money, my DIY standards got to look not up to scratch, not to mention the fact that I was cheerfully donning an apron for a couple of hours a day to clean up after the boys, and doing most of what-all else needed doing for them . . . "

He'd begun to drive too fast and I was wishing very strongly that I'd let sleeping dogs lie. I tried to interrupt, but he raced on, in both senses.

"All of a sudden when you felt like a success, it wasn't good enough any more, the role-reversal thing, you got embarrassed by it. 'What does your husband do?' 'Oh, he makes the fire and bakes the bread and earns his board and – ' "

"Shut up!" I shouted. "I have never in my – "

He suddenly swerved in to the side of the road and threw on the brakes so hard I nearly banged my head on the windscreen. The rain had begun beating down on the car, obliterating the view, giving me a trapped feeling.

"You fucking well did," he said with quiet fury. "I heard you telling one of your mates over the phone that I had a bad back and that in any case I *still* hadn't taken out British citizenship, so how could I expect to get a job? It was the first time I realised how much you wanted me to have one."

"That's simply a lie, or at best a crazy distortion. I've never even thought about it like that!"

He turned in his seat to face me.

"You know something, Sue, this holiday's done something for me. It's given me a chance to look at *us* from just a little distance, our family set-up – all the things, like what we're talking about now, that we never talk about because it's just too close to the bone of our marriage. Listening to Niels talk about *his* marriage and what's wrong with it, and at the same time observing it and seeing what a lot is right with it despite everything, makes me just sick at heart about what's wrong with us. It makes me feel a failure in yet

149

another way. You know why? – because actually our trouble is all about nothing. It's not about anything except you earning and me not earning, and both of us pretending not to mind while actually we mind like hell."

I found I was screwed up into balls of tension, my fists, my feet, my neck, every muscle I had. This was awful – awful, and somehow the very worst was his saying that all our suffering and misery was trivial. No, not trivial, but that it had a trivial cause, that we were over-reacting, like spoilt children.

"I don't mind it," I managed to say. "But if you do, then why don't you apply for citizenship and *get* a bloody job?"

"I'm going to. I'd already decided. I'll go back into banking, or – "

"Oh Christ!" I burst out.

"It can't be worse than hanging around the house now everything in the goddamn place is done!"

"But Cal! If you did get a nine-to-five job I'd have to cope with the children, and I can't! I'm lousy with them, I lose my patience, I – " I stopped. The rain swished down the car windows. Thunder cracked overhead and lightning flashed almost simultaneously. It occurred to me we might be in some danger but it was only a passing thought. "Listen. Today after you went out of their bedroom I tried to kiss George and he *flinched*. He thought I was going to hit him. And that's because in bad moments when they've been fighting and you haven't been around, I've swiped both of them, I've simply lost all control. I've never seen you lose your cool with them before."

"And you know why I did today? – Because Dan threw *money* up at me. Trust Dan to go for the soft underbelly!"

"You've noticed? You never acknowledge their faults, you always make me feel – so guilty and unmaternal when I do."

He didn't speak for a long time. We sat listening to the noise of the storm overhead, watching the flashes lighting up that smug scene of the little white homes and little green fields and gardens. The huge raindrops churned the quiet canals till they were white, as if boiling. At last Cal stirred.

"That's because the boys have been my job," he said. "I

150

have to be very proud of them. I haven't anything else to be very proud of."

I know it sounds ridiculous, but the lightning that whitened the inside of the car just at that moment struck a response in my brain. He'd spoken the words so simply, but after thinking about them, digging them out of himself, and he'd made me understand. A whole area of him and of our marriage, which had been dark and murky, suddenly lit up.

"I see," I said slowly. And then, irresistibly, I added: "In that case I haven't anything at all to be proud of."

He stared at me. "Are you crazy? Your books – "

"Please, Cal," I said painfully. "Don't talk nonsense. My books are such *ultimate* crap I dare not even show them to you."

"They keep us. All of us. I'd think you could be damned proud of that."

After that we didn't speak again for a long time. The storm grumbled and flashed its way off into the distance and the rain began to ease off. Cal at last gave a deep sigh and switched on the ignition and the windscreen wipers. The canals had stopped boiling.

"There must be somewhere around here where we could get a hot drink," he muttered at last.

We drove on. I thought: Something's happened, something's been opened up. Either it'll drain and heal or it'll reinfect. But meanwhile I felt easier than for a very long time.

"There's a place," I said suddenly.

It was a small bungalow with a café sign and some dripping tables and chairs on a patio in front. We drew up. The sun was trying to come out. As we got out and stretched our legs, I saw that on the other side of the road was a field containing a pony. Beyond that was a narrow canal that you could sense rather than see – every dark line on this landscape was a canal.

Cold and wet as it was, I wanted to stay outside. The large proprietress thought I was crazy when I showed her this by sign language, but she shrugged her fat shoulders and came out with a sponge and a cloth and wiped the rain and winter-grime off a white metal table and two chairs, shivering histrionically and asking if we wouldn't die of the cold . . . We sat down and looked at the wet pony across the road, cropping the acid green grass unconcernedly, and after a brief wait the woman came out with a tray of coffee and biscuits. The coffee was very hot and very good and Cal dunked his biscuits and I watched him doing it and remembered how surprised I had been, when we had first met, that a smartly dressed, sleek-looking young banker should dunk biscuits into his coffee at the Pelican (a very posh place next to the Hyde Park Hilton) where he'd taken me, the very first time we went out. He'd had most of his hair then. Well slicked down . . . How had I been percipient enough to recognise the real Cal through his banking disguise? To respond to that hidden person at once, to sense, straight away, that I would love him? Perhaps the dunking had helped, and the snob-waiter's faint look of distaste which we had both caught and giggled about . . .

We ordered more coffee. The sun was right out now; everything glistened and gleamed. It wasn't warm but it was brilliant and I felt oddly blithe, as if nothing were the matter. I sought round in my mind for a subject of conversation which would trigger a response in Cal, be something he wanted to talk about, and not a surface thing; something important, but not about us. Enough about us for now.

"Tell me about Niels," I said as I stirred brown sugar into my coffee. Cal threw me a look of surprise, of appreciation, and I knew that for once my intuition had led me right.

Chapter 16

―――――― ⌇ ――――――

Niels was born in Java, the first child of a Dutch factory owner and his young and pretty wife. His father was a 'black' Dutchman, dark-haired and dark-eyed; his family had been in the Dutch East Indies for three generations and there was some native blood. His mother, whose name was Hendrika, was small, blonde and blue-eyed, with honey-and-roses skin. She was thought to be rather delicate, and her husband, Wim, worried about how she would stand the climate.

She stood it excellently. Her pregnancy, about which Wim also fussed and fretted, passed off without problems; she shot Niels vigorously into the hands of a nursing nun at the local convent after a two-hour labour, and her tiny breasts, which one wouldn't have supposed could suckle a mouse, began to flow with milk.

Niels's first year of life was idyllic, and probably stood him in very good stead later. His father insisted upon a *babu*, a native nursemaid, and the baby spent most of his time on her hip. His mother, having nothing much else to do, made no effort to adjust his rhythms to hers but did the opposite, feeding him on demand. He was adored by all, especially his father whom he physically resembled. The babu used to joke about this resemblance by drawing a little moustache on the baby's downy upper lip with charcoal and holding him up for all to admire, saying in Malay: "Look! He's his Daddy all over again!"

153

Then the war came, and the Japanese, and this happy idyllic life came to an abrupt and permanent end.

Wim would probably have managed to get his wife and baby out of Java in time (he himself felt he owed it to his factory and its workers to stay, a piece of quixotry that in the end did no good to anyone). But Riki was pregnant again, and this pregnancy wasn't going as smoothly as the first. She was sick a lot in the early months, and the doctor's view was that she ought not to be subjected to a long boat journey. So she stayed, and was subjected to a long Japanese occupation instead.

The Dutch colonials, accustomed to having everything their own way, could hardly believe what was happening when the Japanese actually arrived. Wim and Riki lived in Surabaya, which several years later was to be devastated by some of the most ferocious bombing – not by the Japs, but by the Dutch and British, and not against the Japs, but against the Indonesians who wanted independence. During the world war, ironically, there was no destruction because there was no opposition. The Dutch surrendered to the Nipponese invaders with a promptness bordering on alacrity. Many of them fled; others, like Wim, stayed on, and some even stayed out of internment, but at a price – the price of co-operation with the enemy. To do him every justice, this was too high a price for Wim. It must have been a horrendous decision to make. How much easier just to keep his factory functioning!

He didn't produce anything which could be helpful to the enemy war effort – of all things, he manufactured equipment for billiards, including his own patented billiard balls, and the occupiers promised him immunity if he would turn his factory over to them but stay on to manage it. He refused.

There was another 'out' which a lot of Dutch were trampling each other in the stampede to take. After generations of racial snobbery, during which many colonists with Indonesian blood would have died before admitting it, the intelligence that Eurasians would be regarded as Indonesians and spared internment turned their priorities on their heads. To the amazed contempt of the full-blooded Indonesians on whom many of them had looked down, Dutch men and women raced to register their mixed blood. Wim could have done this too, but he didn't.

Why didn't he? Wim, after it was all over, tried to explain to his son – to himself. "I'd always been ashamed of my mixed blood. To exploit this despised aspect of myself after years of craven denial stuck in my craw. Besides, we only had a matter of days to make up our minds. We had neither time nor foreknowledge to allow us to weigh up the pros and cons. Still, I might have done it, but then my partner's mother-in-law, who used to treat her native servants like dirt and put on indescribable airs of superiority, when she saw how the wind was blowing went down to the registration office wearing one of her cook's sarongs, riding in a *batja*. It caused a minor scandal. After that I couldn't. Couldn't bring myself to it. Of course, if I'd known . . . "

This didn't wash with Niels. Because Wim, with another part of his mind, knew a good deal. He had a deep instinctive horror of totalitarianism, and furthermore he knew something of the Japanese. But he, like Willem Dykstra, understood that the war would come to an end and that he would – if still alive – have to face himself and go on living with whatever treacherous compromises he had allowed himself to make.

Wim already knew that the wives of his friends and colleagues had their cases packed, resigned to being marched away to some more or less endurable internment. Their husbands were studiously 'behaving normally' in order not to frighten their wives and children.

It was this passivity which finally drove Wim to plan an escape. There was no question of leaving the island. But there were places high in the hills where a woman and child at least might hide. The *kampong* of a trusted worker . . . Riki, like her fellow white women, was soon quietly packing. Transport in the shape of a pony and cart was arranged. Everyone concerned had been well briefed and well bribed. Then, the day before it was to happen, while Wim and Riki were hastily storing some tinned food and other valuables in the roof-space of their house in case of some unforseeable emergency, the babu came crying upstairs to tell them a message had come from the kampong.

"They no want you, *nonja*," she said. "My people very angry with Dutch people. They think Japanee good, come to help Indonesian be free. They no help Dutch run away from Japanee." So that was that.

They spent their last weeks of freedom as if every day were their last. Wim remembered it, ironically, as something almost beautiful in its intensity. He was later to give his son a battered relic – a copy of James Elroy Flecker's play *Hassan* which had somehow survived the war, and directed him to read with particular sensitivity the scene in which the hero and heroine are making their terrible choice: death by slow torture after a day and a night of love, or surrender to the lust of the caliph. "Your mother and I didn't talk about it so poetically," he said, "but we felt it just as deeply."

They didn't avoid the issue, or the probable outcome. Wim didn't share his colleagues' estimation of their wives' strength of mind. His one obsessive need was to warn Riki.

"When they take me," he said, "it will be only a matter of time before they round you up. You must do anything – take any risk which isn't suicidal, to escape them. The camps won't be bearable, as your acquaintances think. They'll be hell."

One morning he was sitting in his office, looking grimly at the latest list of his workers who, ashamed to be associated with a Dutch enterprise, had fled, when one of his colleagues, looking very pale, came to his door.

"They're here," he said.

Wim was given permission to return to his house to collect the small case of clothes, food and medicines that had been ready for some time. To his utter dismay, Riki, with the babu and Niels, were out. He had to leave a note for her. It was a scribbled message of love and encouragement. It finished with the word, "*Remember*." He knew she would understand that this meant, "Remember to try and elude them." He had no real hope that this would prove possible, especially when he realised that a Japanese soldier was being left on duty at his house when he was marched away.

When Riki came home and saw the soldier, and found the note, she began to scream and run dementedly from room to room. This loss of control was entirely uncharacteristic, and temporary. But it frightened the babu so much that she fled from the house in terror, abandoning her charge. Niels clung to his mother and soon brought her back to herself. By the time the Japanese corporal had mounted the steps to the house and was knocking on the door, Riki had 'remembered'.

The transit camp for white women and children was on the outskirts of Surabaya. After getting that far with a suitcase in one hand, Niels on her other hip, and a six-months' infant churning in her belly, Riki collapsed.

The time was not yet when the sight of a pregnant white woman lying on the bare ground vomiting her soul up would be so commonplace as to leave Japanese officers totally unmoved. The man in charge of the transit camp was disturbed by the sight. He had her picked up by a young soldier and brought to his makeshift office to recover a little.

As she sat there with Niels sobbing on her knee and sweat breaking out all over her body, Riki's mind was hard at work. She had read something of Japan and the mentality of its men. When the officer momentarily left the hut, she carefully set Niels aside, and slid off the cane stool onto her knees. The officer was astonished to find her like that on his return.

Of course he spoke no Dutch or English, but Riki managed to make him understand that the baby would soon be born and that she would need things for the birth, without which she would be a very great trouble to those in charge of her. With the humblest tears and pleadings, she actually persuaded him to let her go back to her home under escort to fetch these things. At first he wanted to keep Niels as surety for her return, but in the end her tears (and Niels's howls) prevailed. The rickety wire gates were unfastened, and Riki with Niels in her arms, and a young Jap soldier whose rifle was almost as tall as himself, were allowed to slip out.

It was a long walk back into town, with the pitiless sun at

its height. Riki began to flag, then to stumble, and soon the young soldier was worrying about the time. He tried to force the pace by walking faster, looking back only every now and then to urge her to hurry. Still Riki lagged behind. But as soon as they entered the narrow streets of the industrial quarter of the town, where Wim's factory was, she mustered her strength. She waited for a backward look, and immediately her escort had turned his head to the front again she darted down a side road and was soon lost to her pursuer in the warren of ramshackle alleys.

The weight of the two children, born and unborn, on her small frame, the fear and the desperation – together with exhaustion and an empty stomach – were almost more than she could support, but panic lent her stamina and after ten minutes of zig-zag flight she reached the back entrance to the factory.

It was not actually part of the factory building itself, but divided from the premises by a narrow unmade lane. Riki cut down this – it was the route taken by trucks coming to collect the billiard equipment – and let herself in through a narrow gateway which the fleeing workers, fortunately, had neglected to lock behind them. She bolted it from inside, staggered across a small courtyard, and, almost blind from running, fell through the door of a building at the far side – a tumbledown shack used as sleeping quarters by factory workers who came from distant kampongs. While Niels, oblivious, hiked himself around the dark and noisome interior on his rump, Riki lay stretched on the cool earth floor, gasping, until the terrible throbbing of her overstrained heart had calmed itself and the flushes of heat and chill had stopped flooding her skin. Then she sat up slowly and took stock of her situation.

By now Niels had fallen asleep on the ground. Leaving him there, she made her way back across the yard, through the gate, across the lane and into the packing sheds. Beyond this section was the open area where the billiard tables, balls and cues were manufactured.

Half-finished tables, rolls of baize, work-benches, pots of furniture glue congealed on woodstoves, turning lathes and other machinery – all the tools of the billiard-maker's craft –

were lying there abandoned. It was as eerie as finding an abandoned ship. The offices, too, were empty, yet with all the evidences of occupancy, down to typewriters stuck with half-finished letters, filing cabinets ajar, a cup of tea chilled to the temperature of the bloodheat air . . . Desperately thirsty, Riki would have drunk even this, had the surface not been fuzzy with drowned insects. Unnerved, she ran back through the echoing premises to the sleeping shacks.

As she went through the gate into the courtward, she stopped. For the first time she noticed something in its middle which fractionally raised her spirits. A well! Running to it, she dragged the crude pail up by a pulley and tipped it against her mouth. The cold water poured down her sweat-soaked dress and her parched throat. If it were contaminated she would soon know it. Meanwhile it tasted like iced champagne. When she'd had enough, she let the bucket fall back into the depths and looked around her. An idea had begun to take shape in her mind.

She began to explore seriously. The stench and the roaring of flies led her to an outhouse. She thought, *The latrines in the camp will be worse*. In one of the huts she found an assortment of floor mats which, heaped up, would make a tolerable mattress. There was a primus stove (though no kerosene), an oil lamp with some oil in it, and a cupboard containing a sordid assortment of utensils for cooking and eating. It also contained bedding. This hardly bore close examination, but as she took it in her hands Riki decided she didn't care what it contained so long as it kept her and Niels warm. The miniature fauna of the East were no strangers to her – like everyone else, even in her protected and privileged home in the white ghetto, she had had to fight off their invasive hoards. Now she would have to get used to sharing her life with them at closer quarters. Looking round the largest of the three little hovel-rooms, with its dirt floor, small grime-opaque windows, ill-fitting doors, makeshift walls and corrugated roof, she thought grimly: *Home. Well, it's better than hell*.

There remained two primary problems: fear, and food.

159

About the first there was little she could do, except learn to live with it and subdue it. At first there was a crippling upsurge of it every time she heard a noise, and every time she looked at Niels, who, at eighteen months, was no longer immobile and was already beginning to explore (with every evidence of approval) his new surroundings. Riki was not afraid that the particular soldiers who had let her go would waste much time searching for her, but there were others. As a white woman she would stand out like a sore thumb when she had to venture out of her hiding-place into the 'native quarter'. Though the invaders had given the factory a cursory once-over and left it, they would certainly be back, probably to occupy it and put it to some use of their own. She might find herself living cheek by jowl with the enemy . . . A thought to terrify anybody.

Meanwhile she sensibly decided to postpone her fears and try to find something to eat. There was nothing in the shacks – the workers had taken everything edible with them. But a second tour of the front part of the factory yielded a number of treasures which she spent the rest of that day transferring to her refuge.

By nightfall she had amassed a good collection of biscuits, coffee, dried milk, sugar, sweets, toilet paper and matches, not to mention some bottles of spirits and packets of cigarettes which held no immediate interest for her but which she knew might come in useful. She also carried over a rug, a chair, a small table, and a portrait of Queen Wilhelmina which she hung, with a combination of practicality and loyalty, over one of the larger knotholes in her wall.

She then went back once more and sat for a short time in Wim's office. Everything on his desk had meaning for her. There was a photograph of herself, another of the three of them. There was one of Wim's familiar notebooks with the firm's letter heading on each page, which she took for a journal. There was the half-drunk cup of tea which Wim had presumably touched. That reminded her to close her eyes and crystalise in her memory the sight of him as she had last seen him – *only that morning!* – anxious and stressed, but safe, loving, familiar, and very dear to her. She mentally examined her face until she pinpointed the exact bit of it he

160

had last kissed – her right temple, just where the bone began its indentation. *That is as together as we can be until this is over*, she thought.

Then she did a thing that struck her afterwards as being a symptom of her underlying state of mind, beneath all the rationality and common sense. She phoned her empty house. It felt like ringing the house of friends who have just died in some sudden cataclysm, hoping against hope that one of them would answer in an ordinary voice, proving the whole tragedy to have been a nightmare. She listened to the vacant ringing for several minutes, then put down the receiver, picked up the cup, the photo, the notebook, and one or two other small items and walked back through the echoing offices and factory, across the lane, and into her own territory. *He would be proud of me*, she thought. It was all she would have to comfort her for the following days of intermittent terror and constant adjustment and devastating loneliness.

The first night, she and Niels were eaten alive by fleas from the mats, and a rat came in under the door. She heard it pattering about and thought, *I'll die, I'll die.* But then she thought, *No I won't.* She sat up and threw a metal cup at it and it scurried out again. Next day she rolled up a spare mat and made a draught-and-rat-excluder. She found a big old biscuit tin with a lid in which to keep her bits of uneaten food. She stuffed up the biggest holes in the walls. Then she made a foray to the factory floor and took some paint and whitewashed the inside of her house . . . It seemed incredible and even exciting that nobody knew she was there. After two days immured, she let Niels out to play in the courtyard. The well-head was too high for him to climb and although the ground was hard and bumpy, as he practised walking he soon gained surefootedness. His nappies were a problem. She solved it by letting him go bare, like the native children, and giving him a wipe with a wet cloth occasionally.

On the fifth day she ran out of biscuits and dried milk and knew she would have to go out.

After some thought, she made a kind of sarong, with a headshawl, out of a pair of curtains from one of the front offices. She carefully stained her hands, feet and face with some paste made of coffee and a little mud, and, keeping the cloth of the headshawl well pulled forward, and her eyes – her tell-tale blue eyes – well down, she walked out by the back drive.

The streets were full of just such furtively scurrying figures as herself. There was an air of fear everywhere. No-one bothered about her. Since she had no money and felt herself lacking either the courage or the skill to shoplift, her best hope was to try to make her way back to her old house. There she might fill a shopping basket with tinned goods and other necessaries. She was afraid to leave the sleeping Niels alone too long and there was no transport, but an unlocked bicycle provided a solution. In a quarter of an hour she was slipping round to her own back door.

Just as she reached it, it flew open.

For one blissful split second, she thought it was Wim. But it wasn't. It was the babu, half demented with terror and hysterical. When she saw Riki she didn't know her in her disguise, and tried to flee past her, but Riki caught her firmly by the arm and dragged her shrieking into the house. There Riki pushed back the head-covering and showed where the 'make-up' stopped. When the babu saw her blonde hair, her eyes nearly popped out, but she stopped shrieking and threw herself into her nonja's arms.

"Ni-roos? Ni-roos?" she asked next, clutching Riki frantically.

"Niels is all right. Come on. Help me collect some food and we'll go to him."

"No food, Nonja! So'dya take or' a food! Now we or' go die!"

"We're not going to die. Come along at once."

She led the way to the top of the house where, under the roof, she and Wim had put their store of tinned goods and other valuables. Babu's mood changed; she danced with delight. Together they packed as much as they could carry into shopping baskets. Riki was secretly terrified to carry so much through streets full of people all worried about the

162

coming of shortages. But there was nothing else for it – she dared not come back here. She was, however, much more sanguine now she had found Babu. Babu could come and go in the streets, to the shops, without fear of attracting attention. And Niels loved her. It would be far easier to manage the new life with two of them.

They reached the factory safely, walking one each side of the laden bike, to be greeted by Niels's outraged bawling; but the quarter was a-hum with human activity and no-one else had noticed.

Babu was shocked to dumbness when she saw how her nonja had been living. In her opinion they ought to return to the 'proper' house immediately. She was a simple girl, utterly devoted and loyal, incapable of grasping what had happened to them and the changes it was bound to cause. For several days she huddled in a corner of the shack covering her face in shame, but inevitably after a while Niels brought her out of it. He was so obviously bursting with life, and Riki so obviously needing help, that Babu at last lifted her head (in an unconscious echo of her mistress) and rose, determined to live, and to fulfil her role. Had she had any foreknowledge of what this would be by the end of the war, she might have kept her blunt little nose pointed into the dead-end corner of the room.

163

Chapter 17

———— m ————

Riki had supposed rightly that the occupying forces would put her husband's factory to some use. She hadn't reckoned on the shock she would get when she found out what.

It was Babu who brought her the news, a fortnight after they had settled in. They had quite a cosy little set-up and had begun to feel almost safe. Babu went out every day or so and did a little trading with the valuables they'd brought from the house, coming back triumphant with food and cash. She did much of the house- and baby-work as before. It meant little to her, once she got accustomed to the scandalous novelty of the situation, that they lived in squalor – for her it was just a reversion to normal after her brief sojourn in paradise.

The stresses of that terrible first day had told on Riki. She knew she must rest, for the new baby's sake, so she stayed indoors. In any case, going out was too risky. On Babu's first venture into the native quarter, she returned with disquieting reports. The Japs were everywhere. They had begun a saturation propaganda campaign against the Dutch. There were even banners and posters in the streets, printed in Malay, which read:

THE BLUE-EYED FOREIGNERS ARE YOUR ENEMIES!

Rewards were offered for the betrayal of anyone in hiding. Riki shuddered whenever she glanced into the broken bit of looking-glass she'd found and set on a cross-beam. She thanked God ten times a day for Niels's Indonesian blood, his black hair and eyes. He looked so unlike a 'blue-eyed foreigner' that Babu could take him into the market on her hip, swathed in her shawl. Fortunately he was not talking much as yet. Riki noted in her diary: "Niels said 'biscuit' today. Thank heaven he said it in Malay!"

She never went into the factory after the first day, but she instructed Babu to walk past the front each time she went out, to see what was happening. And one day Babu came back with a shocked expression which made Riki stiffen for bad news.

"Japanee turn *tuan* fact'y to gir' house."

Riki stared at her, apprehension dawning. "'Girl house'? What do you mean?"

"Gir' house. Rittoo room each have gir'. Sit in window. Japanee high sod'ya come pay money rie on bed with gir'."

Riki put her hands to her face and turned away.

We're lost! she thought. *Oh, Wim!* But she didn't say it aloud. Her watchword was to live from day to day, even from hour to hour. Her thoughts from the first had been a pattern of double-think: she was bound to win through, to bring her babies safe to her husband after the war – at the same time she was bound to be caught. Till now the first had been to the fore. But an officers' brothel on the very doorstep of her refuge! Despair almost toppled her.

Day by day the brothel took shape across the lane. The front offices were turned into rooms for the girls. The factory was partitioned off for the same purpose; the whole place was soon a warren of vice. The stench of it, compounded of cheap perfume, drink, and the sweat of lust, seemed to waft across the lane with the noise of raucous tinned music and other sounds to which Babu, drawing water from the outdoor well, stopped her ears.

"What ir we do, Nonja? I 'fraid go out, maybe they take me, give me to Japanee so'dya!"

"They're not taking girls against their will, they're just rounding up the regular prostitutes. Don't be foolish!"

But Babu panicked and refused to go shopping. Riki said nothing, set her teeth and set about resuming her disguise. Babu, watching her smear her skin with dirt and throw a scarf over her blonde hair, grew horrified, at the degradation more than at the risk. She rushed at Riki, wiping her face, kissing her dirty hands, pulling off the scarf. "I go, you no go, you no make you ugly! You keep nice, not make Ni-roos fright he got Malay mama!" Riki couldn't keep from laughing at Babu's strange notions of ugliness. It was the first time she'd laughed in ages. Babu began to laugh too, hysterically. They hugged each other and Niels joined in. As Babu clutched Riki, she felt the bulge of the new baby, stopped laughing and laid her hand on it.

"What you do when baby come?"

Riki had been thinking about that. She really was terrified of having it here. Babu was an excellent nursemaid, but she was no midwife.

"Is the convent still open?"

Babu understood – she knew where Niels had been born.

"Today I go see."

Then she took a deep breath, picked up her shopping basket and purse of small change, gave Riki one piteous I'll-never-come-back-alive look, and went out as usual.

She returned quite safely. The convent, for the time being, was still functioning, just, though many of the nuns had gone.

The Japanese never crossed the lane which divided their officers' 'gir' house' from what appeared to be the beginning of the native shanty-quarter. But the girls soon found it. In their few idle hours they would wander out at the back, looking for a bit of peace; the little courtyard with its well of cool water was a natural refuge for them, too.

The first time Riki looked out and saw three of them sitting on the well-wall chatting and fanning themselves, she almost fainted. She sent Babu out to chase them away. They ran, but not too fast, giggling and gesturing and cat-calling back at their pursuer. But they were back next day.

From panicky irriation, Riki's reaction to this persistent intrusion modified to nervous resignation. After a few days she forgot to latch the door and Niels, who regarded the courtyard as his garden, toddled out while his mother's back was turned. Inevitably, the girls fell for his dimpled charms and soon made a pet of him.

"Do they notice anything? Don't they see he's white?" she asked Babu anxiously when she had been out and snatched him from their slim arms. "What do they say?"

"Bad gir's think Ni-roos my baby," she said, not without pride.

"So you think it's all right to let them play with him?"

Babu shrugged comprehensively. Riki saw what she meant – maybe it was all right and maybe it wasn't, but either way there was little they could do. It was better not to make a fuss.

Life in the town had returned to some semblance of normality. Trading at least was going on as usual, stimulated if anything by the presence of several thousand Japanese troops, and there were again *batjas*, tricycle rickshaws, plying the streets, chiefly carrying the invaders. The white population had been severely reduced, though some collaborators, essential workers and Germans were still about. Could a 'native' woman in labour get away with riding in a batja all the way to the convent when the time came?

"Bad gir's ride batja," mentioned Babu.

"Do they? But only when they're out with a man, surely?"

"Not onri."

Riki spent days and nights thinking about it. In the convent they were geared for births – it was a nursing order. She and her baby would be safe there, safe from dirt and disease. She must, she must get there! At last, about a week before her time, two helpful things happened. The rains came. And the girls – two of them, anyway – found out about her.

This last happened because of their natural, insatiable curiosity. Two of them, like inquisitive little animals, came creeping right into the shack one day in quest of Niels, who,

167

due to the muddy state of the courtyard, had not gone out. And there was Riki, sitting at the table near the window with her blonde hair falling over her shoulders, writing in her notebook.

Irresistibly drawn, they glided across the floor towards her, their hands outstretched to touch. Her impulse was to flee, to hide, but there was no possibility of that – they had her cornered against the window. Smiling, whispering, they examined her, their tiny hands barely touching, just to verify that she was real. Then, without addressing a word to her, they backed off and pattered away. Riki, running to the door, watched them cross the yard through the rain with their headscarves spread over them between their hands, twittering like native flutes.

"Wait!" she called in Malay.

They stopped in the gateway and turned, shielding their heads and faces. Riki made one universal gesture: she put her finger to her lips. With her other hand she lifted her blonde hair. They looked at each other and then back at her, and nodded in unison. Then they vanished into the lane.

Riki kept Babu at home the next day, and when the girls drifted into the court between downpours she pointed out one of the two who had entered the shack the day before. Babu went out boldly and collared her, sherpherding her into the room where Riki had tea and sweets ready.

Babu sat her down on the pile of mats and engaged her in earnest conversation. Riki had told her what to say. At first the girl seemed unwilling. Babu drew Riki's clothes tight over the baby-bump, to show the girl the situation. After a while, the girl nodded. Babu shot Riki a look of triumph.

"She say yes, she go with you in batja when baby come."

"Will she lend me one of her sarongs?"

The girl nodded solemnly. Riki took some money out of her purse and handed it to the girl, who looked at it for a long time before taking it. Then she said something to Babu.

"She want take sweets too."

"Yes, yes! Give her all of them! Only tell her it's very secret."

"She know that, Nonja. She onri bad. She not stupid."

Riki was not particularly religious, but she believed in God, and now she prayed. During the following week, during the journey to the convent (which passed off without incident, due to the girl's assistance and a providential rainstorm through which the batja driver could barely see the road in front of his feet) and during the birth itself, her most fervent prayer was this: *Let it be dark, Lord. Let it be healthy, and let it be dark.*

The Lord was signally failing to hear or heed a lot of other people's prayers just about then, and Riki was humbly aware of it, so she didn't blame Him when the harassed little nun dumped her newborn daughter into her arms. Riki took one look and knew that this time, fatally, *her* genes, not Wim's, had prevailed. Dark babies are always born with hair. This one was bald. Its tiny face was red; not the puce she remembered from Niels, but the colour of a pink rosebud. The child was going to be fair, blonde, blue-eyed, and a nightmare liability to her.

She hugged it to her breast, in which she felt the premonitory deep prickle and heat as nature did its wonderful work. At least she would not have to worry about feeding it. Perhaps even yet all would be well! She called it Juliana, after the Dutch heir to the throne. But as a private joke, she love-named her daughter Tippi after the little prostitute who had helped her, for *tippelaarster* means a streetwalker in Dutch.

Adinda had not been able to keep the secret from her sister-tarts, of course. They came tip-toeing across the lane with birthing gifts of every sort – flowers, food, little clothes and toys – and were shown the baby, and marvelled at her unearthly foreign beauty. They did everything they could think of to make the little family more comfortable. They became like relatives, and Riki and Babu learnt to trust them. Properly so. None of them ever betrayed Riki, though they might have profited greatly by it.

Tippi was another 'easy baby'. Perhaps the secret of easy babies is simply to carry them everywhere until they learn to crawl – after all, that's what nature programmed them to expect. Niels also neglected to follow the European pattern by showing jealousy – he was uninterested in the newcomer. But then he already enjoyed a complex life of his own. At going-on-two, he had a wide acquaintance and spoke the rudiments of two languages. Riki's fears that he would utter Dutch words in the market were confounded. Only the sight of his mother triggered Dutch; for the rest he responded to the Malay around him.

Even money was not a serious problem. As soon as objects from the house ran out, one of the girls found a job for Riki that she could do without ever leaving shelter. It was sewing gloves at piece rates. Sweatshop labour, but she didn't mind. So much was going on in her head, she didn't even miss having a radio (the tinny music drifting over from the brothel had become quite a congenial accompaniment). In the evenings when it was too difficult to sew, she lit the oil-lamp and sat at her table writing all the things she'd been thinking about during the glove-hours. That was how Niels came to know all that had happened.

One night when Tippi was three months old Riki wrote this:

"Today Adinda came and was very excited. One of her clients is the local quartermaster and he is putting out contracts for gloves for Japanese officers. It would pay much better rates than I get for my ordinary civilian gloves. It was a temptation, but suddenly I saw a picture in my head of that officer who let me leave the camp. He was kind to me that day but somehow I know he's going to stop being kind. In my imagination I saw him do what the girls tell me other officers do. Some of them keep their gloves on in the brothel, out of some strange notion of cleanliness, so when they slap the girls to show who is master, it is the glove that strikes . . . And they do it to prisoners too, I am sure of it. I couldn't sew a glove thinking it might hit my Wim."

It seemed that this idea, of Wim being ill-treated, once it was written down, had power to goad and torment her. A strange urgency came on her, ousting the patient, almost humorous resignation that had sustained her till now. Perhaps they really wouldn't both survive the war . . . Perhaps Wim would never see this beautiful, perfect little girl-child she had made for him. Terrible rumours were abroad about the things the conquerors were doing, the treatment they meted out to their prisoners.

She began to lose sleep, to lose appetite and concentration. She would find herself staring at a wall, or out of her small window – even sometimes at her children – with a grimace of horror on her face. Every atrocity which rumour related to her was instantly made into a sort of horror film in her head, with Wim in the leading role of helpless victim. Her spirits sank and sank, and her health with it. Babu watched with a growing desperation.

"Why Nonja get thin? Why Nonja cry at small thing? Not play nice with Ni-roos?"

"I keep thinking of the tuan, Babu. I think of him all the time. What are they doing to him?" She pressed her fingers suddenly hard against her eyeballs and gritted her teeth. But the ghastly pictures in her head wouldn't go away.

Then one evening after two of the little tarts, enjoying a few hours off, had been sitting in the courtyard sewing and chatting, Babu told Riki a story she had overheard.

One of the prostitutes had also had a nonja, once upon a time, who, being of mixed blood, was still free. The girl had gone to visit her and heard from her that she had been to see her husband in a prison camp. She had taken with her spirits and cigarettes and other valuables with which she had bribed the camp guards not only to let her see her husband alone, but to give him special treatment.

Babu related all this simply as gossip, a tale, a distraction to entertain Riki and bring her out of her despair. Later she would heap herself with unending reproaches; at the time she didn't notice the immediate effect of the story on her listener.

For Riki it was like a flash of light in a dimensionless black cave, light which signalled a way out. She sat up straight, her eyes round and brilliant.

"Perhaps they lied," she said tautly. "The Japanese guards. Perhaps they took the woman's things and then treated him as badly as ever."

171

"No, Nonja," said Babu casually.

"How do you know?"

"The nonja return to camp another time. Her tuan say treat much better now. The Japanee they see drink and cigarette, they do anything."

Riki got down immediately to serious planning. There were numerous imponderables. To begin with, how could she conceivably find Wim? There were reportedly camps hidden in the jungle all over Java. But Riki was not to be put off. She believed that the men from one district might be imprisoned together, or at least might know each other's whereabouts. The other nonja – the Eurasian woman – had, Riki discovered through discreet questioning, been a near neighbour of hers before the occupation. It shouldn't be impossible to tap her, indirectly of course, for information.

"Babu . . . " (very carelessly) "is Adinda planning to visit her old nonja again?"

"Perhaps . . ."

"Ask her to find out where the camp is."

Babu's glance sharpened. "Why ask this?"

"Well, or just see if the nonja is going again to visit. Perhaps her tuan has news of my tuan. Ask Adinda to find out."

Adinda did better than that – or, it might have been, worse. She brought the Eurasian woman back with her.

Babu was beside herself with anger. Her high-pitched abuse shattered the noon quiet. The Eurasian woman – whom Riki vaguely recognised – was standing, bemused, in the courtyard. Adinda was pleading, and Riki could interpret her expression and gestures: It's all right, it's safe, she wouldn't betray her!

Riki dragged Babu indoors and ordered her to be quiet and attend to the baby.

Then she beckoned the other woman inside.

"Tell me," she began without preamble. "About the camp."

The woman told her. She told her about the barbed wire fence, the flimsy huts, the stink of latrines, rotting food, ulcerated flesh. She told her about an old oil barrel, in which men were stuffed for punishment and which was then rolled

172

and kicked and bombarded with rocks. She told her about a prisoner she'd seen hanging from a crosspole in the sun, his back a mass of welts and blackened blood.

Riki listened with no expression. At the end she said, "And your husband?"

The woman smiled an oriental smile.

"He was beaten and starving like the others. But not any more. I go once a month. I take goods for the Japanese. This camp is run by a man who is very greedy, very easily bribed. Now my husband works for him in his office, he doesn't even go out to work with the others."

Riki stood up.

"When you go again, will you ask if my husband is in the same camp?"

Babu was already suspicious. She had begun to guess what was in Riki's mind.

"You not go to tuan, Nonja. It is too dangerous!"

"The other nonja goes."

"Other nonja look like Malay woman. Not 'blue-eyed foreigner'."

Riki said nothing. She merely told Babu to buy cigarettes, good ones. Babu 'forgot'. Riki scolded her, sent her out again. She returned saying she couldn't find any. Riki threatened to go to the market herself. Silently Babu went out and returned with one small packet of English cigarettes. Riki didn't speak an unnecessary word to her for a whole day.

The Eurasian woman visited her again a week later.

"Your husband is not in the same camp," she said. Riki's heart jerked in her breast and she gasped. "But," the woman went on slowly, "I've found out where he is. He's in a camp about twenty miles away. My husband knows where it is. He drew a map for you." She held out a scruffy bit of cardboard with a rough plan on it. Riki almost snatched it from her hand.

"Oh, thank you! Thank you so much!"

Her old neighbour's safely black eyes stared into hers.

"I don't know if I should be thanked. The rumour is that your husband's camp is commanded by a very rigid officer, not like the one I deal with. And it's a lot further away. Are you thinking of going there? Because I wouldn't advise it. It's not safe, certainly not for you."

"You must let me decide," said Riki. She reached out impulsively and embraced the other woman.

When Babu and the girls realised that Riki fully intended not only to go herself to find Wim but to take the baby, they nearly went demented trying to dissuade her. But she was adamant. When she grew weary of them, crying and wringing their hands around her, she turned to them and said simply,

"I must go. The worry is drying up my milk."

They recognised this as a definitive argument. It would be terribly dangerous for Tippi to be weaned on to any of the dubious substitutes available, without proper means to chill or sterilise. Dysentery was rampant. Niels had already had a go of some form of it shortly after Tippi's birth, and Babu had urged Riki to put him back to the breast for a few days. Incredibly she had had enough milk in those 'chest-pimples', as she had jokingly called them, for both children, for the brief time it took Niels to get better. Breast milk was vital, almost sacred. Babu, though filled with fears, gave in and helped prepare her mistress for the journey.

"Stop crying, Babu, please. We'll be all right!" Riki kept saying. She felt carefree, even joyful now she was actually on her way, and Babu's fears seemed absurd.

But Babu couldn't stop. As she tied up food and water and spare clothes, little gifts for Wim, and cigarettes and spirits to bribe the guards, into a big back-bundle, she watered every item with silent tears. Deep in her soul, linked as it was in its sense of duty and destiny with her nonja's, she sensed that she was serving her for the last time.

Just before dawn one morning when the rains had stopped and the country was lush and steaming and even the town, just for once, was dust-laid and clean-smelling, Babu lifted the bundle onto Riki's back, and, after smothering the rosy sleeping face of the baby with kisses, helped to attach her, in her hip-sling, to her mother's body.

At the last moment she clung frenziedly.

"I go with you! I carry the bundoo! I die with you, Nonja!"

"Babu, dear, of course you can't go. Who would look after Niels?"

Babu, caught between fires, wrung her hands, then touched Riki and Tippi again and again for good luck. Riki kissed her and put her firmly away.

"Till we meet. Take care of my little boy."

Babu stood in the middle of the lane, watching with heaving breath till Riki turned the corner. Then she rushed back into the shack, gathered the sleeping Niels in her arms and crept across to the brothel, full of the sounds of well-earned sleep. She found Adinda's box-like cubicle and shook awake the little whore who had become her friend and fellow-servant to her nonja.

"She's gone," she whispered.

The two girls fell into each other's arms and sobbed hopelessly with grief until Niels awoke to their uncontrolled misery and broke into sobs of his own. As well he might. It was the end of his security, the beginning of his inner damage.

The story so far I've told in detail because the details are known. Adinda carefully kept Riki's notebook, and she had some inarticulate recollections of her own to tell Wim when he came back after the war. The rest – which is the really important part, inasmuch as it formed Niels, or deformed that part of him which was to mar his future – has to be told more briefly, because he remembers very little of it and it has to be pieced together.

Wim, then, what was left of him, came back after the liberation, looking for a blonde woman, a dark boy of six and a little fair girl of four. At first he found none of them. When he had exhausted the possibilities of his house (a looted and vandalised shell) he came to what had been his factory. Wandering in bemusement and disgust through the place he had built up, finding it reminded him of an abandoned wasps' nest with its little partitioned cubicles and its stale, sweetish smells, he came upon some 'cells' which were still occupied.

One of them contained a creature really not unlike a wasp. She was wasp-shaped, with her tiny waist and small, round, black head – she even wore a dirty yellowish garment – and she buzzed protestingly at him, or perhaps whined is a better description, when he put his head diffidently round her curtain. It was rather like the sound a wasp makes when it is half-stunned by repeated blows, downed but not yet defeated; one more whack will probably kill it. Wim almost withdrew, but then he saw, lying on the pallet which served as her bed, an urchin who for some reason he could never later explain drew his attention.

Tough, filthy, in rags, this child immediately woke, rolled in one fluid movement off the bed and vanished behind another curtain which shut off a corner of the cubicle. It was the action of a child conditioned to react thus to any intrusion. The little wasp ceased to whine and beckoned Wim in a mockery of invitation, sliding herself onto the rumpled bed the child had vacated. Wim stood staring, not at her, but at the curtain where the urchin had vanished.

It was from Adinda that Wim learnt not only the identity of the child he had glimpsed but also the futility of the hopes and dreams which had kept him going during the terrible years since he had last seen his wife and daughter. Because, by some miracle of endurance and passionate determination, Riki had actually reached him. He had seen her – spoken to her – for a timeless ten minutes (bought with gin and Players Weights) through a wire mesh so fine he could barely touch the tips of his daughter's tiny fingers as she poked them through. Ten minutes. Then days, during which

Riki waited beyond the camp perimeter while Wim's captors laughed and jeered at her, keeping him locked in a distant hut, from which he could just make out her forlorn and unbearably courageous figure standing hour after hour in the blazing heat with the baby in her arms. To the accompaniment of yowls from the Japanese, she even fed the child there, with her back turned but without withdrawing.

Having at last been driven away by soldiers sent out with long canes to chase her off (a process Wim was forced helplessly to watch) she had presumably tried to make her way back to the town. But dangers, which hope and driving will had made somehow harmless to her on her outward journey, now turned inimical. She had seen Wim – seen in his face and on his gaunt, welted, ulcerated body that all her fears were true and that there was nothing she could do to help him. Perhaps she simply lost her will to struggle. She never reached the town.

Of course Wim was heart-wrung to find his son, at least, still alive, although a complete stranger to him, deep-sunk in an alien culture, a life-hardened raggamuffin whose experiences Wim couldn't even guess at. He discovered from questioning Adinda that the babu, who had so feared being forced into the brothel and debauched, eventually drifted into that life of her own accord. The friendship of the girls came to make a whore's life seem not so dreadful as being hungry, not just for food but for companionship. She'd tried to keep Niels apart from the brothel, which she visited, at first, only occasionally to earn money for them both; but soon the boundaries blurred. One night she brought a soldier back to her own bed, because it was less degraded-seeming than the barren cubicles in the transmuted factory (which was still a factory of a sort). The next day the Japs came stamping in, turfed her out of the shacks and turned them into a bath-house. After that she had no option but to move across the lane, taking Niels with her. And from then on, he was a child of the whore-house.

He was not the only child about the place. Several of the

girls had children, and some had no parents to farm them out to. Officially no children were allowed. So Niels grew in a half-hidden sub-community. The furtiveness that ordered his comings and goings, the tasks he was given to do for the girls, the things he saw and heard from his little sleeping corner behind a curtain . . . The fact that, when he was four, his babu disappeared as abruptly as his mother had done (she was carried off by typhus) leaving him in the communal and inevitably slipshod care of some dozen or more different women, who, though they petted him, all had more pressing priorities than himself . . . All this sank deep bore-holes into him which drained the sewage of degradation around him.

Wim's first priority was to get Niels back to Holland, out of the morass and chaos of post-war Java. It must have seemed obvious. He himself could hardly wait to get back to civilisation, not least because Indonesia was in a dangerous mood of pre-revolutionary ferment. The Dutch were taking it for granted that they were going to resume control, if necessary by force and with British help, while the Indonesians were preparing to fight for their independence. Another sort of war was in the making which threatened the tranquillity of those lovely islands as much if not more than the one which had just ended. But Wim couldn't leave yet. He was obsessed with the need to search for his wife, the more so of course after reading her notebook. Learning of her enormous courage and resilience, he couldn't believe she and Tippi were not still alive somewhere, perhaps in one of the kampongs between Surabaya and the camp where he had last seen her.

So he sent Niels home in the charge of yet another woman, a Dutch widow, recently released from a women's camp, who was returning home. She volunteered to accompany the child on the ship and settle him with relatives of Wim's in Rotterdam.

So this six-year-old – who had got used to fending for himself, who knew every fact of life as surely as he knew how to breathe, who had transferred his love from woman to woman to woman until it was largely diffused and de-focused (while taking for granted a constant minimum of physical affection from many different sources) was re-planted in a Western environment without the slightest preparation, on the basis, which most Western-raised people hold as fundamental, that the European way is the right way with children and that its application, however late, and to however damaged a personality, will speedily correct the harm done and set the child back on the high road to normality.

Incredibly again, this is just what seemed to happen.

By the time Wim returned a year later, heartsick and completely thwarted in his quest – no trace of Riki and Tippi was ever found – Niels had become Dutch. Perhaps it started as a protective disguise he assumed, into which he grew as the months passed; perhaps the primary lesson of his begin-nings, adapt or die, had enabled him to triumph over this new and staggering change in his life. Children all over the world were triumphing in the same way. Some more success-fully than others . . . In any contest to judge success in this field, Niels would have won a medal. His mind did wonders for him. It suppressed all remembrance of his mother, of his babu, even of Adinda as an individual to whom his heart was once joined by a two-way conduit of love. He remembers Java only as a hot, wet place in which the darkness of interiors contrasted unbearably with the dazzling brightness outdoors. He remembers certain smells. His passion for Indonesian food must have its roots in his infancy. Certain small, seemingly insignificant incidents he recalled for me when, much later, I was researching. He shows no signs of trauma when the subject comes up – he professes to find it all very interesting, and wishes he could remember more.

But on his wedding night he used his bride as a Japanese officer might have used a whore. He brought his compulsive succession of women back to his own bed. He expected his wife to empathise with his needs, and felt destroyed with confusion and resentment at her jealous rages.

Yet gradually he contrived some measure of control over himself. He learned to make love, to hide the infidelities which gave so much pain.

By the time Cal had finished talking, that day by the pony-field, I didn't know a quarter of all this, which I was to find out later with Niels's cooperation.But I knew enough to know why Cal admired him and respected the marriage. I even knew why he was suddenly so dismayed by us and ours.

Chapter 18

We arrived back at the house to find everyone in a state of excitement. Anna rushed out to meet us, her little snub face alight.

"Come!" she cried. "We are colour the eggs, and Daniel is paint his, *beautiful*!"

The kitchen had been given over entirely to egg-dyeing. On each burner simmered an old saucepan containing a witch's brew of dye, red, blue, yellow and green. The big table was thickly layered with newspapers. As the eggs came out of their dye-vats, they were carefully set to dry in racks which touched only their little-ends. Anna was trying to make purple in a fifth saucepan, but the royal tint was eluding her. Dan was sitting at one end of the table with a paintbox, painting psychedelic designs on a small pile of hardboiled eggs with immense concentration. Niels was sitting out in the conservatory with his back to us, secretively busy about some writing. Every now and then he'd throw over his shoulder at the children what I can only call a fiendish look, which sent the Dutch ones into peals of glee.

"What's your dad doing?" asked Cal.

"Oh, he is writing the notes for the trail!" explained Anna.

I asked what I could do, and Mariolain said that, despite it being Easter next day, we still had to eat supper and could I prepare a table in the big room? Not the dining-room because it wasn't heated. It was getting dusk so I drew the heavy curtains and lit the lamps. The beautiful room had been cleaned and polished and was scented with lemon and pine. Mariolain passed cold platters, salads and baskets of bread and crackers through a hatch from the kitchen and said we could all help ourselves 'as and when' (an expression she'd picked up from me). Her eyes were sparkling. After I'd taken through all the things, I stood on the far side of the hatch, watching the activities in the kitchen, in which Cal had now joined, and I thought what fun it all was and how every ill feeling had been set in abeyance while this engaging ritual was carried out. Trivial, peripheral nonsense, and yet it contained strong magic. Healing magic, or just postponing magic? It hardly seemed to matter.

After a while Cal left the house, and I heard the car start.

"Where's Cal gone?" I asked Mariolain, who had come into the living-room, rainbow-splashed apron covering her from breast to knee. She slumped into the wicker hooded chair which hung from a chain and began twiddling herself round in it, lifting her feet to let it untwiddle, something she was forever telling her children not to do for fear of working out the ceiling-hook. As she spun, the dyes on her apron ran together like a child's spinning-top.

"Your sweet husband," she said, "insist to bring a bottle of wine for supper. That will make supper into dinner I think – isn't that right? Like a cathedral make a town into a city. It will also make me very happy."

"Everyone seems to be extremely happy already," I said. "Is it 'as and when' time for you?" She nodded, letting her curly head fall back against the white wicker. Her face was flushed from the stove and she looked about eighteen. I piled a plate for her and brought it over to her.

"Did you have a nice time today?" she asked brightly.

"Not nice exactly. Interesting. And, I think, possibly important." She looked up questioningly. "A bit of a turning-point, perhaps." She kept the look, so that I found myself going on, quoting, in my awkwardness, a silly couplet from my childhood:

> "Things are not always what they seem,
> And starch looks very much like cream.

– or maybe the other way round."

"Suky, dear, what are you talking about?" she asked. Rolling a translucent tongue of tongue into her mouth, she reminded me for a moment of a Chinese lion.

"Cal and I," I said with difficulty, "have been fighting."

She sat up straight, the last pink morsel sticking out.

"Today? – You mean, just today."

"Not just. For ages."

Her eyes grew round and I thought, she's glad, and who wouldn't understand that? Glad to her bones that we're not the perfect couple she thought we were, that she and Niels aren't the only ones with problems.

"That's what I meant about starch and cream. You've been reckoning we're cream, but actually things have been pretty starchy of late. It was a cat in the original, by the way . . . I remember the picture of it with all its teeth stuck together after lapping up the starch."

"You are in a very obscure mood."

"I enigmatise because I don't want to be disloyal."

She stopped eating.

"Have I been disloyal – about me and Niels? Do you think so?"

"No."

"But I have told you all about us. And you have let me think you and Cal were the model happy couple. Was that so nice of you?"

"It's a writer's bad habit, to listen and not to interrupt even to say 'same here'."

She was giving me a strange look now. "You have in your mind to write about us?"

It was the first time I had thought of it, consciously at least.

"I don't know. The stories of your wars – yours and Niels's – are so incredible, so – please don't misunderstand – full of irony, fascinating, dramatic . . . I might be tempted. But not without consulting you."

"Both of us."

"Yes."

"Niels has told you about him?"

"He told Cal. And Cal told me – today. That's what we did, when we'd finished quarrelling – we sat on a wet seat and drank five cups of coffee and he told me."

"All of it – ? His mother, and the tippelaasters?"

"Yes."

She put her unfinished food aside, and pushed herself thoughtfully, heels and toes, back and forth in the hanging chair, frowning.

"So now you must think that it is not *he* who should have understood *me* and made allowances, but the other way around."

Startled, I said quickly, "That's not the conclusion I reached at all." But now she'd mentioned it, there was something in it.

"What then?" Her eyes came up to mine and there was no brilliant half-artificial smile in them. From looking childlike and fey a moment or two before, she now looked grown-up and deeply serious. It was a vital moment between us, I sensed.

"I'll tell you. Cal's and my problems are of recent origin. Not like yours. Ours could only appear as problems to people like us who've never really been through anything. Today I understood that, and I thought that both you and Niels are very – admirable."

"Are we?"

"Yes. You're still together."

"You and Cal are still together."

"So I should bloody well think," I said. "We've no earthly excuse for not being."

She took her plate back and ate some potato salad. After a long time she said, "If you write about us – if – I ask one thing."

"What?"

"Don't make my mother come badly out of it."

I smiled.

"Mariolain, if you knew what writing fiction is like, you wouldn't worry. You won't really recognise yourself or anybody else by the time I've finished."

184

"But I don't mind. I would like it to be told. I would like a truth to come onto a page about what happened to us and to my mother, a truth against the evasions and lies and en-ig-mat-ics – is that it? – of my father's book."

"Is he still alive?" I asked curiously.

"Yes and no. He breathes, but he is dotty."

"Dotty?"

"In a home. He doesn't know us – me. So I don't go. And Irene's in Brazil."

"Anna told me."

She glanced at me. "So she has been telling family secrets, too. Well. Who am I to blame her? It's a weight on her, about Jan. It was in all the papers and she was ashamed at school."

"What did he do?"

"Confidence tricking. Very clever. He nearly didn't get caught. If not for his mother, he wouldn't have been, perhaps, till now."

"*Irene* turned him in?"

"Anonymously. But I know it was her, she told me she was going to do it."

"Wow," I said, subduedly.

"You think she did wrong? He was robbing hundreds of people with his schemes. So should she keep quiet, or put a stop to him? I think she did right although I know I couldn't do as she did if Pieter was a criminal. But that's because I'm a coward."

"Did Irene say that? That you were a coward?"

"No. She is a psychologist. It is her job not to judge."

"Oho. And yet she judged Jan – and how!"

"He was her special responsibility."

"Of course it's a cliché that shrinks take vast sums of money for straightening everyone's problems while falling into fatal messes themselves."

"She is very successful. She should thank me for it! She got her practice on me."

"When was that?"

"Oh . . . when we were growing up. When we finally talked."

"About – about what happened to you – on 't Gooi?"

She nodded.

"What makes you say you're a coward?" I asked curiously.

"Because I'm always afraid of something. Because I always run away from hurt, not only mine. You see, it was years before I faced that old rape. I never would have faced it, except that my sister forced me to, and there have been many things that I refused to face. If Pieter grew up and was doing crimes I would give one quick thought to what he would feel shut up in prison and then I would shut myself off from the reality. I can't bear pain and I can't bear, only double, to cause pain. I could never hit the children – never – even when I knew that they needed it. I would sense in advance what I would feel after I did it, so I never did do it. That's why Pieter laughs at me and respects only his father. A mother, too, should be strong."

"You faced Niels. You fought him."

"Screaming and hysterics are a kind of mean cowardice. You scream because you can't face facts. It's just another way of escaping. And you saw how I was a coward, the way I told you about all that. I saw that you were put off him."

I flushed. "No, Mariolain – "

"*Yes*, Suky. You were thinking, this horrible man who didn't understand my friend and drove her mad with other women. And I wanted your sympathy. Because the latest woman was just now, just before you all came. All that day you were coming, I didn't speak to him, I just cried into the food I was making for you, and Anna was crying because I was crying, and Pieter locked himself in his room so as not to get drowned in women's tears."

"My God! How well you hid it!"

"And you. We thought, why can't our family be like that?"

"But our kids are so – "

"So what?" she asked in surprise. "They are terrific!"

"So bad mannered," I mumbled. "Fighting and making embarrassing remarks – "

"They are so open! And ours are so – repressed. I think so! You may call if good manners but I think they have no confidence. I think our situation, Niels's and mine, has pushed their feelings down deep and now they just burst out by accident once in a while instead of being naturally on the surface, like with George and Daniel."

I felt a wave of sheer warm gratification flow over my bedrock of guilt, soothing it (for the moment) and even hiding it from my view.

"Oh Mariolain, I do love you!" I said out of the joy of this feeling.

She laughed.

"Well, I'm glad somebody does. But I wish you were a nice *man*, saying that. I sometimes dream a man will say it to me and then I will show Niels what it feels like to come home and find a jockey-strap in the bed, and hairs in his electric razor."

I was laughing. I couldn't help it.

"You wouldn't really, though."

She gave me a very straight look.

"Don't be sure, Suky. I might really, and I may really, if I will get a chance. He thinks that too, that I wouldn't, though he often says, 'Go ahead, let's both be free, then you won't mind what I do.' One day I would love to do it! Now you won't love me any more," she said, like a little girl again.

"But you adore him, really."

"That, unluckily for me, is true, more or less."

"So how could you sleep with another man?"

"I don't know. But I feel I could. My anger with him makes me dream of it so often that now I am sure I could do it 'really'. Just show me a kind, gentle man who likes me, and I will do the things with him (which I must say mean not so very much to me, I always think of something else) and then I will make sure Niels finds out about it, and then we will see. *He* doesn't think I could, and I believe that's because he is, in his bottommost heart, relying on my trauma from when I was a child. He thinks *he* is the only one who I can bear to touch me. But Irene has slept with quite a lot of men, and she told me, the more you do it the more the other business gets covered up. It would be interesting to see if that's true for me. I would like, just once, to see Niels furious and jealous. It would be worth doing just to see that."

The others came tumbling in at that moment, laughing

187

with satisfaction and hunger. Daniel came straight to me, and dragged me again to the open hatch.

"Look, Mum! Look at my eggs! There, in their own rack! Aren't they the best?" he crowed.

Dan's eggs were certainly eye-catching, jagged with brilliant geometric designs like a Mexican rug, and I praised him. But the plain-dyed eggs, lined up in rows, were beautiful too. Someone had polished them with a little wax till they glowed, and the colours were true and deep. Even the puce and mud-coloured ones – Anna's failed-purples – were attractive, setting off the others. I said this too, and was rewarded by a rather watery smile from Anna and a furious scowl from Daniel.

"You always think other people's stuff's better than mine," he muttered. "Anna's are just cruddy, how can you say they're good?"

"Yours are fantastic," I whispered, hugging him. "I can't hurt her feelings." For once I felt his angular, tense little body relax against me, and experienced the fleeting radiance that comes to me every so often when I've done the *right* thing for once. How blissful it must be to be a really good mother! Like a sort of orgasm of the spirit going on all the time instead of the guilt which is so constant one hardly feels it except as a perpetual aching unease.

Cal returned with the wine and we all had a glass, and stood or sat about the living-room among the spring leaves and the birds, eating and drinking. Once or twice I caught Cal's eye and when he topped up my glass, he smiled, his eyes half-closing like a cat's. The wonders of wine, I thought, trying to be cynical. But my heart's knots seemed to be untensing, like Daniel's, and like Dan I wanted to lean against someone warm and loving who would put an arm round me and kiss the side of my head in complete approbation, however temporary.

"What exactly is the programme tomorrow?" Cal was asking Niels.

"Early rising," he replied promptly, in his best O.C. manner. "Breakfast at 8. I will leave first and be on the heath by 9.30 to lay the trail. You will all come along at ten sharp. You see, we aren't the only family which do this, or something like it, so we like to do ours early. Otherwise stupid people can come along and interfere with our trail."

"Will we eat out? A picnic?"

"No. The ground is too wet and it's too cold. We come home for a lunch."

"Who makes it?" I asked, on the alert for female exploitation.

Mariolain laughed. "Most of it's made already! We eat hard boiled eggs."

"Ugh!" chorused George and Daniel. It was one thing to colour them, another to choke them down.

"Don't worry, there will be lots of mayonnaise – "

At the mention of mayonnaise, our two broke into unrestrained sicking-up noises. I forgot my recent benignity and hissed:

"*Will* you two shut up?"

The Dutch pair, forever under a cloud for their faddiness, capered with glee, but Anna took pity and said in a stage whisper, "There are lots of other things too which Mami has made all day when we are out – "

"Beetles in chocolate," said Mariolain. "Toasted worms." Anna only giggled, and beckoned the others, who followed her out of the room with alacrity.

With his third glass of wine, Niels became abruptly silent. He sank onto the lime-green settee, hung his empty glass from a finger-sling between his knees, dropped his head over it, and went into retreat. Mariolain on the other hand became gem-bright. As I watched her scintillating and waving her arms about as she chattered, casting smiles and little jingles of laughter all around her, like the flecks of light scattered by the glass birds nodding on their springs, I was catapulted back to Venice, for she was just like that there. So much so that (and this must have been how the drink took *me*) I suddenly heard myself saying: "Mariolain! Where's your guitar?"

Niels's head came up like a deer who scents a leopard. Mariolain stopped short with her mouth open. For a moment I thought she would say: What guitar? or: What are you talking about? Instead after an oddly electric moment she said, "It's up in the attic."

"In our room, do you mean?"

She nodded. "In your cupboard."

I sprang up, sat down, got up again more carefully.

"I'm going to bring it!" I almost shouted, as if daring Niels or anyone else to stand in my way.

But Niels didn't react at all. His eyes had gone black and slitty, so that I remembered his Indonesian blood. Cal beamed, quite vacuously for him, and then nodded sagely. "Music," he said. "Keep music live." And he drew the third cork with aplomb.

I staggered up the stairs and found the guitar in its case hidden in the back of our wardrobe. Getting it down the ladder was tricky, especially as I was tight as a tick, but I managed it. I met Anna at the bottom of the stairs and she gaped and said, "What's that? You play a guitar?"

"This isn't mine. It's your mummy's."

"That's *Mami's* guitar?"

"Yes," I said in my drunk-loud voice, "it shore is."

By the time I unsteadily regained the living-room I was trailed by kids like the Pied Piper. I marched to Mariolain and placed the instrument in her arms.

She looked at it palely.

"I don't know why you brought it," she said. "I can't play any more." She spoke faintly and her voice wavered.

"Try, Mariolain," I said. "Just try."

The children shouted their enthusiasm. Niels sat motionless, bent over his glass. Mariolain slowly and clumsily took the guitar out of its case and ran her hands over it. Then she took hold of it properly and struck two strong, sweet chords.

There was a silence.

Anna said something in Dutch in a hushed voice of wonder. Mariolain put the guitar down beside her chair.

"That's not playing," she said. "I don't think I can play any more."

"I don't believe it," I said. "One doesn't forget how to play an instrument, one simply gets out of practice. Though why you let it go, something that meant so much to you – " I stopped.

Mariolain looked round at us all. She looked last at Niels, or rather at the top of his head. He didn't move. Anna said,

190

"*Please!*" with great intensity.

"I don't want to try and then find I can play only badly," Mariolain said. "It is terrible to play badly. That's why I put it away years ago, because I was not playing good."

The children were more than disappointed. They were resentful. They grumbled and moped and fell into a collective bad mood, which I realised with deep dismay was spoiling what had been, till then, an exceptional evening. I couldn't bear it. An idyll had been maggot-eaten, and the maggot was me, or at least my sudden impulse.

"Come on," I said, sobering myself up with a sharp effort. "Let's play a game."

Cal twitched visibly. He hates games. *I* hate games. I like *activities*, such as dyeing eggs. But I couldn't think of another activity, and I was driven by a compulsion to redeem the evening.

"What game?" asked Pieter dubiously.

"*Murder*," I said, on a sudden inspiration.

There were no arguments about how to play *Murder* because nobody except me had ever heard of it. I hadn't played it for at least thirty-five years, so I made up the rules as I went along. Fortunately it worked. In fact, it was a riotous success. Only Niels sat out, moody and silent.

I was longing to be the murderer, but I never once drew the Ace of Spades. During one round I was prowling in the dark, wishing I were licensed to kill, when I felt a pair of warm, well-known hands on my neck. Cal's breath, scented not unpleasantly with wine, warmed my face. Instead of screaming straight away I put my own hands up to touch his wrists. For a few seconds we stood like that, close together in the pitch darkness. Then he snarled softly and gently squeezed my windpipe. I felt a sudden upsurge of unreasoning happiness.

"AAAAAAAGH!" I screeched, making the tormented cadences rise and fall and die away into throttled gugglings as I slid bonelessly to the floor. I sensed my killer flitting from the scene of his crime.

Mariolain was the detective. She went about her business unconventionally. Instead of the usual questions ("Where were you standing when you heard the scream?") she would

191

shamefully lead the witness: "Did you know the dead woman had a packet of Polo mints in her pocket? Wouldn't you kill for a mint?" The children were helpless with laughter.

Then she came to Cal.

"Would you kill for love?" she asked.

"For nothing less, sweetheart," he said, being Bogart.

"And did you love the woman you killed?"

"Don't try to trick a trickster, baby."

She bent over me with a professional air, then straightened.

"Her lipstick is smudged. She was kissed before she was killed."

"That's a lie, I never kissed her!"

"Ah!" cried everybody, pointing at him.

Cal conceded his guilt, and hiked me to my feet. As he did it, his eyes were on my lips.

The kids were packed off to bed at last, at about eleven. The four grown-ups built a fire in the lily, made hot chocolate, cleared up the cards and general wreckage left by the game, and had another drink, respectively. Niels was the one who had the drink.

When Cal had the fire going to his satisfaction, he went through to the kitchen to help Mariolain with the hot drinks, and while they were both briefly absent Niels came up behind me and smacked me hard across the bottom.

I was bending down to straighten the rug when he did it, and I jumped up so sharply that the back of my head struck his chin. I can't easily describe my reaction. I was too absolutely astonished to feel anger. I just stared at him open-mouthed, rubbing my sore behind. And I saw at once it had been no misplaced act of flirtation. He had responded to an ungovernable impulse to hurt me.

We were in the back end of the living-room, which wasn't lit; we were also opposite the open hatch, through which, as on a TV screen, we could see Mariolain and Cal in the kitchen. There we stood, Niels and I, glaring at each other in

192

mutual fury. No, not mutual. His was far greater than mine. It had sobered him up.

"What the hell did you do that for?" I hissed.

"You are in *my house*," he hissed back.

"I don't know what you're talking about! What have I done?"

"The guitar."

"What – ?"

"Why did you have to bring her guitar?"

I was staggered.

"Why not? *Why not?*"

"You call yourself her friend! Why can't you help her instead of making things worse?"

Mariolain's face was poking through the hatch.

"Are you two still playing *Murder*?"

Niels and I drew deep sumultaneous sighs and cried, "No, of course not!" in ironic unison. Then I bent again to the rug and Niels moved away towards the fire.

Later, in bed under the skylight, Cal said, "What was going on while we were in the kitchen?"

I was silent.

"Come on, tell me," Cal pressed. "You sounded angry."

"I was."

"You really don't like him, do you?"

"I don't know what to feel about him. He . . ." I hesitated. "He hit me. He smacked my ass."

There was a long pause. Cal was very still.

"Do you mean he made a crude pass at you?" he asked in a tense voice.

"No, Cal, it wasn't like that. He was angry. He wanted to hit me, and he was just drunk enough not to stop himself." I repeated the dialogue as far as I remembered it.

After another long silence, Cal said gruffly, "Christ! I'm having to force down all kinds of primitive feelings when I think of him putting his hands on you – " And he turned suddenly towards me.

It was like picking up a phone when you're tired and

wretched, expecting it to be just another dreary call, and hearing quite unexpectedly the hallo of an old, trusted friend. I couldn't hold out. When he put his arm tentatively across me, I turned in a sudden spasm and pushed myself against him. "Hey . . . " he whispered. Both my arms went round him as I felt his beard rasping against my cheek. He gave a sharp intake of breath and then his lips in their frame of soft hair were seeking out their favourite, familiar places on my face, and on my body. Oh my darling. Where were you all this time when I've been so heartsick and lonely? Yes, yes, settle me under your body in the old way, I want nothing new, no clever tricks or techniques, just what I've grown used to and nearly withered away for lack of . . . Love me again, because I've loved you all the time, and what has this nonsense all been about? There, there, my dearest, what does any of it matter, what idiots we've been, how it all melts away in the sweet fires, now nothing in the world can touch us . . .

Without a word we fell asleep, still intimately entangled. And I dreamed. I dreamed I was watching Riki and Wim making love. I watched, and yet at the same time I *was* her, I let this stranger who was her familiar husband make love to us, and I knew with my special knowledge that tomorrow the Japs would come; she didn't know it and would have been happy, but I whispered inside our head, "Enjoy it, it's for the last time, you'll never be together again!" They, we, began to make love frenziedly, rocking and thrusting and gasping, and I found it was Cal who had swollen up again and was at it like a madman.

"Darling, darling . . . " I murmured, holding him close and looking up at the starlight, grateful to my heart that I'd woken up and was no longer poor Riki with her doom before her. "It's all right . . . "

He climaxed with a stifled cry, I gave him the side of my hand to bite, and he sank down on me, heavy and panting.

"I dreamt you'd died," he muttered. "I dreamt . . . I was fucking you, and you were dead. Oh, Sue! It's been as bad as death. Don't let's ever – You're my love."

"You're mine."

We slept again, this time without dreams.

I don't know to this day what made us make it up, like that, just on that night. Perhaps long quarrels, estrangements, run their term and die like anything else. The problems weren't resolved. When we got home they would be waiting for us. But the horrible bad feelings they'd given rise to had been passed through; like an illness, we'd got well of it. Our marriage was back on the road to health. I suspected it that night as we dropped asleep in each other's arms. I knew it for sure the next morning when we woke up almost at the same moment and lay staring at each other for a long time, communing through our eyes, and the first thing he said was,

"You don't think our boys are too awful, do you? You're not disappointed in them?"

"They're the most marvellous things in my life, except you."

Thus our pre-coital exchange. We were late down to breakfast, and Niels was already leaving for 't Gooi. He was going on his bike, to leave us the two cars. I caught a glimpse of him, his long coat and scarf billowing in the wind and his black hair blown into a crest, flying down the drive like some mad bird pushing before it its bizarre nest of multi-coloured eggs.

Pausing at the gate he glanced back, and saw me framed by the trailing leaves in the window. He gave me a curious look. I related it almost at once to looks I'd seen before, on the faces of my children, when they've misbehaved intolerably and are neither sorry nor defiant but baffled; the look that says, "I couldn't help it so how can it be my fault?" Then he took off again down the Sunday-quiet road.

Chapter 19

———— ~~~ ————

When we reached the heath, the sun had gone in, but the cloud cover was high and there was no threat of rain. The air was laden with moisture and lively with the onset of spring. The children bounded out of the two cars and, led by Pieter, began questing like foxhounds, almost with their noses to the turf, for the first arrows.

Cal, Mariolain and I strolled more sedately away from the carpark.

"Do you know where the trail begins?" Cal asked Mariolain.

"I only know where it will finish," she said.

"So let's leave them to it and walk there by another route."

"Oh . . . ! But we are meant to do the trail too!"

Cal looked at her, mildly appalled.

"What, all the hopping on one leg and singing songs and climbing trees? You've got to be kidding!"

"Not so much, but we must be their audience. Otherwise maybe they will cheat."

"My sons," Cal said loftily, "wouldn't dream of cheating."

"Oh yeah?" I murmured.

One of the 'hounds' gave tongue. He had got the scent. The others rushed to join him and the four of them streamed away from us across the skyline, bumpy with clumps of heather like purple thunderheads, in the direction of the woods.

"By the time we catch up with them they'll be miles ahead anyway," said Cal hopefully.

"I know a shortcut," said Mariolain firmly.

We walked abreast, Cal in the middle. Cal suddenly said, "I've got to say I've fallen for this country."

"It's not very exciting," said Mariolain. "Most foreigners think it's dull and flat."

"That's just what I like," said Cal. "The flatness. You can stretch your eyes. When I first came to England I was afraid even to stretch my legs for fear of stepping into the sea."

"Here you are more likely to do that."

"England is so built up, so crowded."

"Holland is even more."

"One doesn't feel it, somehow. I think it's the wide horizons. It feels like a country with nothing to hide."

Mariolain grunted ironically.

"Listen," I said. "Let's plan a cycling holiday here, next summer, the boys would love it. We could all go together. Maybe we could go right up north, to Friesland." I looked at Mariolain.

"Where my mother came from," she said, looking at the ground and at her feet imprinting the damp sand. "And where she went."

I pricked up my ears and leant forward across Cal. "Went? When? After – "

"Yes. That's where my father took her – that night."

She glanced at Cal, then down again.

"Well," she said, "when you think about it, Suky, what could he have done with our mother? He wanted her removed from his life, and our lives, but where could he take her that she would not come straight back to find her children? The best he could think of was to take her back to Friesland, to her family, and tell them she was a traitor and a collaborator and that she must be kept on the farm of her father and brothers to prevent her disgracing them all and doing more harm to Holland. He told her father that he was finished with her and that if she showed her face again near to him or his children he would not be responsible for what he might do.

197

"Her family were simple people, but very, very patriotic, even chauvinist. They had hidden sharpened farm tools and shotguns ready to attack any Germans who came to take them for work or for the army. And it was not just talk. Later they formed a resistance cell and hid divers, also Jewish children . . . They felt very deeply against the *moffen* and it was to get worse later.

"So that night, when he heard my mother had collaborated, her father knocked her down. Right there on his doorstep when my father tried to hand her over to him. He refused at first to have anything to do with her. But my father simply got back in his car and drove away, leaving her lying there beside the little suitcase he had let her bring. A few clothes and . . . some little souvenirs of us, was all she took away from her marriage . . . Of course her father could not do anything but take her in. And he did it, perhaps also because he hated my father almost as much as the *moffen*.

"But he treated her as an outcast. Her older brother did too. Her other brother was a little nicer to her but they were all afraid that she was a real Nazi and would be dangerous to them and prevent their plans. So they worked her like a slave and gave her just her food and a small place to sleep, an outhouse full of hay and firewood, where they locked her each night like a dog. Poor thing! As if she had anything in her head except getting back to us! And the first chance she got, she stole money from them and came back here. But by then we were gone.

"She reached the door of our old house. My father, when he saw her, just stepped aside and said, 'Come in and look, you won't find them. Never.' And she rushed about the house like a mad woman, hunting everywhere, though she knew it was useless, that he had foreseen all this and had hidden us where she would never find us. And all the time he stood by the door, keeping it shut of course so no neighbours would hear her crying our names, and in the end she fell down at his feet – she'd walked a good part of the way back here and was completely exhausted – and implored him at least to tell her if we were well, and he wouldn't even do that. 'They may be dead for all you will ever know of them,' he said, like ice. Then he opened the door and said, 'Out.'

And she went with her little case and wandered away not knowing where to go."

"And where did she go?"

"Where would you have gone?"

I thought about it as deeply, and as imaginatively, as I could.

"To 'our headquarters'," I said slowly, at last.

"That's right, Suky. And do you know what happened to her then? They sent her to Germany. Germany. *To be safe.* She was not here for the *hongerwinter*. Instead she worked at a lazaret."

"A what?" asked Cal, who, though he must have been bewildered, having not heard the first part of the story, was listening intently as he walked between us.

"A hospital. It was near the eastern front line. She went through bombs, shelling, terror, and she looked after the German wounded, just as a 'dirty-work' helper of course, she was not a nurse. And all the time she was telling herself, 'This is all I ever do, I help people, what is so wrong in that? Why do I have to suffer, why have I lost my children?' She grew very bitter."

"What happened after the war?" asked Cal.

"When the Russians came, and the Americans, the Dutch who had been taken to Germany for forced labour returned back to Holland. And people like my mother went with them. Just to go home, hoping things would be better, not knowing what a hard, sharp line would be drawn between those who had been right during the war and those who had been wrong. Still till now, we talk about those who were 'wrong in the war'. Till today, such people can't live where they are known; they stay together, they move to new towns, or abroad . . . My mother couldn't know that then. She came to the only place she knew, hoping, poor woman, that working with the wounded soldiers under terrible conditions for years and suffering so much would be enough, that she would be forgiven somehow for her crime which she still didn't understand . . .

"Our father had left our old house and moved in with us at Uncle Adriaan's as soon as the liberation came. My mother found our house standing empty. She had nowhere else to go. She broke in and cleaned up a little and camped in the house and waited, not knowing what else to do. And a neighbour who knew her reported to my father that she was back. And he told the new Dutch police, and they came and arrested her for collaboration."

Griet was taken to a concentration camp for those who had – or were reported to have – collaborated with the Germans. The camp – Westerbork – had originally been built as a transit camp for Jews en route to extermination. Now it was full of Dutch men and women of all ages and conditions, from young ones who had fraternised with the enemy in the time-hallowed way, to older ones who had worked for them, and some who had never helped them in any way at all.

They slept in long huts, on wooden bunks, or sometimes on the bare ground, and did fieldwork or other hard labour, ate very poorly, were bitterly cold in winter, had only the most basic medical attention and could not easily keep clean. But all these hardships were endurable. The one unbearable thing was that they were in the charge of people who hated them and spent their time finding new ways to punish, humiliate and degrade them.

The first degradations were the obvious ones, and have an all-too-familiar ring now. They were made to stand naked at roll-call, and some of them were raped. This didn't happen to Griet but she was forced to stand among other women, ringed by a tight jeering circle of guards, while a girl with a shaven head daubed with orange metal-primer was debauched to raucous cries of "*Moffenmeid! Moffenmeid!*" Griet felt two things simultaneously: a sense of comparative virtue ("I would never sleep with any soldier!") and a loathing for the girl's persecutors ("How can they say the Germans were so bad when they can do this?"). These early experiences of her imprisonment merely hardened her and did nothing to convince her that she had been so wrong in her judgement or guilty in her behaviour.

Later some of these early excesses died down, but terrible things still happened. There was rigid curfew during the hours of darkness. Prisoners were forbidden even to go to the latrines. As many of them had bowel disorders (to exacerbate which they were kept deliberately short of water), this was both arbitrary and cruel. It invited infringements which in turn invited punishments. If a woman was forced to creep out to the latrines, which were floodlit, she might be shot at. One at least was killed in this way, a friend of Griet's, one of her only friends.

To frighten the women into staying in their huts, the night-shift – always worse than the guards on duty by day – would fire their rifles through the windows. The mere possibility of these shattering assaults effectively prevented proper sleep. When a girl had been wounded in the leg by one such volley, Griet and two other women spent their free time for several days under the hut scraping out a shallow trench to sleep in. They slept like that throughout November until their scrapes were discovered – by which time the occasional terrors of the night-fusillades were almost welcome by contrast with the wicked cold of that exceptionally severe winter.

Food was in short supply all over Holland for the first year, and prison rations reflected that. The guards, too, had not enough, and often commandeered part of the rations of the prisoners. Sometimes the hot food they did get stank of urine . . . When some women, Griet among them, were bold enough to complain, they were told: "You're lower than beasts. If you want food, crop the grass." They were forced to crawl on all fours and 'mow the lawn' with their teeth.

It was at this point that the iron truly entered Griet's soul.

While Mariolain told us all this, we walked, heads down. Cal and I fell completely silent, no questions, no promptings. At last she stopped, first speaking, then walking.

"I think," she said "that we are lost."

"Who were the guards?" Cal asked.

"We must try to find the children . . . Let's walk to the top of that little rise."

"Who were the guards?" asked Cal again, louder.

"The guards – ?"

201

"Not members of the Resistance, I'd guess?"

"Of course not. Such people don't feel to do such works. No. They were the ones who had a score to settle, or who felt guilty. Because they had not done enough at the time when it counted. Most of them were volunteers, so you can imagine what types they would be, people who wanted to gain credit from being seen to be down on the *moffen* now they were safely gone. And of course some people who will always appear, anywhere, when there is some work of cruelty to be done."

"And when," I asked as we climbed toward a ridge of pinetrees, "did you find out all this?"

"When I was sixteen," she said, "and decided to find my mother. Oh, thank goodness, look – ! I see them! Come on, let's run and catch them, we've missed half the trail, Anna will be furious!"

She took off, flying down the dune-like slope toward the little figures.

Cal took a deep breath and turned to me. "It's not over yet, here," he said. "The war. In England it's over. I didn't realise."

"We weren't occupied," I said.

He stood still for a moment, his thumb gently rubbing my hand as our fingers lay clasped.

"It's not just that. Our involvement in 'Nam will hang on to *us* in the same way."

"Not in the same way," I said. "I don't think so."

"For as long, then," he said. "For just as long. For forty years at least. It's a question of shame."

"Then it's also a question of luck," I said. "It's only luck *we* weren't invaded. All the same things would have happened to us, all the same monsters would have crawled out of holes . . . Evil is so often a matter of occasion."

Later I found out that Griet had said almost the same thing to Mariolain.

Chapter 20

———— ❧ ————

The war ended. Mariolain was eleven. Irene was nearly fourteen. Tante Miep was dead. Uncle Adriaan sold the big house and moved to America to join a cousin in the antique business in Pennsylvania. Willem sold the Hilversum house and they moved into the house where, in the mid-fifties, I stayed when I first came to visit Holland. I remember it as a small quiet place with a sheltered garden. There was a feeling of country living, even though it was in a town.

The profit from the sale of the Hilversum house left Willem sufficiently well off so that, living frugally, he didn't need immediately to return to teaching. He settled down to write his book. The girls went to school where they drank in with every lesson the resonances of the recent past, the version of the victors. Every child who had a parent who had been in the Resistance was made to feel superior to every child who had not. Children whose parents had been 'wrong in the war' kept deathly quiet about it. Irene boasted about her father, about her own role as the little postman, and was a local heroine. Mariolain said less but basked in reflected glory. When anyone asked them about their mother, they said, "We haven't got a mother." Of course the assumption was that she was dead, and before long Mariolain picked up this habit of thought. She had no mother. It was infinitely better not to have a mother than to have one who had been wrong. She and Irene no longer remembered 'Julie'.

That was why it was such a horrendous shock when the letter came. It was crumpled and in a cheap little envelope which had been opened by a censor. It was addressed to Irene and had been forwarded after some delay from the old house. It was sparsely worded, with grim undertones:

My dear daughter, I am in a *camp* for "traitors". We are treated very [censored]. I sleep on the *ground* and do farm-work. The farmer is *very* hard on me. I hope you are well and Mariolain too, and that you have enough to eat. These are *very bad times*. I ask you to come and see me. You are fifteen now and can come if you choose. If you can come please bring me some *cigarettes* and if possible a little meat. I send you my love. Mami.

Irene panicked when she read this. It was as if the ground had opened under her feet. Crying and distraught, she instinctively took the letter straight to the only authority she recognised as powerful enough to cope with this mythical emergence. Her father. He glanced through it stony-faced and ripped it to pieces.

Then he told Irene to wash her face and he took her out with him for the whole day, allowing her to miss lessons. He was probably afraid to let her go to school in the state she was in, for fear she should blurt something out. They spent a reasonably agreeable, and certainly effectively distracting day visiting relatives, coming home late to a furiously jealous Mariolain who was given no reason for this unwonted departure from justice and even-handedness. That night Mariolain nagged Irene into telling her about the letter, and was struck dumb. She promptly put it from her.

Subsequently there were other letters. They mingled complaint and muted reproach with pitiful appeals. Irene read them more rationally now, and she didn't show them to her father unless he saw one arrive and demanded to have it. (She lost two unread like that.) When she got a letter from a small coastal town not thirty miles away, telling her that her mother had been released ("for good behaviour, so you see I am not as bad as you seem to think me") and had found a position as housekeeper to a doctor ("a wonderful man, a better Christian than many who go to church each week") Irene at last wrote to her, though in utter secrecy and in deep fear that her father would find out.

Mother,
    You must try to understand what the war has meant. I know you are my mother but I hardly remember you and – [she crossed the last five words out, but they could still be read] – Papi has not allowed me to write to you or come to see you. I'm glad you are free and have a good home. Mariolain is well. Please don't write any more. Irene.

The letters stopped.

Irene had always got on better with Willem than Mariolain had. Mariolain, as she grew older, strove to love him and be loved by him, but she failed. The truth, which she couldn't acknowledge then, was that she feared and disliked him. Since the war he was subject to fits of cold rage of which she was nearly always the butt. (Irene, though more devious and calculating in her dealings with him, seemed to get away with everything and still be given such occasional bits of affection as he was capable of, as long as she lived at home.) Willem would summon Mariolain to his study with a frozen face and in a voice which filled her with quaking dread, though he never hurt her physically. He would stride up and down the little room, his stiff arms trembling with suppressed fury, and, rolling the finely-wrought phrases off his tongue, would tell her how she had disappointed him, angered him, made him ashamed of her. Half the time he wouldn't even tell her why.

"But what have I done, Papi?" she would sob frantically.

He would stop and face her, his cold grey eyes seeming to bore into her soul. "You know perfectly well what you've done!" he would roar, as if she had driven him past all restraint. "Don't put on this act of stupid innocence! Go to your room, you sicken me!" Sometimes he would not speak to her for days on end . . . She would have nightmares revolving around these searing scenes. A single eye, bent on her and burning like hot ice, would appear out of darkness and dissolve her with a mixture of helplessness and terror.

Unsurprisingly, she became religious. She had a girlfriend who was a Catholic, with whom she sometimes went home to tea. The mother of this child was, for Mariolain, a paradigm of mothers. When the girls arrived home from school, she would be sitting there, waiting, with a teapot in front of her. She would kiss her daughter and ask routine – but, to Mariolain, unbearably poignant – questions about her day. Mariolain timidly asked if she could have one of the holy pictures she saw sticking in the edge of her friend's mirror. At home, she hid it near her bed and said her prayers to it. The face she saw on the increasingly dogeared card was that of her friend's mother, to whom, in reality, she was too shy to make a single confidence.

Irene left home at seventeen to go to university in Leiden. Mariolain missed her terribly at times, but at other times had a sneaking sense of relief. But now she became conscious that their house was cold. Its arrangements were all austere and masculine. Their housekeeping was done by a series of women who 'came in'. One of them was a little special: she would bring flowers in from the garden, occasionally bake a cake, sing while she cleaned and even chat to Mariolain. Inevitably, she grated on Willem's nerves and was let go.

This led to a cataclysmic quarrel. Mariolain roused herself to accuse her father of sending the kindly housekeeper away on purpose because she, Mariolain, had liked her. Willem was furious at the imputation and tried to banish her to her room. Foreseeing the onset of the one punishment she could not bear – days of withdrawn silence – she grew desperately bold.

"I'm lucky in one thing!" she cried as she backed towards the door, away from the power of those basilisk eyes. "I've got someone I can tell it all to, someone who understands what you're like because she knows you!"

She had the momentary satisfaction of seeing her father's

skin go from an angry flush to putty grey. He rose to his feet, staring at her.

"Who are you talking about?" he demanded in a voice thick with menace.

"The Holy Mother!" Mariolain shot back, confident, for the moment, of heavenly protection. To her astonishment and chagrin, her father relaxed back into his chair and burst out laughing.

"You silly girl!" he exclaimed. "Nonsense. Get along with you!"

She heard him chuckling still as she closed the door. It was a long time before she realised the cause of his relief.

Mariolain's 'little illnesses' now began to show themselves. Migraine, occasional fainting fits, backache, upset stomach, strange allergies the cause of which couldn't be traced. She gradually became 'delicate' and assumed the status of a semi-invalid, though in between attacks she was quite normal. She was late starting her periods. Willem, who knew his duty, discovered this and took her to a doctor.

The doctor was a woman. She asked Mariolain the usual questions and made an examination. Mariolain became aware from her stance that something was wrong. The doctor probed. Mariolain flinched, then cried out. The doctor straightened up, her face full of veiled distress. She gently told Mariolain to get dressed, and left the room.

On the way home Willem was stiff and silent. It was several days before he could bring himself to the point. Then one night he came in to her room and sat down on the bed. He appeared haggard and ill. He didn't look at her, but suddenly took her hand, a thing so unusual that she was frightened and drew it back.

"The doctor told me someone hurt you once, when you were little," he said with difficulty at last. "She said I should talk to you about it. Do you remember who it was?"

Her mind was a shining blank. She shook her head, her teeth locked as if to shut in any words that wanted to come out.

"I want you to think back, to try to remember," said her father. "It's not good to bury bad things that happen, they can cause trouble later. Someone hurt you when you were a

207

little girl. I think . . . . " he swallowed and his jaw hardened. "I think I know who it may have been. But you must try to think of it yourself. I want you to know one thing. I am sometimes angry with you but about this I promise I won't be angry. Whatever was done, whatever happened, it was no fault of yours. Remember that."

Mariolain was fifteen. She had a boyfriend, her first. He was a good-looking boy from a wealthy but, like her own, a broken home, and he liked her; he had specially chosen her to cycle home from school with, to sit by in a movie. Soon, she sensed it, he would want to kiss her. She feared this (she had become aware of an aversion to being touched) and yet the undamaged part of herself told her she should welcome it and might enjoy it if she could overcome some hidden unwillingness. It was suddenly very important not to think about what her father wanted her to think about. But he wouldn't let it alone.

Every few days he would seek her out to ask, quietly but persistently: "Have you remembered?"

She would bite her lips and shake her head.

Irene came home for a visit. Willem spoke to her privately.

"Do you know that your sister was sexually molested during the war?"

To his utter consternation, Irene, after only a brief silence, replied steadily: "Probably at the same time that I was."

"What – ? What are you saying?"

"It was that man who was living in our house. He raped me one day on 't Gooi. Didn't you know?"

Willem, white as ashes, almost reeled out of the room and she heard him stumbling up the stairs. He didn't come down for hours and the two sisters made themselves supper together in the kitchen.

"What's wrong with Papi?"

"He asked me what had happened to you in the war, and I told him."

Mariolain seemed to freeze.

"You'd better not stop stirring that egg, it'll burn," remarked Irene, taking the wooden spoon out of her hand.

After a while, seeing that Mariolain was numb with shock, she became more kindly.

"Had you forgotten?" she asked. "I'm sorry."

Mariolain began to shout.

"I don't remember! I don't remember!"

Irene was by now a girl of strong, even ruthless, character, very direct and with little natural patience. But some instinct made her do the appropriate thing. She turned off the stove, took Mariolain by the arm and led her briskly out into the garden. As she had expected, being outdoors, where neighbours might hear, restrained Mariolain and she calmed down, superficially at least. Irene led her to a garden seat and they sat together, sheltered by high shrubs and trees.

"We'd better talk about it," said Irene. "God knows why we never have."

She did most of the talking. But by degrees Mariolain was persuaded to join in. Perhaps, as the 'session' went on, Irene was consciously looking ahead to her own future as a successful therapist, aware that she had a talent for this kind of thing . . . Out it all came. Mariolain forgot the neighbours and the oncoming chill and darkness. She wept and cried, and Irene, perhaps with as much budding professionalism as sisterly empathy, comforted her unsentimentally and efficiently. Eventually she took Mariolain, shivering with cold and reaction, back into the house and went on with cooking the supper. Later she went and knocked on her father's door with an unusually firm hand.

"We've talked it out. She'll be better now."

Willem was slumped at his desk. The face he raised was puffy-eyed and ravaged; he looked, literally, ten years older.

"Why didn't you tell me? *Why didn't you tell me*?"

"What's the use of getting into a state about it now, Papi? And it's certainly no use getting mad at *me* about it."

"That bloody, bloody swine! I knew he was a damned degenerate, I knew . . . "

"You knew he was a *political* degenerate, but I don't think you knew anything else, or, to be fair to you, you'd have done something about getting rid of him quicker than you did. It wasn't you who brought him into the house."

Her father's face, loose with shock and grief, abruptly

settled into the strong harsh lines of implacable hatred.

"I know who brought him," he said.

"I suppose you're going to use this as another reason for hating Mother," said Irene. Under less extreme circumstances such a remark would have called for immense daring, but now she sensed it was safe.

Her father stood up, unbearably agitated, his fists clenched at his chest.

"If I'd known this, I'd have killed her, I swear it, I'd have killed her like vermin!"

Irene's patience snapped. She was eighteen, she'd lived away from home, she'd got some perspective on all this and she had grown up. She stood up, too. She was a tall girl, taller than he was, and she had much of his strength when she was roused.

"Don't talk like that," she said. "If she was so bad, you shouldn't have married her. You were in the house at the time too, perhaps you should take some of the blame on yourself for not noticing what had happened to us. You were always too busy working for the national good to notice what was under your nose. I think Mother was guilty and I never want to see her again, but whether she deserved the punishment she got for her mistakes is something else. I certainly don't think you should talk about her as if she was a – a cockroach."

For a moment they faced each other and she saw such outrage in his face that she almost quailed in the old way. But she didn't. And she saw him go slack and sink into his chair with his head in his hands.

"Don't turn against me," he muttered. "Not you! Don't you know I always did my best?" She had never heard self-pity in his voice before. It made her shiver, but she stiffened herself.

"Yes, Papi," she said. "The terrible thing is that perhaps she did too."

Chapter 21

———— ⁓ ————

Mariolain duly got her first kiss. She didn't get any physical thrill from the experience but her personal satisfaction, the confidence it gave her, more than made up for that. The doctor had told her that the damage done to her reproductory system was not of a kind which would prevent her living a normal life. Mariolain was 'tidied up' under a general anaesthetic. (There was quite a lot of such tidying going on in Holland at that time.) A short while later she began to menstruate.

It was this event and the deep, liberating relief it brought – together, probably, with her 'session' with Irene – which triggered off the action she took shortly before her sixteenth birthday. There was to be a party. Planning the guest-list with her, Martin, her boyfriend, remarked, "What a shame you haven't got a mother."

Mariolain stared at him, startled, for a moment, and suddenly the thought surfaced: *But I have a mother*. She didn't say it aloud. But she didn't spend very long thinking about it before she acted – the subconscious thinking must have been going on for a long time.

She telephoned Irene in her digs in Leiden.

"I want Mami's address."

"Are you crazy?"

"I'm going to see her."

"You are crazy."

"It's my business."

"Don't do it."

"I intend to. I've a right."

There was a silence. Then Irene said, "I can't help you to do something I think is so wrong. Just don't poke about among my things looking for the letters, that's all."

Five minutes after this conversation ended, the letters, found at once in Irene's 'secret drawer' under her rolled-up spare stockings, were in Mariolain's hands. Whether Irene meant her to find them or not she was never sure.

She read them avidly. The early ones, from the camp, wrung her heart. It angered and agonised her to think that these piteous pleas had gone unanswered, even though the brief messages gave only a hint of what her mother had actually undergone. The ache of total abandonment transferred itself, from between the lines of the notes, straight to Mariolain's imagination.

She came to the last letter, written after her mother's release. The address was in a small town half-an-hour's bus-ride away. She literally clutched this to her chest, her breath coming short. Half a little hour, and she could see her, be with her, open her heart to her – offer her some recompense for the years of injustice and neglect and cruelty! She felt a compensating, invigorating fury, even hatred, rising in her against her father. It would be a positive delight to deceive him!

"Irene's invited me to Leiden. I'm going on Friday afternoon."

"Will you stay overnight?"

"N-no . . . I'll come back in the evening."

"How absurd. It's not worth the expense."

But he didn't try to interfere with her plans.

On the way to the bus station, Mariolain was palpitating with intense nervous excitement, exalted with a sense of destiny. She had conjured up a mental picture of her mother as she remembered her – tall, slim in her dark dress and white collar, but big-boned and comfortable, her pale face and severe brown hair softened by one of her rare maternal smiles. Her features were smudged like those of the madonna on the much-handled holy picture.

Mariolain had sent a brief note in advance: "I am coming on Friday next to see you. Please expect me at tea-time. Love, Mariolain." Love . . . Yes, she would love her! She would have a mother again. Someone to talk to, to care about her new, womanly problems. All the years . . . all that had happened . . . In a confused way, because of her difficult relationship with her father, Mariolain felt confident that she could take her mother's side, that her sufferings must have more than made up for any wrong she had done. Was it right to go on paying forever? The Catholics didn't think so. When Mariolain once read about a criminal sentenced to jail, she said, "Oh, the poor thing – to be punished so hard, shut up for so long – " Her father, and Irene too, laughed at her and said scornfully, "What about the people he harmed? What about *them*? You're wasting your pity on the wrong ones!"

At the other end of her journey Mariolain asked the way, and then walked. It was further than she'd thought. The district was a comfortable one, large, even opulent, full of houses with gravel drives set well back amid trees. Professionals' homes.

She found the house. She was tired now, her head was aching. Looking at the shining black front door at the end of the drive she felt her feet sticking to the pavement, unwilling to carry her forward. She felt frightened. There was a movement at the front window, a face flickering among the plants . . . A moment later, the black door opened.

A woman stood there. It was not her mother but a complete stranger. She was old, with greying hair and a thick, slightly stooped body. Mariolain approached without horror at first because she was sure this was a servant who had come to let her in and take her to her mother, who would be sitting in a beautiful living-room behind a table laid for tea . . .

She came up the steps.

In the space of a few seconds, two terrible things happened. She recognised her mother in this old, stout, ravaged woman. And she was seized and clasped irresistibly to the body of the stranger.

Her strongest impulse was to struggle, to free herself, even to run. But she thought frantically: *I mustn't! It's her, she's been waiting, she loves me, she'll be so hurt!* So she submitted to a kind of claustrophobic nightmare, long moments of confinement, hugged so she could hardly breathe, feeling the utterly unfamiliar body against the length of her own (she was unused to being hugged, no-one had ever held her like that) – her shallow, imprisoned breaths taking in a strange, even repulsive smell . . .

At last, at last she was released. With agonised reluctance she looked into Griet's face. She was just past forty at that time but she looked twenty years older. Terrible, terrible were the sufferings Mariolain could see written in her face. The smile of welcome, even of rapture, only underscored the lines of old anguish.

"Come in, my dearest, come in!"

Mariolain walked as if in a trance into the high-ceilinged hall and then into the drawing-room. This was all she had expected – an elegant room, all its appointments in sound conservative taste. On a low round table by an open fire, tea was indeed laid out, a lavish meal with plenty to eat. In the midst of it, a tall teapot, Mariolain's private symbol of motherhood, stood regally like a chess-queen upon its warming throne. From below glowed the little light, which seemed to summon Mariolain from her abyss of dismay.

"Sit down, my little girl. Look how nice, it's all for you! How grown-up you are! If you knew – how I've dreamt of this moment –"

Mariolain sank down on a brocaded armchair. She was cold all over and reached her hands to the fire. It seemed legitimate to look at the flames instead of at her mother. And Griet was stumbling, both her words and her hands, pouring tea, admiring Mariolain's hair and clothes, pressing her to eat. Mariolain glanced at her and away again hastily, appalled by the tears in those hollow eyes. But the loving pity she had experienced so warmly in her imagination now seemed frozen.

"How are you, Mami?" she managed to say.

"How am I? I'm better. I'm almost human again now. The doctor saved me. No, that's no exaggeration. I don't think I'd be alive now if he hadn't taken me in." Her voice was strained and she tossed her head as if defiant. "They say the

Germans were so bad. They say anyone who helped them was a monster, to be treated like an animal – worse than that! Well, I want you to meet the doctor. He's waiting to meet you. Then you can tell all the 'right' people that not all the ones they call 'wrong' are so bad!" She nodded her heavy face and got up.

Mariolain sat, still frozen. She was now to meet a real 'NSB-er', one of those men her father, and others, talked about with a hatred and contempt which seemed to go so deep that all the time in the world, and all the punishment, could never assuage it. If Adolf Hitler himself had been about to walk into this sedate, comfortable room she could not have been more apprehensive.

The man who entered was small, rather stout, bald, with thick-lensed glasses and a genial expression. He walked up to her, his well-polished shoes clacking on the woodblock floor between the rugs. She half expected him to click his heels and bow when he reached her. Instead he extended his hand. She shook it numbly.

"I'm delighted to meet you," he said. "It's quite time you came to see your mother." Was there – ? Yes, there was – a hint of *reproach* in his tone. "I will tell you frankly, young lady, I've sometimes thought hardly of you for not coming. But then I thought, well, she's only very young, surely when she grows up she will realise . . . We must all try our best to break free of prejudice, to judge cases on their merits. And you should consider . . . " He turned aside briefly to help himself to a biscuit, and kept his round shiny head averted. The firelight flashed off his glasses. He didn't tell her at once what she ought to consider, but instead, biscuit in hand, pointed to a large gilt-framed landscape in oils above the fireplace.

"What d'you think of that?" he asked.

"It's – pretty," she said faintly.

"Pretty? It's superb! Know what that is? Luneberg Heath, where our Wehrmacht used to train."

Mariolain's veins ran ice. She was in the presence of the devil. But he had now turned his face and was positively twinkling at her. He had said it on purpose!

215

"Don't be alarmed, my dear. I am making a point. If things had gone otherwise . . . who would have been the outcasts then, eh? And war is such a lottery. Such a lottery . . . Perhaps being young and naive, inexperienced, you think whole nations are worse than other whole nations? That 'our' side was fated to lose because God was against us, because we were some sort of anti-Christ? That all the evil was gathered in us and all the virtue in you? Listen to your mother, let her tell you her story. It is, in part, your story, too – you'll never wholly escape it. Listen with your heart and mind as well as your ears. It will shock you out of your simple judgements. And you will be all the better for it!" He popped the last half of the biscuit into his mouth, picked up another one, and patted Griet on the shoulder. "I will leave you now, I have calls to make. My patients don't ask me to take my shoes off to see if I have cloven hoofs before they alow me to use my skills on them . . . I hope to see you *very regularly*." He gave her a penetrating look, nodded, and left the room, crunching his biscuit.

Mariolain's head swung round and she gazed at the painting.

'Our' Wehrmacht . . . *How could he*? It was as if the Germans were still here.

"What do you think of him?" Griet was asking eagerly as soon as he'd gone. She lit a cigarette. Her hands trembled. "Such a fine man! A clever man . . . you heard how he talks! A widower . . . But he has never – don't imagine he has ever behaved in the slightest way disrespectfully toward me. There were guards in the camp who didn't respect womanhood as he does, 'good' Dutchmen your father would call them, 'on the right side', and you should have seen how they behaved, the things they did! *Animals* . . . But don't let's talk about those terrible things now. I want to just sit and look at you, and hear what you're doing, how you're feeling . . . What made you decide to come . . . Your sister would never come, though I wrote such begging letters to her . . . You have no idea how far I had to be driven, to risk the snub she gave me . . . Don't tell me, she has gone on to your father's side! The side of the winners, that's the easy way.

But you're here, my little one, you've come to see me, I mustn't complain. I know people whose whole families . . . who, for doing nothing but trying to help others, for believing what they were told, have had their lives, their health, their – well! Self-respect, that's the first thing to go, the last to come back. Terrible, terrible, what war does! And your father and sister are still at war with me! – Does he know you're here?"

"No."

"No. I thought not. I knew you wouldn't be able to tell him. I don't blame you for being afraid, not able to stand up to him. I never could . . . never! Even when he turned me out of my own house, stole my children and hid them, turned my own father and brothers into my enemies . . . *They* won't speak to me, would you believe it, until today . . . Well, your grandfather's dead, but he held out to the end, it was his last wish that your uncles would keep up the hate. Just imagine a man dying with such a wish on his lips! That's how deep it goes. I knew, when your uncle Piet told me that, that I had nothing to hope for, that I must make a new life. But it's hard, so very hard . . . "

She was trying to staunch tears, but it was useless, they were running down her face; she kept giving deep sniffs and blowing her nose as she talked, puffing at one cigarette after another.

Mariolain couldn't bear to watch. She felt oppressed, intolerably uncomfortable. The more her mother cried and talked, the uglier she became. Mariolain could feel no warmth, no daughterliness . . . She just sat there, numb, chilled; the pity had run away unused; there was nothing else, nothing.

After what seemed an eternity she was able to leave. The doctor, thank God, didn't reappear, but she still had to endure a further long, claustrophobic embrace before she heard herself promise to come again soon and was free to go. She forced herself to walk steadily down the crunching gravel drive, knowing that Griet was watching her. But the moment she was out of sight of the house she broke into a run.

She didn't go home that night. She was afraid her father would see the state she was in and guess at the reason – she couldn't have borne any more that day. She spent the night with a friend, and helplessly poured out her story of bewilderment and disillusion . . . She swore her friend to utter secrecy. But the next morning, coming down rather late to breakfast, she detected instantly a change in the atmosphere. Her friend's parents did not meet her eye. Conversation at table was stilted. She left, vowing never, never again in her life to trust any living soul with the secret of her mother's shame. "*It is your story too,*" the doctor had said. "*You will never escape it.*" That brief hour at her friend's breakfast table had taught her that this at least was one of the primary truths of her future.

Chapter 22

The trail was fun in the end. Even Cal enjoyed it, the way he can when he can forget his natural sense of dignity and be boyish and free. Niels had certainly thought up some fiendish things for us to do. At one point we had to pretend a certain tree was an Indian totem-pole, and do a war-dance around it, complete with loud whoops. Mariolain's were the loudest, and her barbaric leaps the highest – our boys paused in their somewhat inhibited progress to gape at her, half in admiration, half in dismay.

We caught up with Niels at last. The final arrow had pointed up a slight hill, and there we saw him, sitting in the branches of a stunted leafless oak, with his arms folded, grinning like a leprechaun. Cal, who'd brought a camera, took a shot of him which I am looking at as I write this, and others of the children, looking so different from their present, grown-up selves, in their coloured anoraks and 'flares', their cheeks rosy from exertion, their grins echoing Niels's triumphant one; and there's one of Mariolain, her henna-red hair like an upside-down chrysanthemum on her head, in an exuberant pose with both arms raised in the boxer's victory salute. There's another of the four children with their hands full of coloured eggs, which, in between shots, they'd rushed about, like hunting dogs once again, to find hidden among the heather, or almost buried – just a little bright spot of primary colour showing like an elf's window in the sand. From the cries of excitement when one was found you'd have thought they'd been made of solid gold, or at least solid chocolate. But it was the sheer joy of the chase. It was something they remembered and talked about for years. It also marked the end of their hatred of hard-boiled eggs – they ate the lot.

Well fed, well entertained and thoroughly at peace with the world, we eventually strolled back to the cars, Niels wheeling his bike beside me.

Remembering last night and its painful denouement made conversation difficult for me, but I carried it off by congratulating him on organising a wonderful morning.

"It was almost as good as your *Murder* game," he reciprocated generously. And after a moment, "We must play it again, the children will insist. Next time I shall try to be sober enough to play."

"You were a bit far gone," I admitted.

"You are trying to say you forgive me," he said in a low voice.

"I forgave you the minute it stopped stinging," I said. (The minute Cal said he was feeling primitive, the minute he took me in his arms.)

"I was awake all night. I don't know what came over me. Sometimes I just act . . . It was terrible of me to hit you. I am really, truly sorry."

The sky had darkened; there would be rain. At last he said, "I know she's been telling you everything."

Well, that explained a lot.

"So it wasn't the guitar?"

"It was mainly that. You know, you asked me, in your car that day, whether she still played, and I pretended I didn't know she ever had. But of course I remember how she played and sang, so beautifully, till the kids were four or five. And how her voice grew rough one time from shouting at me – it was just a little hoarseness, it would have gone away again, but while she had it she did a school – "

"What do you mean?"

"Didn't you know she used to sing professionally? She had a whole one-woman show she used to do at church functions, schools and so on. Nothing so big, but she loved it, and so did the people she sang for. She got and gave a lot of pleasure. And this time, when she had been screaming at me over some silly woman I cared nothing for, she had to do a school the next day, and she refused to cancel, and her voice kept breaking as she tried to sing, and she forced it, and did to her throat some real damage. So she had to stop, the doctors told her she would lose her voice if she didn't. Of course I thought it was only for a while, to rest it, but when I asked her, after a couple of weeks – the other business had completely blown over as you say – 'When are you going to sing?' and she said, 'Never' – I was shocked. I didn't believe her, her music meant too much to her, I thought it was just a gesture, to punish me. But then I began looking for the guitar. I looked all over the house for it. I couldn't find it. I thought she'd sold it or given it away. I was absolutely . . . What can I say? I was horrorstruck, guilt-struck. Also angry, deeply angry, too much to talk to her about it. I thought, if she wants to cut her nose to hurt her face, let her. I refused to show how she'd hurt me, how it went on hurting every time the phone calls came – "

"Phone calls?"

"To invite her to perform. If I took them, I'd leave a note on the pad, and then wait and wait for her to say something. At the beginning I'd have to ask. 'Aren't you going?' 'Where to?' 'The church coffee meeting wants you to sing, I wrote it.' Then she'd say, quietly, sadly and yet brightly, the way she is sometimes, 'I can't sing any more.' Once I said, 'Is this doctor's orders, or is it your orders?' 'It's nobody's orders,' she said. 'It is just fact.' Once I did talk. I said, 'It's good for the children to have music: they used to love it. I know they miss it now.' It was true. The house had lost something. She gave me a strange look. 'You're right. I'll buy them a radio . . . ' "

We walked on in silence, broken only by the bike making its clicking wheel-song. How subtle women are . . . She had some of Willem's cruelty after all.

"I didn't know till last night that she never gave the guitar away, that she had it all the time. It was like a ghost when you walked into the room with it. *You* . . . After all these years . . . For *me* she wouldn't. 'Never.'"

I wanted to take his arm, but I didn't. Instead I said, "Maybe if *you*'d asked her – you know, for yourself, not for the children or the church ladies – maybe she was waiting for that?"

"Sometimes things matter so much you can't say anything."

He glanced at me out of his handsome black eyes and for a moment I thought of Wim and Riki and felt such heartache for all of them that I had to draw a deep, groaning breath.

"Why do you sigh like that?"

"I'm sorry I added to your hurt," I said.

Then he said, with such sincerity I couldn't be offended:

"I'm so glad you don't attract me physically. This frees me to appreciate you very much as a person."

The kids, with hardboiled eggs coming out of their ears, were indifferent to lunch, but we weren't. After they'd pushed off to Pieter's room (he'd relented about the trains), we four grown-ups ate on our own for a change – very civilised. Some subtle change had taken place in the general chemistry. We had a thoroughly good, if at times flippant conversation, across the table and around it, drawing the meal out until mid-afternoon with fresh pears and slivers of cheese and lots of coffee kept warm on the warmer. Outside it grew darker and darker as a storm approached, and soon the little nightlight which fuelled the warmer was gleaming like Portia's good deed in a naughty world.

"It's a fantastic bonus to be able to take the kids abroad," Cal said enthusiastically. "I couldn't stand it if they grew up insular."

"Yes," I agreed. "Like, when I was little, we just went to the same seaside place year after year – Felpham, it was called. We knew every rock and breakwater and tree, we used to meet all the same children every year – there were donkeys on the beach and a peripatetic icecream man who dribbled coloured syrups on the cornets – "

"How revolting," said Cal. "Did he keep little vials of

raspberry and peppermint up his nose, or what?"

"Don't be so clever . . . All I want," I said, "is for the boys not to be boorish, and to have something going on in their heads. It's obvious things are never going to be the same, ever, since the oil crisis. There's going to be massive unemployment. They'll have to make themselves mentally independent of work, not feel bad or be bad if they haven't any. They'll have to study leisure and I don't care if they're not university material. They can knit for all I care. I shall *never* nag them to break their heart looking for jobs just for the sake of it, if there aren't any."

"What if you're poor and can't keep them?" said Niels. "Our children will get the best education there is. If we are ruined for it. Even if they don't want it. In addition Anna is learning the piano. She doesn't like it but she must do it. And Pieter is taking Italian. It's not in children's nature to learn, the way people think, you have to force them. They won't thank you at twenty-five for letting them be lazy at twelve."

"One thing I'm glad of," said Mariolain, "is that here in Holland we have not given up national service. I wish only that it was also for girls, but at least our boys have to face up to it."

"God," I said, shocked, and Cal echoed me. "I'd die if George or Daniel had to go to Northern Ireland."

"Pieter will look beautiful in his uniform, and he won't have to shoot anyone," said Mariolain firmly.

"All I hope is that none of them gets married too early," I said.

"You *are* keen to keep them with you forever," said Niels. "I have a picture in my head of you with grey hair – "

"It's starting – "

"Really grey, white then, and Cal with a white beard like St Claus, living still with your boys who are now middle-aged men, with no education, and no jobs, and no wives. George is sitting in a rocking-chair knitting and Daniel . . . Daniel is dribbling on a cornet."

I let out a snort of laughter. "All right, touché. Now let me look in the crystal ball . . . Ah! I see Anna, chained to a piano in a concert hall banging out concertos while gnashing

223

her teeth. She's wearing blue stockings. And Pieter . . . Pieter's standing at the doors of the hall, the most intellectual-looking sergeant major you've ever seen, with three degrees and a rifle with a fixed bayonet. He's there to stop people leaving."

"And are ours married? – because I don't mind if they get married young," said Niels.

"Then, yes, they're both married. That's why I don't see their mother at the concert. She's at home going round the twist babysitting for all the grandchildren."

"No, thank you," said Mariolain. "I would be the world's worst grandma. Though I would like the weddings – I'm longing for the weddings! Did you two have a nice one?"

Cal and I looked at each other wryly. We had rushed off to a registry office of course. I'd worn a fairly ordinary dress, not white or anything, and he, newly released from his banking days and their attendant formality, had defiantly worn an open-necked shirt. We hadn't had any photos taken, something for which the boys have not forgiven us. They sometimes appear to doubt we ever had got married, seeing there was none of the customary evidence. Cal thought wedding rings were bourgeois and bought me a beautiful medallion instead, which was nice, but my mother couldn't bear me going around pre-George, bulging and bare-handed, and thus I am probably the only woman living who sports a wedding ring bought by her mother. This is one of my best stories and Mariolain and Niels enjoyed it. Then I asked about their wedding, and we moved into the living-room so Mariolain could show me their photos. Cal opted out of this feminine enterprise and followed Niels out to his study, where there was to be a run-through of some of Niels's old commercials on his Betamax for the kids.

"They're amazingly good," Cal was to tell me later, to my absolute astonishment, and proceed to describe several of them in frame-by-frame detail, like works of art. Really, male friendship is a wondrous thing.

Chapter 23

———— ⁓ ————

Mariolain produced a large album and we sat together by the fire.

"See," she said. "Here's Niels . . . Doesn't he look sweet? His hair is so nice, it wouldn't lie down, every time he took off his top hat it popped up again!"

Niels looked not so much sweet as ridiculously young. About sixteen. Mariolain wore one of those curious bell-skirted short wedding dresses popular in fashion history for such a brief moment that I could date her marriage almost to the month – the winter of 1959–60. On her head was a little pillbox hat and a short, perky veil, on her feet white satin shoes with winkle-picker toes. She looked enchanting, but dated, though I remembered wearing such clothes and thinking them delicious.

"Who are these others?" I asked. "Oh, look – that must be Niels's father – Wim!"

"Yes. And that's his second wife, a very nice woman, and his children, Niels's half-sisters, they were my bridesmaids."

"I didn't know he'd remarried."

"Yes. He was a sensible man."

"He's dead now?"

"Yes. He died in his early fifties. Malaria. Well, that was part of it. Lots of people who were in camps, who seemed to survive, died young, after all."

"And where's Irene?"

There was a brief pause. Mariolain turned a page.

"She didn't come," she said flatly.

"Didn't come? To your wedding? Why on earth not – was she abroad?"

"Yes. She went abroad that morning. The morning of my wedding. She made sure to go."

"I don't understand."

"Look, here we cut the cake – a beautiful one! And here's my father."

Momentarily distracted, I bent and gazed, then took the album from her hands to see him better.

"He's not looking very festive. Didn't he approve of Niels?"

"He had nothing against Niels."

"So why's he scowling like that?"

"Can't you guess the reason?"

I guessed at once, and looked for Griet in the photographs.

"But she's not here."

Mariolain produced another album from the settee at her side, a much smaller one. She laid it in my lap.

"Look at these."

I opened it. The first picture was fixed to the middle of the page. It showed a snowscene which was so picturesque, so incongruous with the figures in the foreground, that for a moment I thought it was a studio backdrop. But no – I could see it was real. There was Mariolain in her brief wedding dress and her little pointed satin shoes and her perky veil, even with her bouquet, standing on a frozen lake on thin snow. The air was misty with frost; the bare trees lightly stencilled against a grey sky. At her side was Niels in his morning suit, smiling bravely but evidently numb with cold. And on her other side was Griet.

She wore a winter coat embellished with a fur collar, and a turban-like fur-fabric hat. She was made up and had a jewelled pin on her lapel – she had obviously done her utmost for the occasion. Her smile was a rictus, the fixed grimace of a nervous subject in a posed photograph. She clung to Mariolain's bare arm with both gloved hands as if trying to keep her warm.

"My God," I said. "You must have been frozen!"

"Just outside the picture is my warm coat. I took it off, hung it over the bonnet of the car, ran to the place, stood for just long enough and ran back."

"But where is this?"

"It's about five miles from where the wedding was held. I made the photographer drive us there after the other photos were taken while everyone waited at the reception."

I turned over the pages. There were two other shots of the three of them in slightly different positions, taken, I guessed, within seconds of each other.

Mariolain put her elbows on the open pages of the heavy album and leant towards the fire, her chin on her fists. Her eyes opalised in the firelight. I felt emanating from her, an almost tangible smell of her past as she slipped back into it.

"The week before my wedding, I went to Irene and told her. 'Mami's coming.' She was twenty-eight years old, a trained practising psychotherapist, a good one. She had helped me so much, and now she was helping others. But when I said that to her, she was like a mad woman. For a moment she was silent and then it burst. She screamed at me: 'You have dared to ask the woman who let us be raped? Who sided with the cursed *moffen*? Haven't you understood yet that to have such a person in your family is a disgrace?'

"When she was a little calmer she said, 'Do as you like. It's your wedding. But if she comes, I will not.' I begged her. I rang her up every day until the wedding, and on the night before, when I should have been happy, she told me, 'Tomorrow I am going to France.' I cried into the night. You can't think how I cried. How could I be married without Irene? But I had to."

The tears were falling now.

"And she had made me so afraid. What if no-one would speak to Mami, what if Niels's family, or Papi's family, cut her? It was my day to be happy, for all the long time I had not been, but I was too nervous. Well," she said, sitting up and blowing her nose, "in the end they were well-behaved. They could all understand it was my choice and my right to choose, but they all believed I had chosen wrong, and as much as they could they avoided her. Only Niels' father came to her and said, such a sweet, gentle thing: 'Niels' mother couldn't be here. I am glad Mariolain's mother could.' I loved him for that. But he was the only one. Papi didn't even look at her. And Irene . . . Irene's empty place was like a hole in my wedding."

I looked in silence again at the photographs. The conventional family group on the church steps, with the bridesmaids, the other relatives, the friends, all warmly wrapped in winter coats and smiles. And the few others, the ones on the lake, so bleak, so isolated, so chill and lonely. I thought that I had never in my life seen such a poignant evocation of family schism.

After that first visit to her mother, Mariolain didn't go back for a long time. She couldn't. She thought about it every day and nagged herself to go, but she was unable to force herself – every time she thought about her mother, she felt she was suffocating in her unwanted embrace.

And then one day, just as she was beginning to push the whole incident behind her, the doctor telephoned.

The sound of his voice was like a policeman's knock. As she listened to his few words, shivers of fear and remorse were running over her. What he said cut a recording in her brain which she played back to me, she claimed, word for word:

"Do not think you can pick your mother up and drop her again like a toy. She has suffered enough. She was not what you expected? That is too bad. She is your mother. You owe her your life and you owe her your loyalty, no matter how hard it is for you." Then he paused, and added, like a command: "Friday?"

And she whispered, "Yes."

Because, as she told me ruefully, "What that Nazi said to me was right."

Being with her mother didn't at once become easier. In

some ways it never did. But there were worse and better times. The worst was the way Griet talked about the war – half defensive, half attacking. This used to irritate Mariolain terribly, because she could sense, as with someone endlessly tugging her sleeve, the recurring bids for her sympathy.

And sometimes – but only sometimes – she learnt that she could give sympathy. These moments came when Griet lost her sense of grievance and of her mission to rehabilitate herself in her daughter's eyes. When, as Mariolain put it, she was "just remembering". For instance, there was a story about a young boy she had nursed in the lazaret on the Eastern front. He was shell-shocked and couldn't speak properly, and she would sit with him trying to coax him to tell her about his family, to bring his voice back. And suddenly one night he began to talk perfectly normally in a low, desperate way, and she listened in amazement because she realised he was Dutch. He had only been pretending to lose his speech so no-one would ask him questions. He told her that he had joined the German army when he was seventeen; convinced by their propaganda, he volunteered. And gradually he saw what they were. On the Russian front he had to take part in operations against Jews and partisans. He was terribly ashamed, shocked, opposed. But he was afraid, too, of what would happen to him if he didn't join in.

And then one night he was set to guard some partisan prisoners who were to be shot in the morning, and he let them escape, and felt clean, but after an hour he became so afraid of what would happen to him that he tried to run after them, to join them.

A sentry shot him in the leg, and so he was sent to the lazaret. He was terrified they would send him to a concentration camp as soon as he was better, and he kept picking his dressings off and refusing to drink in the hope of getting fever. Griet told him he could go back home after the war and that everything would be all right, that people would understand he made a mistake because he was young. She believed it. But he knew better than she did what awaited people like him, and like her. "They will never," he told her prophetically, "let us forget."

"He managed to die," Mariolain told me, "from his not at

all fatal wound. He died in her arms. She always spoke of him so tenderly . . . I asked her to tell me that story several times. It wasn't that I liked to hear it so much, but that when she told it I could feel I loved her a little."

For the first time in all Mariolain's long, broken-up, tragic story, I felt tears come into my own eyes.

"Of course," she went on, "my father didn't know where I went, those times. I invented new things so he wouldn't get suspicious. Lying to him became my second nature. I came to enjoy it, it was my first victory over him, a triumph.

"My mother didn't know about the struggles I had about my father – not *with* him, about him. In my head only . . . I had no courage to have struggles with him, she was right about that. But she didn't make things easier for me. She hated him, she hated that I was living with him; she didn't spare me or hold back what she felt. Sometimes it was as if she was trying to win me from him. I think she hoped some day I would arrive at the doctor's house with a suitcase and tell her I'd left home! Come over to her side for good. Of course I couldn't. Habit was too strong. Besides, I could never bear the doctor, he gave me goose's skin just to be in a room with him.

"Once it got so strong I burst out with it. He'd come in, as he usually did during my visits, to 'inspect' me, to say some little moral thing, what's that word, a homily, to eat up some biscuits, make sure we knew whose house we were in, whose tea we ate. He went strutting out on his little polished feet and I burst. 'How can you live with that Nazi?'

"She was furious. She scolded me like a child for an hour. She asked me, 'What is important in life? The most important thing is kindness, helping people. On 'Axe-Day', when people here thought the Allies were coming, they said they were going to chop off our heads! Is that so civilised? And they call the Germans barbarians! Was it Nazis or anti-Nazis who made me eat grass? Well, I know the Germans better than you! I walked nearly all the way back from the Eastern front, and on the way I met with a lot of kindness from the ordinary *volk*, more than I've found here where my own family won't speak to me!

" 'The doctor took me in when I was ill, broken, desperate, after the terrible years in that camp where none of you would visit me . . . where I was sent on the word of that man your father. You ask how I can live with the doctor, who never asked anything from me but loyalty and some housework. I ask you, how can you live with that man your father? Tell me the truth now, have you found one soft spot in his heart anywhere? Can you say you love him? He's incapable of love. The doctor has more heart for his patients, and he does more good in the world, than your father, for all his patriotism and his iron principles. And I'll tell you something else – " '

Here Mariolain stopped and looked at me.

"What did she tell you?"

"That my father was once on the point of joining the NSB. Oh, long before the war, in the middle thirties. She told me he actually remarked, 'I wish we had in Holland a man like this Herr Hitler! He would soon straighten out our political system with all its silly time-wasting factions, and begin to get things done.' 'Yes,' Mami said, seeing how I was shocked. 'He was not so against them then.'

"Yet he was against evil. Not just rigidly, cruelly, destroying my mother's life. But bravely, and heroically. He wrote his book and he named names and he didn't hide. And for that I was able to respect him. At last."

Willem's book – called in Dutch *De Ondersgrondse Wereld*, in English *The Nether World*, a reference to the Netherlands, the Underground and Hell – came out at last just about two years before my first visit to Holland in the mid-fifties. It caused a sensation. The publishers had been deeply alarmed, not about the bulk of the book, in which personal experience was brilliantly woven together with wider events, the whole illuminated by hindsight and years of scholarly research, but about a lengthy epilogue which Willem insisted upon adding. At first they refused to publish it; but he threatened to withdraw the book and publish it first abroad, so in the end they yielded, though with many misgivings. They knew they had a bestseller. They chanced the lawsuits, which in the event never came.

This shocking epilogue tells of exploitation of the young, idealistic, mainly socialist resistance workers by more right-wing elements who took them over in the name of unity and co-ordination, who ordered them to risk their lives – which they willingly did – transporting parcels and messages, even carrying out executions, only to discover later that the parcels contained black-market liquor or other contraband, that the messages had little to do with the war-effort. Those they had been ordered to kill were not invariably Nazis or dangerous infiltrators or informers; instead they could be people who knew of the activities of certain men who, while claiming to be in the Resistance, were using this as a cover to enrich themselves, who, while their countrymen starved, were observed by their young couriers drinking heavily and smoking cigars.

It tells of plotting by the Dutch government-in-exile, who, near the end of the war, infiltrated new underground leaders into occupied Holland, officially to unify the disparate elements of the Resistance to facilitate the Allies' advance when it came, but unofficially to sow seeds of dissension between, for example, Catholics on the one hand and Communists on the other – opposing factions, 'natural enemies', who during the course of the war had made common cause and found out each other's virtues. This hardly suited the purposes of the exiled establishment, who were accustomed to the Churches keeping the radicals in check and who were secretly working for a return to the status quo ante, to facilitate their rule when the war should end.

It tells of small, sinister post-war episodes. Young resistance workers receiving 'rewards' in the form of gold watches, which turned out to have Jewish names engraved on them. Parties to celebrate the liberation, at which men from whom others had received their orders were heard boasting, in their cups, of having killed 'capitalist' Jews. Commissions of enquiry utterly failing to uncover the truth, rejecting evidence, having on their panels men who were themselves suspect. Youngsters who had risked their lives a hundred times during the Occupation, now threatened, intimidated, even shot at, because they had been horribly disil-;

lusioned and were trying to bring the truth to light.

In short, Willem exposed a 'nether world' beneath the Underground, or rather, with it and on its fringes. It made villains of heroes, it stained reputations, debunked myths, exposed sores which had been left festering under cosmetic patches for ten years. He named names. He 'stirred the dirty pot', and the noxious gases that rose from it proved dangerous also to him.

He found himself – not greatly to his own surprise, but very much to the surprise of Mariolain and Irene, who, as usual, had been told nothing in advance – the centre of a national scandal. The girls were harassed by the press, sent hate-mail, followed in the streets. It was now that Jan became unmanageable, that Irene's marriage cracked, and that she turned against her father, feeling he was to blame. It was now that Mariolain, still living at home with him, became once again prey to the 'little illnesses' which, for the previous five years, had almost stopped. But it was also at this point that her entrenched dislike of her father began to modify.

The lies she had grown used to telling him to cover her visits to her mother stopped being a secret pleasure to her and became a burden. When she examined this change and looked for a reason, she realised that for the first time she, as distinct from others, perceived her father in a role she could acknowledge as noble.

Not that she admired or approved of the main part of the book. She hated it. She despised it for the things left out, the deception, Willem's elevation of himself to the role of Resistance hero without a mention of what it had cost those closest to him. But the epilogue redeemed it. The honesty and fairness in Mariolain's nature showed her now a man struggling to expose an evil at whatever cost to himself. Unlike Irene, who profoundly resented what it was costing her, Mariolain almost perversely felt proud and defiant. She bore the harassment stoically and showed a loyal face, even going on a radio programme to stand up for her father. And for the first time she sensed that he needed her support and was grateful for it. They didn't exactly become close; but there was some degree of mutual respect, and this, for her, was healing.

Mariolain's religion, over the years, had modified. She was no longer on the fringes of Catholicism. She had begun to believe in a complicated kind of reincarnation, in which one had to work out, over a series of visits to earth, relationships which had been botched or had caused damage. Death as such was not the important thing; what mattered was not to die – or let anyone close to one die – until all unfinished business had been dealt with. Otherwise one was liable to find oneself reborn and struggling again with the same person.

Where she came by these ideas I don't know. She merely outlined them to me rather diffidently, as if afraid of my reaction. I decided that this odd faith – abstruse and unlinked to any orthodox creed as it seemed to me – had been worked out by herself to satisfy the deepest needs of her nature and reconcile the ironies and dichotomies of her family.

This has to be understood to know why she sprang the news about her 'perfidy', her 'betrayal', on her father when he lay in hospital, laid low not only physically but morally and spiritually by a piece of violence which had overtaken him.

One day, months after the book came out, when the fuss was beginning to die down, Willem went out to meet someone and while he was standing beside a low wall, waiting, he heard the screech of car tyres. Turning sharply, he saw the car driving straight at him. He dived headlong over the wall, but not quickly enough to avoid a glancing blow from the bumper which caught his foot as he jerked it to safety. The car went into reverse with a grinding of gears – a sound which afterwards always brought him out in a sweat; and as he lay on the ground beyond the wall, agonised as much by the fall on his elbow as by the injury to his foot, he heard the car speed away. Then he fainted.

He was in far worse condition than his hurts strictly explained. He seemed to have suffered a slight heart-attack, and for a few days there was fear for his life.

Irene relented to the extent of visiting him in hospital, but in her heart she believed he had invited this disaster. It was Mariolain who gave him comfort.

She sat with him by the hour and, while she sat there, partly at least from a strong sense of duty, she found herself passionately willing him to live. She traced this not so much to daughterly feelings as to a half-mystical fear, based on her belief that if they didn't sort out their relationship now, they would have to do it in a future life. This was terrible to contemplate ... She became obsessed with the idea, rehearsing in her mind the endless possibilities of other relationships – husband and wife, brother and sister, perhaps even mother and son – in which she could, in a reincarnation, find herself locked with him, striving for understanding and reconciliation. She had appalling headaches while she sat there, so that she cried silently from the pain, never thinking to ask the nurses for a pain-killer – for it didn't seem to be physical. It was the pressure of all the years of anger, bitterness, hatred, resentment, striving in her head to get out, together with a longing to be free and cleansed.

And so, when he was over the worst and sitting up a little, she could hold herself back no longer. One day she arrived for her visit, said: "Hallo, Papi," as always as she entered the private ward, and before she had even reached the bedside said: "I want you to know that for three years I've been going to see Mami."

Willem's colour changed so startlingly that she was terrified. His hand went to his chest, his eyes almost started from his head. "Don't!" she cried. "Don't, Papi! Nothing will change it." And slowly he seemed to get control over himself. His hand sank back, his breathing became normal and his face lost its deathly look.

(When she told me about this, she used a curious comparison. "Did you ever read about torture, how there are certain kinds of pain so bad that afterwards if they do something less to you, which usually would make you scream, you hardly notice it? I told him at a strange time, a wrong time you might think, when he was weak and in pain. But his anger and horror that a fellow Dutchman should try to kill him, that was what tortured him. My 'betrayal' was a lesser thing. It couldn't make him cry after that.")

At first, Willem tried to maintain his former stance – unrelenting opposition, even outrage. But he couldn't keep it up. The new 'post-book' relationship had drained some of his venom. Mariolain's slow, deliberate, remorseless persistence – and his own weakness – finally forced him to be silent, to listen.

Keeping reproach out of her narrative with an effort, she simply told him how she herself felt about her mother's sufferings; how, without being won over in any way to her ideological point of view (which hadn't substantially changed with the years – the doctor's influence, no doubt), she could see why her mother had done what she had done. It was useless, she said quietly, to expect a quart out of a pint pot. Her mother was a person with limitations. Not everyone could be clever. The German propaganda at the beginning of the war had been very convincing . . . She watched her father's hard face sag, as if its stony features were being worn down by the steady, ineluctable drop, drop, drop of details. At last he escaped into sleep . . .

Mariolain left it at that. She had done what she had to do. When her father came home, she quietly continued her visits to her mother without subterfuge, and he had to accept it. Eventually she revealed to him her other secret, that when she was away from home she used her mother's maiden name of Jansen. This shocked and wounded him, but he said nothing beyond: "Is my name not good enough?" But it was a shadowy riposte.

He had aged. His sight was failing; he had to wear the thick pebble-glasses I remembered. And the bad limp from his injured foot never really improved. In due course, he went back to the university. And Mariolain settled down to the quiet, semi-sequestered life she was living when I visited her first, the life, almost, of an invalid, which was only to change when she appeared on Dutch television, singing and playing a song of her own. A young man who was in the same building as the studio saw her on a monitor and wrote her a fan-letter. It was Niels.

That was our last day, the Sunday of the trail, of the attenuated lunch, of the wedding photos. The next morning we got up early to a gloomy, rainswept vista from our attic window. We packed. The children were overtired, fractious and tiresome. It was time to leave.

I carried some of the luggage down the stairs (a perilous operation, both flights being like precipices) and stood in the hall for a minute to get my breath. I found myself gazing at Mariolain's mural. I'd looked at it numerous times since we got here but I always noticed something new. This time it was a couple of people lurking under a tree near the hen-house (hen-house? Evidently a thing of the past, like the cats). The woman was rather plump and wore a blue skirt and a coloured bandeau round her hair. I also do that, especially when I travel, to keep my flyaway hair in place. The man was the same height as the woman. He was bald and had a beard. I frowned suddenly and peered closer. I could smell the fresh paint.

"Mariolain!" I called. Or rather, yelled.

She emerged from the kitchen where she'd been filling our thermos. A picture of innocence.

"What," I asked, pointing grimly, "have you been up to?" She grinned impishly.

"Do you like it? I did it early this morning. I wanted to do the boys too, but I took too long over you two. I'll put them in, though, don't be afraid."

I swallowed. "That – fat – creature – that's meant to be me?"

She stood as far back as the hall allowed and looked critically at her painting.

"I wouldn't say fat! Do you think you look fat? I'll paint some grass in round your hips and make them smaller. What do you think of Cal?"

"Cal's all right," I said shortly. I couldn't take my eyes off that rotund little figure. I must, I thought grimly, diet. No wonder Niels, who goes for anything in skirts, was willing to make an exception of me.

"Why don't you put yourself in?" I asked, somewhat sourly I fear.

"I was in." She pointed. "See? Under that flowerbed. You can just see my outline."

I peered. "With a guitar. Was that why you painted yourself out?" I couldn't help smiling to see that she had

237

turned what had been her head into an oversized pompom
dahlia.

"I can't remember. Perhaps I'll put myself back."

"I would," I said. "Guitar and all."

Stifling my bruised vanity, I went to hurry the boys along.
As I shepherded them down the stairs with their duffle-bags
I caught sight of Anna, beckoning to me mysteriously from
her door. She shut it behind me and placed a little parcel in
my hand.

"What's this?"

"It's a present."

"How sweet of you!"

"Open!"

The paper revealed a small box containing an odd little
contraption with a handle. I turned it. It produced a tinkly
rendering of a familiar tune – of all things, the *Internationale.*

"Oh, Anna! Thank you darling, it's gorgeous!"

"You should put it near the toilet. Then no-one can hear
that you make peepee."

I hugged her, and she held me round the neck.

"You will come back again?"

I drew back and looked into her pointed face. So much
had gone into the making of her, so much that it was her
right to know, but that I hoped with intense urgency she
would never find out. So many scars, of all kinds, haunted
the genealogy of this seemingly perfect little human female.
Behind those slanting dark eyes, as striking as her brown
hair was commonplace, was a Malayan great-grandmother
whose contribution to her genes could have saved her grandmother's life. "He married again," Mariolain had said of
Wim. "A sensible man." Yes, sensible, practical, a realist –
when it was too late. I wondered briefly about Niels's half-
sisters. Did they, like Niels, bear some scars, not of their
very own but inherited from their father? Would they, like
this strange little girl clinging to me so passionately, inherit
soul-damage?

Because she was damaged, I could see it as she stared up
at me. She was afraid; afraid of how things would be, again,
when we were gone. She adored both her parents, but what

was between them, what had formed them, the harm it had done them and their marriage, had affected their children. Naturally. How could it be otherwise? Should traumatised people then eschew parenthood? Should just plain lousy mother-material, like me?

"Of course we'll come back," I said.

"You promise?"

"I promise."

And in a flurry of hugs and goodbyes, we set off for home.

Epilogue

—————— ∿ ——————

But it was to be seven long, full years before that promise was kept.

Pieter and George would be going on twenty, Anna and Daniel eighteen. Beautiful strangers, as much, in a sense, to their parents as to each other . . . Pieter, so uptight and hidebound as a child between his eruptions of bottled-up nervous energy, would have evolved into a six-foot drop-out with a pirate's pigtail and earring, a penchant for aggressively shabby clothes which exposed his arms to the shoulders, revealing both to be luridly tatooed. He had been rejected by the Dutch army on grounds of health – his mother called it chronic sinus trouble, but he himself was at pains to tell everyone: "I am psychologically unsuitable."

And my Anna! Strange, withdrawn, unsmiling, sworn to veganism and celibacy, her pretty fussy room with its myriad feminine fancies reduced to a minimalist shrine where she spent hours meditating . . . She had no plans for a career, in music or otherwise, and would 'obviously' never marry. Her sect believed that the world was going to end in the year 1992, not with a whimper but a bang, making it pointless and irresponsible to produce children.

Our two, meanwhile, would have been transformed into short, stocky youths, deep-sunk in the pop culture and with little of any other sort to boast of; short on manners and long on hedonism, but open, friendly enough, with plenty to say for themselves and no discernible hang-ups. Daniel's only commitment so far was to his appearance and to the pursuit of girls; his only ambition to own a car as different as possible from the modest one that we owned; but he had been heard to say that, if all else failed, he could always join the army. He seemed to think it would be good for his image, and even, if he could get posted to a hot country, his spotty complexion. George – to his father's incredulous dismay, but his American grandfather's exuberant gratification – was expressing an interest in banking.

The musical toy, after three of the seven years, had been carefully unscrewed from the tiles near our Wembley loo, and reaffixed to the pine cladding (a much more effective sounding-board) in the one in our next house. We moved into this when Cal got his job making sets for television commercials. You can tell when a visitor is relieving himself because you can hear the brave, resonant tinkling-out of the *Internationale*. No stranger can resist trying it; and I can never hear it without thinking of our week in Holland. Not that I needed reminding, because Mariolain developed into a first-class correspondent.

When she wrote to me about her affair, I couldn't help laughing. It was a wildly exuberant, witty letter, about five years ago. Her lover was the music teacher Niels had coerced her into going to, to relearn the guitar. She wrote that "he has music in every part of him, especially *that* part, which makes my body sing. If he could give me music like that in my fingers I would play like Segovia."

But the music-maker was firmly married, and, having driven Niels almost out of his wits with jealousy (and incidentally set Mariolain back on the church-and-schools circuit), he faded from the picture, leaving Mariolain only a little bit forlorn for only a very short time before Niels, after threatening to divorce her, discovered he was madly in love with her and couldn't live without her. Which I suppose goes to prove that my ridiculous romances are not all total rubbish after all.

The occasion of our return to Holland was that I was going to write this book and needed to talk to both Mariolain and Niels again. We spent most of last summer with them, and had our cycling holiday, better late than never. Pieter didn't come; he wanted the house to himself to give an unending series of parties in, and only the projected horrors of this upon Anna's now hypersensitive soul drove her to accompany us. I'm glad to say she became a little less wan and elegiac en route; her all-white get-up (mark of whatever sect she adhered to) got grubby, her pale face tanned and her hair came loose from its anti-sex-league restraints. She wouldn't soil her mouth with any 'dead animals' though, and by the end of the trip George had been converted, not to the sect, thank God, but to veganism. It doesn't look as if he's going to get over it, either.

Dan was a bloody nuisance for three days and finally we put him on a train, bike and all, back to join Pieter's perpetual pop festival – much more to his taste than hard cycling in the open air and a lot of different beds. Shortly afterwards George and Anna took off at a tangent and were last seen pedalling away in diminishing perspective along one of those classic Dutch avenues of trees.

That left the adults, with several times the stamina and enthusiasm of our young, to enjoy a superb tour. We spent the nights in a variety of inns and youth hostels and ate our meals sitting by waterways or on boats or in markets, and I plied my new pocket tape recorder throughout to great effect. I got incredible co-operation from both my friends, although I had to get each alone before they would talk about their wars.

"I'll have to read this book of yours to find out about my wife," Niels said several times. "You know her better than I do."

One glorious evening of wide acquamarine skies, Mariolain and I were nursing mugs of cocoa on a bench at the back of a Friesland youth hostel. The wooden wall at our backs was still warm; all the sounds around us were benign and soothing. We'd spent the day exploring the region of her grandparents' homes – both sets – and she was in contemplative mood.

"I suppose your father isn't alive any more," I said diffidently.

She shook her head, staring away to the west in the direction both of the setting sun, and of her 'ancestral homes', one grand one with a coat-of-arms over the door, and one stolid farmstead in the midst of green acres where she had stood for long minutes testing the rusty lock on the door of an outbuilding full of bales of straw.

"How did you feel when he died?"

After a moment's pause she turned to me.

"As a prisoner when he hears he has a sentence many lifetimes long."

"You really think he and you will have to come back, and sort everything out?" She nodded. "But you got it all off your chest, your feelings about how he treated your mother."

"But he cheated us. He robbed us of her, of our normal childhood. I never talked to him about that, he never apologised, he never explained."

"And your mother . . . ?"

"That was more terrible, even. Because with her it was the rape. I never mentioned it. I never asked her if she knew about it, we never, ever mentioned Dirk, though sometimes his name trembled in my mouth. She was always so busy defending herself, and about *that* I could think of no defence she could make except to deny any knowledge of it, or memory. And if she'd said that, I wouldn't have believed. I couldn't bring myself to accuse her, and hear her lie. So she left the world with all that unresolved. She will have to come back and make amends to me. Not because I want it. I shall hate it. But that's the only kind of justice I can believe in."

"By that rule, you'll have to meet van Sluis again, too."

She stared at me, wide-eyed.

"Oh, no!"

"Why not?"

"No," she said, shaking her head vehemently. "No, Suky. Not him. He is not important. He is nothing to do with me. His soul is too thin to come back. It will just – blow away."

FOR THE BEST IN PAPERBACKS, LOOK FOR THE

In every corner of the world, on every subject under the sun, Penguin represents quality and variety – the very best in publishing today.

For complete information about books available from Penguin – including Pelicans, Puffins, Peregrines and Penguin Classics – and how to order them, write to us at the appropriate address below. Please note that for copyright reasons the selection of books varies from country to country.

In the United Kingdom: For a complete list of books available from Penguin in the U.K., please write to *Dept E.P., Penguin Books Ltd, Harmondsworth, Middlesex, UB7 0DA*

In the United States: For a complete list of books available from Penguin in the U.S., please write to *Dept BA, Penguin, 299 Murray Hill Parkway, East Rutherford, New Jersey 07073*

In Canada: For a complete list of books available from Penguin in Canada, please write to *Penguin Books Canada Ltd, 2801 John Street, Markham, Ontario L3R 1B4*

In Australia: For a complete list of books available from Penguin in Australia, please write to the *Marketing Department, Penguin Books Australia Ltd, P.O. Box 257, Ringwood, Victoria 3134*

In New Zealand: For a complete list of books available from Penguin in New Zealand, please write to the *Marketing Department, Penguin Books (NZ) Ltd, Private Bag, Takapuna, Auckland 9*

In India: For a complete list of books available from Penguin, please write to *Penguin Overseas Ltd, 706 Eros Apartments, 56 Nehru Place, New Delhi, 110019*

In Holland: For a complete list of books available from Penguin in Holland, please write to *Penguin Books Nederland B.V., Postbus 195, NL–1380AD Weesp, Netherlands*

In Germany: For a complete list of books available from Penguin, please write to *Penguin Books Ltd, Friedrichstrasse 10 – 12, D–6000 Frankfurt Main 1, Federal Republic of Germany*

In Spain: For a complete list of books available from Penguin in Spain, please write to *Longman Penguin España, Calle San Nicolas 15, E–28013 Madrid, Spain*

A CHOICE OF PENGUIN FICTION

Other Women   Lisa Alther

From the bestselling author of *Kinflicks* comes this compelling novel of today's woman – and a heroine with whom millions of women will identify.

Your Lover Just Called   John Updike

Stories of Joan and Richard Maple – a couple multiplied by love and divided by lovers. Here is the portrait of a modern American marriage in all its mundane moments and highs and lows of love as only John Updike could draw it.

Mr Love and Justice   Colin MacInnes

Frankie Love took up his career as a ponce about the same time as Edward Justice became vice-squad detective. Except that neither man was particularly suited for his job, all they had in common was an interest in crime. But, as any ponce or copper will tell you, appearances are not always what they seem. Provocative and honest and acidly funny, *Mr Love and Justice* is the final volume of Colin MacInnes's famous London trilogy.

An Ice-Cream War   William Boyd

As millions are slaughtered on the Western Front, a ridiculous and little-reported campaign is being waged in East Africa – a war they continued after the Armistice because no one told them to stop. 'A towering achievement' – John Carey, Chairman of the Judges of the 1982 Booker Prize, for which this novel was nominated.

Every Day is Mother's Day   Hilary Mantel

An outrageous story of lust, adultery, madness, death and the social services. 'Strange . . . rather mad . . . extremely funny . . . she sometimes reminded me of the early Muriel Spark' – Auberon Waugh

1982 Janine   Alasdair Gray

Set inside the head of an ageing, divorced, alcoholic, insomniac supervisor of security installations who is tippling in the bedroom of a small Scottish hotel – this is a most brilliant and controversial novel.

A CHOICE OF PENGUIN FICTION

Family Myths and Legends Patricia Ferguson

Gareth was just beginning to believe that he really enjoyed his relatives these days. And then Gareth's grandmother turns up in Gareth's hospital – and he is up to his upwardly-mobile neck in family once more. 'Great funniness and perception, and stunning originality' – *Daily Telegraph*

The Beans of Egypt, Maine Carolyn Chute

Out of the hidden heart of America comes this uncompromising novel of what life is like for people who have nothing left to them except their own pain, humiliation and rage. 'It's loving, terrible and funny and written as deftly as stitching on a quilt . . . a lovely, truthful book' – *Observer*

City of Spades Colin MacInnes

'A splendid novel, sparklingly written, warm, wise and funny' – *Daily Mail*. *City of Spades*, *Absolute Beginners* and *Mr Love and Justice* make up Colin MacInnes's trilogy on London street life from the inside out.

The Anatomy Lesson Philip Roth

The hilarious story of Nathan Zuckerman, the famous forty-year-old writer who decides to give it all up and become a doctor – and a pornographer – instead. 'The finest, boldest and funniest piece of fiction which Philip Roth has yet produced' – *Spectator*

The Rachel Papers Martin Amis

A stylish, sexy and ribaldly funny novel by the author of *Money*. 'Remark-able' – *Listener*. 'Irreverent' – *Daily Telegraph*. 'Very funny indeed' – *Spectator*

Scandal A. N. Wilson

Sexual peccadilloes, treason and blackmail are all ingredients on the boil in A. N. Wilson's new, *cordon noir* comedy. 'Drily witty, deliciously nasty' – *Sunday Telegraph*

Also by Lynne Reid Banks in Penguin

HER POIGNANT TRILOGY

The L-Shaped Room

Unmarried and pregnant, Jane Graham is cast out of her suburban home.
Lighting dejectedly on a bug-ridden room in a squalid house in Fulham,
she gradually comes to find a new and positive faith in life.

The Backward Shadow

After the birth of her son, Jane exchanges the L-shaped room for a remote country cottage. She is joined by Dottie, and together they embark
upon an enterprise that is to change both their lives.

Two is Lonely

Now the mother of an eight-year-old, Jane finds she has to grapple with
the increasing problems of single parenthood.

and

Children at the Gate

Gerda is a Jewish-Canadian divorcee alone in a miserable room in the
Arab quarter of Acre. She is thirty-nine but looks far older: emotionally
her life is a shambles. Her sole comforts are drink and an Arab friend,
Kofi, about whom there is considerable mystery.

An End to Running

Seeking refuge from the domination of his sister and from his own Jewish-
ness, Aaron Franks turns to Martha, his secretary. Together they travel to
Israel and a kibbutz – Martha with strong misgivings, Aaron full of
anticipation.

Also published

The Warning Bell
Dark Quartet: The Story of the Brontës
Path to the Silent Country: Charlotte Brontë's Years of Fame